Praise for *My Five Sisters* by Pam Franklin

"When I opened the book My [...] feeling of being pulled into Pam [...] was compelled to read to find wh[...] How she made it to adulthood int[...] and determination. Those of us w[...] ... and teenagers would be wise to take this book to neart. We don't know what each of them deals with every day. This book will stay in my mind for a long time."

—Mary Grace Murphy, retired middle school teacher and Author of the Noshes Up North Culinary Mystery Series

"Powerfully written, Pam Franklin's story of sibling abuse demonstrates how one can come through Hell and yet create a productive adult life."

—Dr. Bonnie Nussbaum, Licensed Psychologist and Holistic Coach

"A sad, tragic tale of growing up in the South during the 50s, a childhood of abuse, fear and insecurity as seen through the eyes of the child and the strength to not only survive but ultimately achieve great success and happiness in life. A compelling message of hope for lives that have been touched by mental illness."

—Robin Klamfoth, Film Journal International

"Pam Franklin's book, **My Five Sisters***, is written from the point of view of a young girl in a family tortured by abuse and untreated mental illness. Each of these circumstances, individually, can destroy a person and a family. Together, they are devastating. The significance of Ms. Franklin's touching story shows that traumas can bleed across generations. In her search for treatment and resolution, her story serves not only as a depiction of life inside a family's chaos (a kind of chaos that too many families must live through), but also as an example of how one person can survive, seek help, and stop the cycle of intergenerational trauma."*

—Charles McDaniel, MD, Assistant Clinical Professor, Department of Psychiatry and Biobehavioral Sciences, UCLA David Geffen School of Medicine

My Five Sisters

A Psychological Thriller based on a true story about multiple personalities

PAM FRANKLIN

Freality
Publications

Editing: Brittiany Koren/Written Dreams
Cover Design/Layout: Eddie Vincent
Cover illustration Tim Lantz/EddieVincent
Cover photos Shutterstock.com
Author Photo courtesy of Terri Zollinger Photography.
Photograph of Patra, age nine, courtesy of the Franklin Family.
Photographs reprinted with permission.

Category: Psychological Thriller
ISBN:978-0-9962531-0-9
Printed in the United States.
First Printing
0 1 2 3 4 5 6 7 8 9

This book is dedicated to my husband Bobby,
my daughter Whitney Windham, and my grandsons,
Teague Hendrickson and Crews Hendrickson.

Patra, age 9

Preface

I'm not exaggerating when I say that movies saved my life. Ever since I was a young southern girl in Jackson, Mississippi, I've gone to the movies at least once a week. My favorite show time is three o'clock in the afternoon, fifth row, center seat. Most of the time I am all alone in the cool dark theatre. The minute I sit down in that seat with my hot dog, diet Coke and candy, my life outside that room ceases to exist. I'm in my own little world where I feel happiest, safest, and most comfortable. I love to sit there and enter other people's lives for a few hours and forget about everything else.

It's no wonder that Franklin Designs, the business I founded in 1990 with my husband, Bobby, is all about movies. And that I live in Celebration, Florida, the town that Disney built on Disney property. I call it freality, *a place somewhere between fantasy and reality.*

Even when I was a little girl, I loved the dark interior of the Paramount Theatre on Capitol Street in Jackson, Mississippi. It was nothing like the pitch black I experienced when I was trapped in a closet. Just the opposite. In the darkness of the theatre, no one could get to me. Not my mother, whom I loved dearly, but who seemed not to notice what was going on inside our house. Not my father. And especially not my sister, Angela.

The majesty of movies has always made me believe that there is a better world out there. I'll never forget the first time I saw Gone With the Wind. I loved it, especially the scene when Scarlett O'Hara returned home to find her mother dead and Tara in ruins. I felt a strong connection with her—she knew plenty of heartache, too.

I vividly recall how she staggered up the hillside to an old garden area, looking as tired as I felt, even though I was only seven years old. She was so hungry she dug up a gnarly, old root with her hands. When it made her sick, she fell down on the ground, crying. But not for long. She struggled to her feet and made a fist toward the heavens, declaring, "As God is my witness, I'll never be hungry again."

I got goosebumps (and still do) because she gave me hope. Not just her words, but the emotion in her words. From that

11

first time I heard her say that, I knew everything I did from that day forward would be because of Scarlett O'Hara.

Today I work to make movie theatres comfortable and attractive. We don't build the bricks and sticks, as Bobby calls it, but we supply and install everything inside after the building is complete. We are partners in the largest movie theatre management company in the U.S., Phoenix Big Cinemas, and a theatre management company that operates over 150 screens nationwide. We also partnered with some friends to save an icon—the oldest screening room in the L.A. area, The Aidikoff Screening Room at 150 Rodeo Drive in Beverly Hills. What a joy to be so connected to something I love so much. I tell everyone I live a blessed life.

Now.

When I was a young girl, life didn't seem so bright. It was more like the ending in Gone With the Wind, *under dark, ominous skies. Something about the last scene, as much as I love that movie, always made me shiver. Scarlett, dressed all in black, crying again, hears voices—her father, Rhett Butler, and Ashley Wilkes—telling her to go home to Tara. The music swells, and she begins to accept the wisdom of their words. She now wants to return home, vowing, "After all, tomorrow is another day."*

Back then, I didn't ever want to go home. I wanted to stay safe inside the comfort of the Paramount Theatre. I never knew if I would have another tomorrow.

Prologue

The Oven

"Get in the oven, now."

"No," I shake my head, "I don't want to die."

She shoves me toward the oven, hard, then sneers at me. "Asshole, you will die either way if you don't listen to me, so what choice do you have?"

None, and I never have a choice. I am terrified. I touch the oven with my tiny fingers to see if it's hot. It's not, but I still back away.

My sister looks at me with a face full of hate. Without takin' her eyes off of me, she leans over, pulls the wire racks from the oven, and puts them on the floor against the wall. She turns on the gas, walks behind me and shouts, "Get in!"

At six years old, I'm thinkin' I'm small enough to climb inside the oven and she can still shut the door. When I start to cry, she kicks me in the hiney, and I stumble to the floor on my hands and knees in front of the oven. My heart is poundin' so hard in my chest I can feel it, and I am so scared I can hardly breathe. With wet tears streamin' down my face, tremblin', I slowly climb inside.

From behind me, I hear her strike a match. I hear the boom. The next thing I know, I am flyin' through the air. I hit the wall, and then everythin' goes black.

When I wake up, my sister is sittin' next to me on the floor with tears in her eyes. I am still stunned and I can't figure out where I am or why my face feels like it's on fire. I try to open my eyes but my eyelashes are stuck together, and I can barely open them. The smell of burnt hair fills the room. I think for a minute the apartment is on fire.

I try to stand, but my legs aren't strong enough to hold me up, so I'm sittin' here on the kitchen floor in a daze. After a few minutes, she helps me half-walk/half-crawl to the bathroom. I slowly pull my long melted eyelashes apart before I look into the mirror. My eyebrows and bangs are burnt off. My face is red, and when I look down there is no hair left on my arms or legs.

I sorta remember Angela makin' me climb into the oven in Cheyenne's grandmother's house, and her strikin' the match. My first thought is that this will not be easy to explain to Mommy. She is scared to death of fires and has told me a hundred times not to play with matches. I know immediately I will have to take all of the blame for playin' with fire. Angela has made it perfectly clear what she will do to me if I tattle on her for anything, and her wrath is not something I want, even if it means lyin' to Mommy.

Even though my dress is singed and I am burnt from head to toe, she tells me we have to go. It's almost five o'clock and we're still at my best friend Cheyenne's house. We have to get home before Mommy gets there. In my confusion, I can't imagine why that is so important.

She drags me out the door of the apartment, down the old wooden stairs, around to the front of the house, down nineteen steps to the sidewalk and makes me run all the way home down the busy street. It is hot outside and the swelterin' summer heat is like a blast from a furnace on my already scorched skin. All I want to do is scream from the pain.

But I don't. I don't ever cry when she hurts me.

Cheyenne and her grandmother's boardin' house is only two blocks from mine, but it feels like we have been runnin' forever. I keep tryin' to pull my burnt hand away from her, but she won't let go of me. She keeps pullin' me faster and faster along with her.

Suddenly I just stop runnin'. I stumble on my own two feet and fall down on the curb of the sidewalk. I sit up cryin', askin' her why she is draggin' me down the street when I am burnt to a crisp.

She looks straight at me and says, "I don't know how long I can keep her from switchin', Patra."

I get up and start runnin' as fast as I can.

When we get home, she takes me into the bathroom and starts takin' my clothes off. I look into the mirror and I am shocked at what I see, but my skin is burnin' too bad for me to care. My dark waist-length hair is singed and stickin' out in every direction. My clothes are scorched and tattered. My face and body glow bright red. It looks like I've been burnt with a blowtorch, like the one Daddy uses at the restaurant to caramelize the top of his *crème brûlées*.

In the bathroom, she frantically searches under the sink and finally finds some sunburn lotion Mommy bought at the beach last summer; she puts it on my arms and legs. With a cool wash-rag, she carefully cleans my scorched face before she gently smooths on the lotion. She takes me into the living room naked and sits me on a towel on the couch. With knots in my stomach, we wait for Mommy.

Before long, Mommy walks in the door. I am so happy to see her even though I know I'm in big trouble.

When she looks at me, her face kinda crumbles, and I think she is gonna cry 'cause I look like a huge pile of rubble. I have bald spots from her combin' my bangs and pullin' out clumps of hair. My eyebrows and eyelashes are burnt off. My face is the color of ripe strawberries.

I sit on the overstuffed couch with painful hot tears runnin' down my roasted face, afraid to say a word. Waitin'.

I can tell Mommy don't want to touch my burnt skin, so she sits down on the floor in front of me cross-legged and asks what happened. I bawl harder.

"It's okay. We can talk about it later, Patra," she says, her voice more soothin' than any lotion.

Mommy leads me down the hallway to the bathroom, runs a tub of cold water and tells me to get in. I climb into the big claw-foot tub and ease myself into the water. I sit there coolin' my body down tryin' to decide what kinda lie I will tell her about what happened.

After I have been sittin' there a little while, she brings in a tray of ice cubes and dumps it into the water my tortured body has turned lukewarm. There's a catch in her voice when she says, "Please don't tell Mom what happened. It will cause a heap of trouble."

I turn and look at her, but all I can think about is how wonderful the ice feels on my hot skin.

After what seems like hours of soakin' in the soothin' water, Mommy helps me out of the tub and carefully dries me off.

I tell her I don't think I can put any clothes on, and she says, "Okay, you don't need any right now. Let's go into the dining room."

Mommy tells me she doesn't have a way to take me to the doctor 'cause the buses have stopped runnin', so she lies me down on the dining room table and covers my body with the whipped egg whites she beat in a glass bowl in the kitchen. The cool egg whites feel wonderful on my skin, but I imagine I must look like a lemon ice-box pie. Through her tears, she tells me the burns on my body didn't blister or break the skin, and she thinks I will be okay in a couple of days.

It is the first day of summer, and this is what my days will be like for the next three months. After all, who is goin' to believe a twelve-year-old girl put her six-year-old sister into an oven and tried to kill her?

1

Multiple Sister

My name is Patra and I'm six years old. I live in a nightmare that lasted for as long as I can remember. I live in a beautiful southern town where people are friendly and the days are long, hot and lazy. My home in Jackson, Mississippi looks like most middle class houses in the south in the 1950s, with swayin' trees in the summer breeze, emerald green yards and flowers bloomin' everywhere. Heavy scents from the magnolias and sweet olive bushes constantly fill the air. But my story inside the house is not a happy one. I am small for my age with long dark brown hair that hangs in curls to my waist. Big blue eyes, long eyelashes, and a perfect oval face complete a look my eleven year old sister hates with a vengeance. My sister, Angela is pretty, but everyone says, 'she can't compare to little Patra'. Angela was the baby and the apple of everyone's eye until I was born when she was five and a half years old. Then everythin' changed for her. I became the enemy the day I was born.

Angry is the smartest and meanest sister trapped inside Angela's head, kinda like the bad witch in the fairy tales in our storybooks. Her face looks like a mask from the Wicked Witch of the West from the *Wizard of Oz*, cruel and full of hate and grimaces. She is capable of almost anything.

From the first time I saw it happen sittin' on my bed in our room on Gallatin Street, I knew from a place deep down inside that Angry could switch anytime she wanted, but Angela can't change back to herself. She doesn't even know Angry exists. I've watched them day after day to see if I can catch Angry the minute she switches with Angela, but since I turned six I have only seen it a few times.

When they switch, it's like watchin' something out of a scary movie.

The moment Angry appears, her face changes. Her mouth pulls down at the corners in an upside-down grin. Wrinkles appear, and there are lines on her face that are not normally on her forehead and in the space between her eyes. Her neck stretches longer and her dark blue eyes darken to black. Her voice gets higher when she talks, like she is in pain. And that's when she starts screamin'.

I shiver every time I see the change, and it happens so fast sometimes I miss it. The first time I saw Angela switch to Angry, she was nervous for a few minutes. Runnin' through the rooms in the big old house to see if anyone else was home, she searched all closets in the bedrooms, under the beds, and in the bathroom. She even searched under the sink. She looked out the windows and locked all the doors. She looked petrified, and she acted like she was afraid someone would find out she was here. She darted around the house like a bird out of a cage.

I could tell Angry saw through Normal's eyes, 'cause she was not a stranger in the house.

Angry knew where everythin' was, but she didn't look like she was searchin' for anything in particular. And then she ran to the pantry. Sugar! The only food she wanted was sweet. She ate things Normal would not think of eatin', probably 'cause Normal knew Mommy wouldn't let us have it. Normal tries to follow the rules. But Angry sat in the pantry and ate sugar right out of the sugar bowl, and honey out of the jar. She ate cookies, candy, cake, and anything else in the pantry that had sugar in it. She knocked food off of the shelves and left it on the floor.

I knew Mommy was goin' to have a fit when she got home from work and found all of the snacks gone, and the pantry a big mess. I knew I would get blamed for it. I don't know why, but I was always the one who got in trouble. I tried so hard to be good, but Angry always twisted things around and made me look bad. She had a knack for wrappin' Mommy around her little finger and silently laughin' and makin' faces behind Mommy's back when she walked away.

After she ate herself sick that day, Angry threw up all over the floor and left it there. Then she ran into the living room, flopped down on the couch, and yelled at me to turn on TV. When I walked in front of her, she kicked me in the hinny and said, "Go get me one of Daddy's cigarettes."

I asked what for. She jumped up off of the couch, threw me down on the floor, straddled me, and choked me until I almost passed out. I was too afraid to move or say anything and all I wanted to do was skedaddle out of the room.

She glared into my eyes and said, "To smoke, dumbass, and don't ever question anything I tell you to do again, or I will kill you."

It was the first time she threatened to kill me, but it wouldn't be the last. Angry hated me something fierce.

I was so confused. I didn't know who this person was or where she came from or how she had replaced Angela. But I did know if she was here to stay, my life would never be the same again.

After Angry choked her way through the cigarette, she walked into our bedroom. I am curious about the way she is actin', so I trail slowly behind her hopin' she wouldn't notice me. I slipped around to my side of the room and sat down on the bed without makin' a peep. She walked around Angela's side of the room and touched all of the girlie stuff on the bed and looked at it with disgust.

I could tell she didn't like Angela very much, but I could also see she was very happy to be here by the evil grin on her face. It makes me shiver.

Just lookin' at her distorted face scared me half to death. I knew I needed to get out of the room. Now! I tried to get around her to get out the door, but she stepped in front of me and slapped me hard across the face and knocked me out of kilter.

"Where do you think you're goin', moron? I didn't say you could leave," she growled at me.

I'm shocked; I had never been slapped before. My face burned; I saw stars. "Who are you," I asked, "and why are you doin' this to me?"

She put her face so close to mine I could smell her stale cigarette breath. "I am your worst nightmare, and I am here to torture you for the rest of your life!"

I started to cry, but she kept talkin'. "Oh no, little miss shit, you don't get to cry around me, ever!" She punched me in the stomach and dragged me to the closet. She opened the door, threw me in, and told me if I ever came out, she would beat me within an inch of my life.

My first day in the dark closet was the worst. I hated the dark, and the closet was so small I could barely sit down. When she closed the door, I couldn't breathe at first—the cramped, dark space terrified me. But I didn't cry. I never cried when she put me in the closet. I was too afraid of what she would do to me if I did.

After a while, I started playin' little games. It helped. I'd count to 100 forward and then backwards. I told myself stories about all of the books Mommy read to me. And I'd recite nursery rhymes. I had to whisper, 'cause if Angry thought I was havin' fun, she would open the door, kick me, and slam the door shut.

The second time Angry switched, she put me in the closet and dared me to come out. She sat outside the door and sang country songs for hours. I begged her to let me go to the bathroom, and she said, "Pee on yourself, you stink anyway." And then she laughed really loud like a wicked witch. When I asked for water, she would just beat on the door and say, "Shut up, you idiot!"

I spent a lot of time in the closet those first few years. Sometimes she would tie me up or put me in there naked. Other times she would tell me to stand up and not sit down; she said she'd open the door and if I was sittin' down, she'd beat the livin' daylights out of me. Sometimes she would open the door and beat me with her fist just for fun, then slam the door shut again.

I was so lonely sittin' in the tiny dark closet day after day. I sat there with my heart breakin', prayin' with silent tears rollin' down my face wishin' for someone to talk to. Then one day Teddy Long appeared out of nowhere. He was sweet and kind, and he was always on my side. He held my hand and wiped my tears away. I don't know how he got into the closet with me or where he possibly could have come from, but I didn't care. All I knew was he was like a big handsome teddy bear, and he comforted me when I was alone. I think God knew I was at my wits end that day and may have answered my prayers and sent me a friend.

After the first switch, Angry started showin' up every few days. It was like she was comin' out to play. Sometimes she ignored me completely, and other times she beat the crap out of me for no reason at all. I could tell she was tryin' to figure out this new world she had found her way into. I could tell how pleased she was with herself for doin' it, and how she planned to stay here forever. And that scared me something awful.

Hero   Kind   Normal   Sad   Angry

I figured out that Angela has five sisters who live inside her head. I call them The Sisters. I don't know how they got there, or why. I don't know when each of them will switch to the other, or how they do it. I just know who she is by lookin' at their faces when they have switched. One of them loves me, Kind. One of them protects me, Hero. Two of them could care less about me, Normal and Sad. And one of them wants me dead, Angry.

Kind only comes out when I'm in a lot of pain. Most of the time, Angela switches to Kind after Angry has hurt me bad enough that I need help. I think Kind has a hard time switchin' with Angry, so she waits for Angela to return to herself before she tries to help me.

Kind cleans me up and puts Band-Aids on my boo-boos after Angry hurts me. To make up for the things Angry does to me, Kind takes me to the store and buys my favorites: Hostess Twinkies, Almond Joys and Cokes. She babies me something awful. I always know the next time I see Angry I will pay for Kind bein' nice to me with a kick or a punch, 'cause Angry knows everythin' Kind does. It makes Angry mad for anyone to be nice to me, and by now I was way too familiar with what happens when Angry gets mad.

Sad has the face of an angel, but she always has tears in her eyes. I think she knows how Angry treats me, but she doesn't know how to help or maybe she doesn't really care. Sad is almost as strong as Angry, and they seem to know about each other, 'cause I hear them arguin' sometimes. Sad looks like the clown I saw at the circus, the one with the saddest face in the world. She hurts herself a lot, and she draws pictures of tortured people in her art books. She spends a lot of time sayin' she wants to die. I feel bad for Sad.

God only knows what Hero endures. She protects me; she's the only reason I am still alive. Hero steps in and takes my place when Daddy comes for me, and she tries to stop Angry from killin' me. She is not as strong as Angry, but I know she tries to fight her evil ways.

And then there is Normal. Angela and Normal are the same person, but Angry, Kind, Hero and Sad are totally different people. I just call Angela Normal 'cause when the Other Sisters appear, a lot of Angela disappears. Angela was always jealous of me, but not the way Normal is. Angela used to be more like my older sisters, Stella and Lola. But Normal is moody and withdrawn, probably 'cause she has no idea what is goin' on in her own head now that she shares her brain with the Other Sisters. She hides her new self from everyone in the family but me, just like the rest of the troubled Sisters.

I'm still scared to death of them, but I feel much better when Teddy Long is nearby. I think grown-ups would wonder why I don't tell someone about them, but Angry has made it perfectly clear: not only would she kill me, she would kill mommy, my brother, and both of my other sisters all while they were sleepin'. So I have no choice. I will never tell.

To make sure I don't, she takes the big knife out of the kitchen drawer and holds it in front of me while she tells me what I call *The Story*.

"I will kill sisters Stella and Lola first 'cause they are the weakest, and then I will kill our brother David," she hisses at me, spit hittin' my cheeks and eyes. "Mommy dies last 'cause you love her the most. Oh, and did I mention that I will tie you up and make you stand beside the bed and watch me kill all of them?

"Let's see," she adds, "I will cut our sisters' throats, since they sleep together. I will stab David in the back 'cause I don't like to look at his face. And Mommy? I'll stab her through the heart 'cause of the things she lets Daddy do to me. I want her to know her own daughter killed her. And you—I'll kill you last."

2

Patra

I've never known a month or a week or even a day when one of The Sisters livin' inside Angela hasn't tried to kill me. Angry has hit, slapped, punched, kicked me and flung me across the room by my hair. I know one day Angry will kill me 'cause she tells me so every day of my life. She makes no bones about it—she wants me dead.

When Mommy is at work, I am the maid, the cook, and whatever else Angry wants me to be. She uses me as a punchin' bag; she ties me up and locks me outside in the cold and the rain. She dares me to tell anyone anything about who she is or what she does.

This is my story—the story I was never allowed to tell.

I am six years old, and during the summer, I get up around nine o'clock and fix Normal's breakfast. I do this every morning Monday through Thursday, and on Saturday when Mommy goes to work. She works at Greco's Spaghetti House six days a week and has to catch the 8:30 bus downtown to start work by 9:30. She has retinitis pigmentosa, an incurable eye disease that gradually makes you go blind. She has never driven a car and never will. She can see well enough to get around, but eventually she will be totally blind. No one knows when that will happen and we pray every day it will be a long time before it does. It makes life hard for us 'cause we have to ride the bus everywhere we go.

On Fridays, our maid, Mamie comes, and she does all of the cookin' and cleanin' so I don't have to make Normal's breakfast that day. Today I am up in our bright yellow kitchen with big open windows tryin' not to rattle around too much and wake Normal up. I stand on a wobbly chair in front of the gas stove stirrin' a pot of grits. She likes them made with milk instead of water, and I have to stir them constantly to keep them from boilin' over. I find the longest wooden spoon in the kitchen drawer 'cause the bubblin' grits erupt like hot lava, and if I am not careful, it will pop out of the pot and make blisters on my hands. Then Mommy will know I have been cookin'.

She also likes her eggs over easy, so I have to wait until I hear her walkin' across the bare wooden floor of our bedroom before I pull the black cast iron skillet from the bottom of the oven. I pour just enough bacon grease from the blue Maxwell House coffee can Mommy keeps on the stove to keep the eggs from stickin' to the bottom of the skillet and wait for her to sit down at the kitchen table before I start fryin' the eggs.

Normal expects her coffee the minute she wakes up. I turn on the percolator at nine o'clock when I first get up 'cause it takes thirty whole minutes for the coffee to percolate. I even have a cup myself before she gets up. I like mine with lots of milk and sugar, and by lots of, I mean half a cup of milk and four heapin' teaspoons of sugar so it's nice and sweet. I also like to spoon the heavy cream off the top of the glass milk bottle into my cup, but I have to be careful and not take too much or someone will notice. Mommy would kill both of us if she knew we were drinkin' coffee, but I am very careful about cleanin' the pot and havin' it ready to turn on just before she gets home from work in the afternoon.

After my coffee, I sweep the floors and dust the furniture. In the summer heat, we leave our screened windows open to keep the mosquitoes out, and we keep the attic fan runnin' all day and all night so it stays halfway cool. We live on a busy street, and there is a fine layer of dust on the hardwood floors and all of the end tables in the morning that I gotta wipe and sweep away.

Cleanin' is supposed to be Angela's job, but Normal makes me do it every day except Friday when the maid comes. Normal takes credit for everythin' I do. Not just the cleanin', but the cookin' and the washin'. Mommy hugs her and thanks her for bein' such a big help. She tells her what a good sister she is for babysittin' me, and what a good daughter she is for cleanin' the house for her while she works. When I complain to Normal about all of the work, she tells me it's the big sister's right to boss the little sister around and make her do stuff. I guess I should be thankful that she don't hit me or punch me the way Angry does.

If I have all of the chores done by the time Normal gets up, she will let me go to Cheyenne's house to play. Cheyenne is my best friend, named after Cheyenne, Wyoming, where her daddy grew up. Accordin' to her daddy, he named her Cheyenne to have a daily reminder of home, so he would never forget growin' up on a ranch with open spaces and lots of fresh air. He wears a cowboy hat and has a belt buckle with a bull on it he won in a rodeo. He told us one day that his only mistake was fallin' in love with a southern girl, 'cause everyone knows Southern Belles never leave the South.

Cheyenne is taller than me and long and lanky like her daddy. She has short, bouncy blonde hair and sparkly brown eyes, and her smiley face always makes me happy. My mommy says she is just as beautiful on the inside as she is on the outside.

We met on the first day of school in first grade when she sat down in the desk next to me in the back of the classroom. She smiled and said hi, and we became instant friends. After that, we spent all our time together on the playground at recess, and we walked home after school holdin' hands. We were so excited when we figured out we lived just two blocks away from each other. The day after we met I asked Cheyenne why she wanted to be my friend.

"'Cause I can see in your eyes that you need me," she said. Even now, I think it's pretty wonderful that another six year old girl could see that clearly.

On that first day we stopped in front of Cheyenne's house, it was the biggest house I've ever seen up close. I counted nineteen steps up to her front yard, and then there was a sidewalk between five more steps to the two-story front porch that ran all the way across the front of the house. It's painted white with brown shutters, and it looks just like a big, old Gingerbread house.

Cheyenne says that they don't live in all of it, and that it's called a boarding house. Cheyenne, her mommy, daddy and little brother live upstairs in an apartment, and her Grand—her word for grandmother—and Grandfather live downstairs. Grand rents eight other apartments to strangers, and that is how she makes her money.

The second weekend after we met Cheyenne asks if I can spend the night at her house with her. I said yes and we're both excited, but my mommy says she will have to meet her mommy first.

I know there's gonna be a problem when Mommy and I walk up the narrow stairs to Cheyenne's apartment. Mommy says she don't want me sleepin' upstairs 'cause if the house catches on fire, they might forget I'm there and I'd burn up.

Cheyenne and I hide behind the door where we can hear them while our mommies and Grand talk. We keep our fingers crossed. Grand says she understands her concerns, and if I can spend the night she would love to have us sleep downstairs in her guest bedroom. I'd never heard of a guest bedroom before I met Cheyenne.

When I get there for my first slumber party, I see the bedroom has its own front door, so I can easily run outside if the house catches on fire. I sure hope it don't 'cause this room is so beautiful.

First I notice the wallpaper has big pink flowers with tiny green leaves and yellow polka dots. The room has high ceilings and long green, silky curtains, with a bedspread that matches them. I've never seen so many fluffy pillows on such a big, soft bed so tall you have to use a step stool to climb up to it. And there's the gentle breeze from a ceiling fan blowin' to keep us cool during the night. I look around the room and know when I grow up I want a bedroom just like this one. Hope wells up inside me 'cause it makes me determined to survive the gut wrenchin' way I am forced to live every day, and I'm so glad Cheyenne asked me to be her friend.

No one else but us uses the bathroom next to the bedroom; it's just for guests. It has bubble bath, and soap that smells like roses, and soft white fluffy towels. Grand puts out matchin' pajamas for us to sleep in, and a pair of soft slippers. She says they will keep our feet warm when we walk on the cold linoleum floors during the winter night.

After our bath, Grand makes us hot chocolate with marshmallows and lets us watch the Ed Sullivan show with Grandpa. He is the nicest grandpa in the world. I always feel like a princess when I am at Grand's house.

I never stop wantin' to be at Cheyenne's house, and today, while Normal is in a good mood, I ask if I can go play if I promise to be back before Mommy gets home from work. She says I better be home before "American Bandstand" starts. I promise her I will.

When I get to Cheyenne's, she's waitin' for me on the front porch. She tells me our favorite apartment is empty, so we can play in it. But when we get there the door is locked, and we have to walk around and find one that is open. Most of the apartments are furnished with everythin' anyone could possibly need. Grand boasts that they're "move-in ready."

We find a door that is open and go inside. We love to pretend it's our apartment and we're all grown up. This one is an efficiency on the back of the house. Grand calls it that 'cause the living room, bedroom and kitchen are all in one room. It's not my favorite 'cause it don't have a TV to watch soap operas on, and it has a brown sofa and chair and looks like an old man would live here. No frills, Grand would say. But we are happy just being together. We take our baby dolls and all of the doll clothes Mommy made for me, and we play all day long.

I have always felt safe here at Cheyenne's house. Until today.

Today I play too long and forget about the time, and Angry, not Normal, had to come lookin' for me. She is red-faced and screechin' like an owl, and I know I'm in big trouble. Grand told her we were playin' in one of the apartments, but she had no idea which one. She says there are several that are vacant right now, and Angela would just have to walk around to find us.

I know when she walks in it is Angry and not Normal lookin' for me.

When Angry finds us, she is livid, and in her loud voice says she's been lookin' for me for over an hour. I can tell by her screwed up face she is furious. Cheyenne sees her face, too, and knows it's time for her to leave. I'm in a lot of trouble. That's when Angry screams, *"Get in the oven."*

3

The Siblings

*B*esides Angela, I have three other siblings. I love my
sisters, Lola and Stella, but I have always been crazy
about David, my oldest sibling. I recall how when I was a little
girl I told everyone who would listen to me that he was the
smartest, most handsome boy in the world, tall with beautiful
blue eyes and black hair. I always felt we had a special bond.

I've often heard that if just one person in your early life
represents love and sanity, you have a much better chance
of overcoming abuse. Fortunately, I had more than one, but
David was a big part of my life. He'd let me sleep with him
when I was scared, and without complaining, he'd carry me
ten blocks from the movie theatre when I was too tired to walk
home. He also let me sit in his lap when no one else wanted to
be bothered. I felt safe with him.

After my father disappeared, David became "the man of
the house." My mom, my sisters and I were all so grateful to
have him in that role. He worked with my mom at Aunt Lena's
restaurant, Greco's Spaghetti House, and he helped keep us
afloat even after he joined the military.

When David joined the Air National Guard, and though I
didn't cry every day the way I told everyone I would, I sure
missed him. My middle sister, Lola, felt the same way about
David. When he came home on leave, she tried to monopolize
his time, and she pretty much succeeded. He was so kind,
he'd take her wherever she asked him to go—to dances on

the roof of the Heidelberg Hotel or to the movies. I'm a little embarrassed to admit this, but I was jealous of Lola, at least when it came to David.

For as long as I can remember, Lola wanted to be a nurse, and I knew she was stubborn enough to get what she wanted. Even when we were kids she volunteered as a candy-striper at the Baptist Hospital and looked so happy in her red-and-white-striped uniform. She'd come home and tell me about all the blood and other cases she worked on that day, but Normal claimed all she did was empty bed pans. That cynicism was rampant in our household; no one ever got to be herself or himself without a chorus of critics, though I suppose that's true in every family.

When I was young, before The Sisters appeared, I thought I had the best family in the world. I had a devoted father who was the best chef in the finest restaurant in Jackson, Mississippi. And I had a loving mother who spent her days taking care of me and my siblings. My brother David and sister Stella adored me, and although Lola and Angela paid a little less attention to me, it was obvious they loved me, too.

* * * * *

Stella, the next to the oldest, was always sweet and pretty, and accordin' to everyone who met her, had a heart of gold. I can't recall her ever sayin' anything bad about anyone. When our mother had to go to work, which back then was considered unusual, Stella acted like a second mommy to me. But when she began spendin' more time with her boyfriend, James, everythin' felt off. By then, Daddy was gone. David had left for the Air National Guard. And when Stella married and moved to Chicago, it left me with way too much time alone with Angela.

Angela is five-and-a-half years older than me, and she and Stella were best friends. It always puzzled me why Stella liked her so much, but then I don't think she knew the same Angela I did. They spent hours together in Stella and Lola's bedroom with the door closed, laughin' and talkin'. Stella took Angela everywhere with her, always leavin' me at home. The only place she didn't take her was on dates with James, which stirred up all kinds of hate in Angela. I found pictures she'd drawn of James with horns on his head and a forked tail on his butt. And I saw where she had stuck pins in his heart hopin' he would die a slow, horrible death.

At first it really confused me 'cause when James came to the house, Angela would be so sweet to him. Of course later, nothing she did surprised me.

Angela was always jealous of me and picked on me constantly. Mom would dismiss it, tellin' me it was not unusual for an older sister to pick on her little sister, but she didn't realize that the *pickin' on* had turned into much more.

I was five years old when I started seein' the other person inside Angela's head. At first she stopped talkin' to me, and most of the time she acted like I wasn't there. When my Mom explained she'd have to babysit me while she worked, Angela acted happy. I thought maybe we could be friends again. Angela wasn't lookin' for a friend, though. No, she wanted a servant, and my life went downhill from there.

It started with tiny flares of anger in her eyes when I did something wrong. Then the kickin' and punchin' began.

At first, she didn't hit me or punch me too hard. But I was scared that at any time she could change and really hurt me. If I asked her why she was bein' so mean, she looked at me as though I were crazy. Like it was my fault. Sometimes I wondered if she even remembered hittin' me. Other times I felt her hatred as sure as a hot red poker.

Like that time I was sound asleep when I heard a thud, then something heavy landin' on me. When I opened my eyes, I saw my wide-eyed crazy sister sittin' on my chest, pinnin' me down with her knees.

I asked her what she was doin', but she just beat me with a hairbrush, laughin' as I cried and whackin' me even harder. Then she jumped up and raced out of my room.

I look back at those times when I was alone in the house with Angela, and I see how terribly frightened I was. After one of those beatings, I'd sneak around to find her, and more often than not, she'd just be sittin' alone in a room, starin' at the wall as though nothing had happened. Calm and uncarin'. From that day she beat me with the hairbrush, I called this sister Normal.

4

Daddy

The small fan by my bed blows directly on me in the dark room. My hair moves in the breeze, but I'm still hot. I sleep in just my panties 'cause of the stiflin' heat, and my skin is damp from sweatin'. I try to keep my long hair pulled up and over the pillow to keep it dry, but it's wet and sticks to my face. It's July in Mississippi, and the summer nights are miserable.

All of a sudden I'm wide awake and my body freezes.

I think the monsters lurkin' under the bed have come out and are touchin' me. I lay still and hope it's a dream and that I will wake up. Or, the monsters will go away.

I feel something tuggin' at the legs of my panties and I can't breathe. I wonder why the monsters are touchin' me there. For some reason I smell my daddy's spicy cologne and the alcohol on his breath. My mind screams, "Why would daddy be touchin' my panties?"

I squirm and he knows I'm awake. He whispers into my ear, "It's okay. You are my favorite little girl and I love you so much." He strokes my hair.

I ask myself what he is doin' in my room. I squeeze my eyes shut and stay silent.

"I just want to make you happy," he says, but I don't feel happy. I feel sick and I think I am gonna throw up. I open my eyes and turn my head to look at him, but his eyes are closed.

I hear someone cough in the room. I look up and see Normal standin' at the foot of my bed. Daddy turns around and stares at her, and she slowly shakes her head no. Then she disappears into the darkness, like a ghost who appears in the dark and then vanishes.

Daddy tries to get up off of his knees, but he loses his balance and falls face first onto the floor, where he stays for a minute or two. Then he gets up and stumbles out of my room. But before he goes, he whispers, "Don't tell anyone; this is our little secret. OK?"

I try to speak, but nothing comes out. I'm so stiff I can't move my arms or legs. I can feel my heart slammin' against my chest, but I can't breathe. I feel like I might suffocate.

David's room is closest to mine, and when I can finally move, I sneak inside and climb in bed with him. I tell him about the monsters in my room, and that's why I need to sleep with him.

"Okay, you can sleep with me," he says, "but be still, and go to sleep."

My mind is racin' in a thousand different directions. His room is hot like an oven, but I shiver, or maybe it's my skin crawlin'. I can't tell. I snuggle as close to him as possible, hopin' to calm down, but it doesn't work. I wish I could tell David the truth about the monsters. I shake so hard my teeth chatter just thinkin' about it. I stay awake a long time.

I try to convince myself Daddy didn't come to my room, that it was all a bad dream. I want to blame my terror on monsters under the bed. But in the end I know it happened. I can still smell the icky, spicy cologne on my body.

I give up tryin' to sleep and ease out of David's bed. Back in my room, I look for a clean pair of panties, hopin' to get away from the smell of Daddy's cologne and his stinkin' beer breath. I go into the bathroom down the hall, but I don't turn on the light. I'm afraid someone will catch me and then figure out what Daddy tried to do.

The light from the full moon is shinin' through the open window, givin' me enough light to find what I need. A tiny breeze blows through the window and the curtain moves slightly above my head. I stand there feelin' the coolness of the midnight air on my face. For a minute everythin' seems okay, but it's not. My daddy is the monster under my bed.

I run a wash-rag under the hot water in the sink and rub soap on it. I want to wring it out, but my hands are too small. When I try to wash myself the water drips down my legs and puddles on the floor around my feet. I scrub and scrub to get the cologne off my body, but it doesn't work; the nasty smell still clings to me and I finally give up.

Earlier in my bed I was so hot, but now there are goose bumps on my wet skin runnin' from my arms all the way down around my legs to my ankles. I dry myself off with the towel I find hangin' over the bath tub. Then I cover my body with the jar of cream Mommy uses on her face at night. It's Pond's Cold Cream, and it smells like cherries. I almost smile. Almost.

I am so confused about what happened. I don't understand if it is right or wrong. I know if something feels this bad it can't be right, but why would Daddy do something so wrong. I sit alone in the bathroom on the floor beside the commode with my arms wrapped around my knees and cry my eyes out.

The next morning, Mommy comes into the bathroom and finds me under the sink curled up in a ball. I wrapped myself up in a towel and used my arms as a pillow. At some point I had found a dry towel and hid in the safest place I could find.

She asks me what I was doin' asleep on the floor in the bathroom. I just look at her and say, "I don't remember."

She picks me up, carries me to my bed and covers me up with my sheet. I roll over and wish I could make it all be a nightmare I dreamt up.

After that first night, I can tell Daddy is watchin' me, hopin' to catch me alone. I can see it in his eyes and it makes my skin crawl. When he stares at me, he looks like he has just stolen a candy bar from the Tote-Sum-Store. I refuse to go to bed alone. I plead with everyone to let me sleep with them. Except for Mommy, 'cause that's where Daddy is. I tell David and my sisters about monsters under my bed, or I tell them I'll die if I have to sleep in my room alone in my tiny bed by the door. Finally, after all my beggin', one of them says yes, but just for tonight.

I never sit in Daddy's lap anymore; there are no more hugs and kisses. I don't leave the house with him alone for any reason, and I never look into his eyes after that night.

I have always been Daddy's little girl. I wanted to go everywhere he did, and most of the time I did. I thought he was the most wonderful man in the world, a man who could do almost anything. I thought he hung the moon in the sky. He was kind and gentle; he was more fun than a barrel of monkeys. Now I spend my days tryin' to stay far away from Daddy and Normal.

Daddy worked part-time at the cafe down the street from the house when he wasn't cookin' at the Rotisserie Restaurant. He spent most days sittin' on a bar stool in a small bar next to the cafe drinkin' beer with the rest of the alcoholics in the neighborhood. Sometimes, when I still thought he was such a special daddy, he'd take me with him. And sometimes, he'd stand me up on the bar and call out, "Look at my beautiful, little daughter."

Everyone in the bar clapped and whistled, and I'd smile and curtsey like a good little girl. Daddy ordered a Coke and candy for me. He would make sure the bartender put cherry juice and a cherry in my Coke, and refill my glass every time it got empty.

I felt very special, and I loved Daddy so much. Sometimes, we sat in the bar all afternoon. He'd let me play music on the jukebox. Patsy Cline was his favorite, and he'd play her songs over and over until someone would complain. Then we'd get up and leave.

On the way home he'd stumble down the sidewalk holdin' my hand to keep from fallin' down. Once we were in the house, he'd crawl into his bed and immediately fall asleep. Then I'd take his shoes off and cover him up with a blanket before I'd sneak out of the room and shut the door.

A few weeks after his first visit to my room, I was takin' a nap and

Daddy came into the room and said he was goin' to take a nap with me. I tried to get up, but he grabbed me by the arm and wouldn't let me. I could tell he was drunk, so I started to cry. Then Normal came in. She showed no emotion whatsoever on her face, and without a word, she took his hand and led him out of the room.

I sit there on the bed, tremblin'. There is a knot in my throat not allowin' me to swallow. Too scared to get up, I realize she knows the truth, but what if she tells Mommy? How much trouble will I be in? Will Mommy hate me? Or is this my fault?

After a very long time, I force myself to get up and leave the bedroom. I slowly walk down the hall and into the living room. Normal is on the couch watchin' TV. I ask her where Daddy is. Without lookin' away from the TV, she says, "Gone."

Normal sits in front of the TV all afternoon without sayin' a word to me. I ask her if she wants anything to eat but she doesn't answer. I find a box of graham crackers in the pantry, and after closin' the door I sit on the floor and eat the whole box.

Normal never said anything to me about what she saw or what happened when she and Daddy left the room. But after that day, Daddy never came near me again. I don't know how or why she stopped him, but she did.

The way Normal felt about me changed that day. She never looked at me or wanted to talk to me anymore. No more help with my homework, and she never read books to me like she used to. She took care of me when she had to, but she didn't act like my older sister. She never hugged me or held my hand when we crossed the street. I knew for sure she didn't love me anymore. I know from the way she acted she didn't remember exactly what happened with Daddy 'cause one of the others inside her switched with her. Still, I could tell she was confused and in pain. I didn't understand why.

Normal started actin' like a stranger around everyone else, too. Speakin' only when someone spoke to her. Because she didn't smile, she looked sad most of the time. When she sat alone in our room starin' into space for hours I knew she was confused by what was happening to her. Her dark blue eyes once looked like sparkly *Safire*, but her eyes were hollow now. When I tried to talk to her, they often filled with tears. Her skin no longer had a rosy glow that other people noticed and even commented on. My big sister was gone, and I could only guess who had replaced her. It made me sad.

Mommy would say to Angela: "Would you please go comb your hair," or, "Would you please go take a bath? You don't look like you've had one for days." Normal would ignore her or walk away. She started dressin' funny, too. Before, she wore short shorts and spaghetti strapped tops, but then she started wearin' David's shirts—ones that were way too big for her—and Lola's pants which she had to roll up at the waist. Angela also started rollin' her shirtsleeves down just enough to cover the cut marks on her wrists. Mommy said she was going through a phase. I knew it was not a phase. My sister was like broken glass, all shattered inside. And she was tryin' to disappear by buryin' herself in the big clothes.

Back then, I didn't realize that the person who shook her head at Daddy that night in my bedroom wasn't Normal but a completely new person who was quiet and rarely spoke. She'd glide in and take over and always had a determined look on her face. She was my savior, like in the Bible. She protected me from Daddy and tried to protect me from anyone else who hurt me. But she had no control over Angry. I call her Hero.

5

Mamie

Mamie, our maid, comes every Friday at eight o'clock sharp. She is short and as big as Santa Claus with a round face and a big smile. Today I ask her, "Mamie, why do you smile so much?" and she said, "'Cause the Lawd loves me, and he loves you, too." I don't tell her this, but I'm not sure the Lord even knows I'm alive. I pray to him all the time, but he doesn't listen. If he did exist, would he really let me be tortured every day of my life without helpin'? I don't think so.

Mamie wears a bandanna with bright-colored flowers on it around her head. She makes them out of flour sacks she collects from the white people she works for. She adds the cutest little bow on the front, right at the top of her forehead, and ties a knot at the back of her head. Everyone who sees her wearin' it wants one, and she makes and sells them in the colored quarters for twenty-five cents apiece. (That's what Mommy calls where Mamie lives—the colored quarters, which are just across the railroad tracks.) If you want a special one, you can give her buttons and bows, and she will sew them on for you for no extra charge.

I ask Mommy if I can get a bandanna, too, but she laughs. "Patra, white people don't wear bandannas."

So I ask Mamie if she would make me one for my doll. She says, "Chile, I will make yo sweet lit'l self as many as you wont." I just love that woman.

The next Friday Mamie brings me matchin' bandannas for me and my baby doll. Our bandannas are red, white and blue, just like the Fourth of July. She put lace all around the edges and a star on the front instead of a bow.

When she gives me mine she says, "Dahlin', I makes this one specially for you, even if yo mamma ain't gonna let you wear it."

I tell her I have all day, all summer long to wear it when Mommy is at work. She looks a little worried. "Chile, don't go gettin' me fired over no bandanna."

Mamie doesn't have a sewin' machine at home, so Mommy lets her use our sewin' machine to make her bandannas for a few hours after she finishes the cleanin', and cookin' supper. Mommy knows how much Mamie loves sewin'. It makes me happy that Mamie stays late on Friday 'cause she will be here until Mommy gets home from work.

Mommy found out Mamie could sew when she asked her if she could hem some pants for her. Mamie told her, "Ma'am, I can sew the britches off a sewin' machine."

So now Mamie checks our clothes before she washes them to be sure they don't need fixin'. She hems our dresses and pants, too. Mommy says it's a good trade. "I don't have time to sew anymore, and I can barely see the needle anyway," she tells me, "and Mamie can make some extra money making and selling her bandannas."

Mamie lives across the railroad tracks in the colored quarters where all the colored people in Jackson live together away from the white people. I ask Mommy why they have to live in a place that is fallin' down.

"They live on their side of the tracks, and we live on ours, Patra."

I don't think that is a very good answer, so the next Friday I ask Mamie, and she says, "Crimination, little girl," and shakes her head side to side. I see a tear roll down her dark round cheek and I feel sad for her.

All the colored people I know work for white people. Well, I don't really know that many colored people, but the ones I do know are nice to me. That's more than I can say for most white people.

My grandmother's maid is colored, Miss Hattie, but she is more like family than hired help. Willie works at my grandmother's restaurant, The Hamburger House, and has been workin' there since he was eleven years old. He started out cleanin' tables and washin' dishes. His mother has twelve children, that's almost double what I have in my family, and she takes in washin' to support them. She won't let Willie drop out of school to help support the family, but she will let him work after school as long as he has finished his homework and keeps his grades up. Willie's daddy died in a tractor accident a few years ago, and now Willie is the man of the house just like David. I think Grandmother feels like he is family, too.

This morning Mamie came in singin' her church songs and smilin' like a Cheshire cat. "The Lawd be wif us all de time," she tells us, "and we haf to praise his name every day."

I love listenin' to her sing, but The Sisters hate it. Mamie knows how they feel about her singin', but it don't stop her. She looks at them and says, "The Lawd works in sterious ways." But if she thinks Angry cares anything about the Lord, she is sadly mistaken.

I hear someone get up and slam the bedroom door. Mamie just smiles and goes into the kitchen. She asks me, "Dahlin', what yo wont for breakfus?" "Pancakes."

Mamie makes the best pancakes in the world; she puts in a little cornmeal, her secret ingredient. She tells me every time. Next, she adds eggs, buttermilk, sugar, and vanilla extract. I think the vanilla extract is a secret ingredient, too, 'cause vanilla makes everythin' taste better.

As she flips the last pancake, she says to me, "Go wake yo sista up to see if she wont to eat breakfus."

That puts a chill down my spine. "I ain't wakin' her up," I tell Mamie. "She'll kill me!"

So Mamie walks to the bedroom door and walks in. I think, what is she thinkin'? Then I hear something hit the door, and Angry screams, "Get your ass out of my room, nigger."

Mamie walks back into the kitchen shakin' her head. "I guess dat one ain't nobody to mess wif in the morning. I feels like the debil done run up inside dat girl with so much hate, he don't see daylight."

Angry doesn't care if Mamie sees her or knows about her craziness. No matter what she does, she knows Mamie don't have the right to talk bad about white people. Sad comes out when Mamie is here, too, but I think she just likes it when Mamie gives her a big hug and calls her a pretty little girl. Sad never lets anyone touch her but Mamie. I guess her Godliness shines through and makes Sad feel safe.

Mamie tells me she knows all about "dem other peoples, what live in Angela." And she says she prays for her every day. "I thinks the demons so deep inside her, they eatin' her alive."

After I am full of the best pancakes, bacon, fried eggs and sliced watermelon in the world, I'm ready to help Mamie clean the house. But Mamie says, "Go on and git, Pitty Pat," her pet name for me. "Go play with yo friends. I reckon I can clean dis house all by myself."

So I go. Besides, Mamie has a ritual. She washes the clothes first, and then she changes all of the beds except Normal's, 'cause Normal is still in it. She sweeps, mops, and cleans the bathrooms and dusts the whole house, all by noon. It drives me crazy that she cleans the kitchen last, but she says, "I will have to clean it agin after lunch so why be wastin' the time doin' it twice?"

I guess it makes sense to her, but I hate a messy kitchen. I can't stand dirty dishes sittin' in the sink.

Mamie cleans the house for a dollar a day, and she gets five cents apiece for ironin' clothes. My Mommy even likes the sheets and pillowcases ironed. Mamie charges ten cents for the sheets but five cents for two pillowcases. I don't understand why Mommy wants the sheets and pillowcases ironed 'cause no one sees them once they are on the bed under the bedspread, but Mamie says, "If dat what the Missis wont, then dat what the Missis gits."

Mommy told me her mother didn't have an electric iron and she still ironed her sheets every week. "My mother would put the iron on the eye of the wood burning stove to get it hot, then she'd iron a little bit and put it back on the stove eye again." She said sometimes it took her all day to do the sheets, but she didn't care how long it took. "There is nothing like getting into bed with clean, crisp, fresh-smelling sheets," her mommy always said.

Well, I can promise you one thing: I will never iron sheets in my house when I grow up. I will cover them up with the bedspread and be done with it.

I know Mamie will be cleanin' nonstop until noon, and Normal won't get out of bed until I wake her up for lunch. That means I have about two hours to sneak off and play with Mamie's daughter, Mayze. I met Mayze one day when Mamie brought her to my house with her 'cause she was sick and couldn't go to school. She told Mommy that Mayze ain't contagious; she just had a headache and needed to rest that day. Mommy said it was okay because I was leaving for school soon anyway.

At first it was kinda strange being around her 'cause neither one of us had ever been that close to a child of a different color before. We just stared at each other, and all I wanted to do was touch her hair. We don't know what to say. Before I left for school we were friends. She told me where she lived in the quarters, and I promised her I would come play with her one day.

Mayze has two brothers, but Mamie will not let them miss school for anything. She says, "Dat school ain't much, but least dey learn to read an write. And dat's moren I ever got."

Today, as I run across the backyard as fast as I can, I know Mommy will tan my hide if I get caught goin' to the colored quarters. But I figure what's a butt beating compared to the beatings I get from Angry every day? I'll have two hours of freedom playin' with Mayze.

I jump over the ditch and run across ten or twelve tracks toward the colored quarters. Mayze lives on the far side of the quarters, so I have to pass rows and rows of shotgun shacks before I find the right one. They all look alike, but I remember Mayze tellin' me she lived on the corner of 3rd and Bloom. And that her house had a red swing on the front porch and a broken down car sittin' up on cinder blocks in the front yard. I guess Mamie tried to dress the yard up 'cause there are flowers flowin' out of homemade wooden planters in the windows of the car. There are tires everywhere that have been painted bright colors. They have been sliced and reversed so they look like alligator teeth, and they are filled with tall sunflowers and tomato plants. There are at least a dozen of them spread out all over the front yard.

I walk up toward the shack, but there is no door for me to knock on. I wonder how in the world they keep the mosquitos out at night, or during the day for that matter. Peepin' inside the open doorway, I see a man sleepin' on the couch in nothing but his tighty-whitey underwear.

I back off of the porch real slow, careful not to make any noise gettin' off of the porch. I don't think that's Mayze's daddy, 'cause I remember hearin' Mayze tell me that "Mamma ran Daddy's sorry ass off a long time ago 'cause all he did was get drunk, spend her money, and get her heavy with child."

Mamie is a very religious woman and she would wash Mayze's mouth out with soap if she heard her talkin' like that. I know 'cause I hear Mamie say this every time Normal cusses: "I wants to wash dem dirty words right outta your mouth. De Lawd be watchin' you, girl."

Normal just laughs and says, "Shut up, stupid nigger; you can't tell me what to do."

Angry calls all colored people niggers, and she calls the little ones nigglets. Mommy tells her to call them Negros, but I'm a good speller and I know they are both wrong. The women are Negras and the men are Negros. But when I tell Normal that, she just looks at me and says, "Shut up, dumbass. I will call them whatever suits my fancy. No one can stop me."

When I get to the back of the house, I see Mayze there chasin' a calico kitten up the tree and remember Cheyenne tellin' me all calico cats are girls. I call out Mayze's name and she turns around with a big grin on her face. Her dark eyes get as round as saucers when she sees me. She has two-dozen pigtails with at least that many different-colored rags at the end of each one. Her two front teeth are missin' and the gap is as wide as Capitol Street.

She runs toward me and hugs me and says, "What yo doin' hea?"

I tell her her mommy is at my house so I know I won't get caught, and she better not tell.

"I ain't tellin' nobody nothing," she says, "and we best stay out back so we don't get caught."

She is happy to see me 'cause she doesn't have any sisters to play with her. I tell her she is lucky she has only brothers. I know her brothers think the world of her and would never hurt her the way Angry hurts me.

When we get to the backyard, Leroy, Mayze's oldest brother, is up in the tree building a treehouse out of a pile of scrap wood. He looks down and sees me and almost falls out of the tree. "White girl, what you doin' round hea? You know yo mamma beat you within a inch yo life she catches yo hea."

"That's why I'm not gettin' caught," I said. "I will be back home before anyone misses me, or I sure hope I am."

Leroy is twelve years old. It's his job during the summer to take care of Lonnie and Mayze while Mamie works. Lonnie is ten, and he's perched on top of an old refrigerator next to the vegetable garden, watchin' Leroy build the treehouse.

Next to the garden sits a fresh-picked basket full of turnip greens, squash, okra, and tomatoes. The tomatoes are big, round, and juicy lookin', and

I'm sure they are much better than the ones you buy at the Jitney Jungle where Mommy shops. A peach tree full of green peaches shades the back of the yard, with a tree full of almost-ripe plums right next to it. There's no grass to mow in the whole backyard, just dirt and a few patches of dead weeds here and there.

Lonnie jumps down off of the refrigerator and chases the chickens roamin' around the yard.

"I didn't know you could have chickens inside the city limits," I said.

Mayze gives me a look and says, "Girl, colored town don't got no limits. We don't got no cops round here."

"Who keeps the peace?" I asked.

"We ain't got no peace, either."

I shake my head and think to myself that colored town and Jackson are as different as night and day.

In the way back of the yard is an outhouse, where Mayze says they do their "bizness." I already know about that 'cause my grandmother lives in the country and people there have outhouses, too. Mayze's outhouse has a moon carved in the wood and bold letters that says, "THE PIT." My grandmother says you can tell you are in the country when your toilet paper has page numbers on it from the Sears & Roebuck catalog.

In the other corner of the yard there is a wooden pen with two big dogs in it and a litter of the cutest puppies I've ever seen. I ask Mayze if we can play with them, and she says no, they have the *mange*. I don't know what that is but it sounds really bad, so I don't go near that part of the backyard.

Instead, I walk over to the back porch to pet a big white cat sittin' on the steps, but before I do I ask Mayze if it has the mange.

She laughs and says, "Patra, cats don't get the mange." I don't know if people get the mange, but I am goin' to steer clear of all the animals around here.

There's no back door on the house, but there is a screen door. You can see all the way from the back of the house out the front door. I see makeshift beds lined up, down the hall to the end from the front door to the back door. I ask Mayze why their beds are in the hallway instead of in bedrooms.

"So at night we can catch a breeze runnin' through the house, so we don't roast our ass off," she says, as though I'm stupid. I guess there are no ceiling fans in colored town either.

Leroy comes down from the tree, lookin' tall and skinny as a telephone pole. His hair sticks out like a Brillo pad and his teeth stick out like big, crooked white kernels of corn. But he has kind eyes. He walks up to me and says, "Little un, it time you go on home 'fore you get in a heap of trouble. I gone walk you back to de tracks now."

Mayze jumps up and says, "I wont to go, too!"

Leroy shakes his head. "Mamma whup my ass I let you walk to de tracks, little gal." Then he turns to me and says, "Gal, let's go."

On the way back to the tracks I think that for church-goin' Christians they sure do swear a lot.

6

The Debil

When I get back home, Mamie has lunch ready—egg salad sandwiches and tea cakes for dessert. There is a big pitcher of just-made iced sweet tea on the table next to fresh lemon slices on a plate. I am really thirsty. I didn't know if Mayze had runnin' water at her house, so I was afraid to ask for a cup of water. I climb up to the table and pour myself a glass of iced tea without lemon, 'cause I don't like lemon in my tea.

Mamie has put the egg salad sandwiches on a plate and put a saucer of sweet baby jerkin pickles next to it. A large bowl of fried potato slices sprinkled with dried parsley and the warm homemade sugar-coated tea cakes are piled high on a platter all in the middle of the table. It's like we're havin' a Sunday feast. Mamie makes every meal look special, 'cause she says, "The Lawd done provided dis for us, like he always do." But I know the Lord didn't prepare this food in my mommy's kitchen, Mamie did.

Mamie puts her sandwich and potato slices on her special plate that she keeps in a cupboard. She keeps her plate, fork, and a glass in a place separate from ours 'cause she ain't allowed to eat off our dishes. I don't understand why she has to eat off of special dishes since she touches everythin' we eat when she fixes it. It don't make sense to me. She loads up her plate and heads to the back porch to eat by herself. I beg her to eat with me, but she says, "It ain't proper for me to eat at the table with white folk."

I am sittin' there eatin' my lunch when Angry walks into the dining room. She looks at the table and screams out to Mamie, "You idiot, I don't eat boiled eggs." All I can think is that Angry hates the smell of boiled eggs. She won't even let me crack them when she's in the house.

Mamie shuffles into the dining room from the back porch, but doesn't look at Angry's face. She mumbles, "Miss Angela, you love my egg salad." But Mamie has no idea she's talkin' to Angry. She probably thought she was talkin' to Normal.

Angry walks over to Mamie and looks her right in the eyes. She has her mean face on, and I can tell Mamie doesn't know what to do. Angry puts her finger in her face and says, "You big, fat dumbass. Get in the kitchen and fix me some lunch."

I stand up from my chair at the end of the table and tell her not to be so nasty to Mamie. Angry turns around, walks up to me, hits me upside the head with her fist, and I fly backwards over the chair. I fall to the floor on my back.

Then Angry goes to the kitchen, grabs a kitchen knife off of the counter and comes toward me. She looks at me on the floor and screams, "I told you to never talk back to me!"

I look up at her stunned. The fall knocked the breath out of me and I can't breathe.

I hear Mamie runnin' up behind Angry. She stops just before she gets to us, cryin', "Please don't stab dat baby."

Angry turns to Mamie. "Stay out of this; it's none of your damn business."

Angry turns back around and looks at me with fire in her eyes. She throws the knife, but she misses me and it sticks in the floor beside my head.

Mamie screams, "The debil done come out dis chile. Lawd, what I gona do? If I touch dis chile, I be hangin' by morning."

"Stupid bitch," Angry says, "get out of my house."

Mamie cries even harder now. She looks at Angry and says, "I can't watch you kill dis baby! Lawd, what I gona do, what I gona do?"

Angry turns and kicks at Mamie. She misses her and kicks the table. "Shit," she yells, and jumps on top of me. She starts beatin' me in the face and chokin' me.

Mamie squeals, "Help me, Lawd, for what I do. I can't put my hands on a white chile. God help me."

As she walks over to us, a determined look on her face, I think to myself this is the hardest thing she will ever do.

Mamie pulls Angry off of me and pushes her across the room against the wall. Thank God Mamie is a big woman and outweighs her by at least a hundred pounds. Angry is so mad her face is red and distorted, and she is cussin' a blue streak. I look at Mamie. Her face looks like she is strugglin' with God Almighty himself, tryin' to convince him that what she is about to do is the right thing. She holds Angry against the wall and pushes her large body against her so she can't move. Angry is screamin' and threatenin' to kill both of us if she don't let go of her.

Mamie looks at me and says, "Run baby girl, run next door and call yo mamma. Yo sister done gone crazy."

I tell her I can call from here, but she says, "NO! Go next door. I don't know how long I kin hold her here like dis."

I run next door to my neighbor's house and beat hard on the door. When Mr. Robertson answers, I tell him we need help, that my sister has gone crazy. We run across the back yard, up the back steps and into the house. It seems awfully quiet inside and I am afraid someone is goin' to be dead when we get back to the kitchen.

We run across the hall into the dining room. Mamie is sittin' in a chair leanin' over with her hands on her knees, exhausted with sweat runnin' down her round face. She is pantin' like she needs air. I am afraid she is havin' a heart attack. I run into the kitchen to get her a glass of water. She takes the water and drinks the glass before I realize I gave her one of our glasses, but I don't care. I wet a dish-rag and put it on her forehead, and she smiles a weak smile. I wonder if I will have to throw the rag away since it touched her face.

I panic and look around for the knife Angry threw at me a few minutes earlier, but it is no longer stickin' out of the dining room floor. The chair is upright and our lunch is still perfect on the table just like we left it. I am flabbergasted that so much turmoil could have happened in this room just minutes before, and now nothing is out of place.

Normal is sittin' on the floor with her legs crossed, cryin' silently. I look at Mamie, and she just looks me in the eye and shakes her head slowly back and forth when Mr. Robertson wasn't lookin'. Then Mamie looks at Mr. Robertson and says, "Everythin' is all right, Mr. Robertson. Angela is OK. She must have had a brain shake."

He looks at me and asks me if she has seizures, and I nod my head yes. A big necessary lie to protect Mamie, 'cause I don't even know what a seizure is.

Mr. Robertson and I help Normal get up off of the floor and into the bedroom. We put her into bed and she closes her eyes like she is asleep. I cover her up with her blanket, and we walk out of the room and close the door. I tell him I will let her sleep for a while.

When I take him to the front door, he asks if this has happened before when we are alone.

I said no.

He asks if he should call a doctor, and I tell him no again. I tell him if she isn't any better when she wakes up, I will call Mommy. I tell him Mamie will be there with us until she gets home from work, and then I thank him for helpin' us.

He nods and tells me if I need him, he will be next door.

I can tell that he don't want to leave us, and I am sure he is goin' to ask Mommy about it later when she gets home. I'm already dreadin' I will have to tell her something; I just don't know what kinda story I will make up. I will probably just lie and say she fell backwards on the chair.

Mommy is always tellin' her if she doesn't stop leaning back in the chair she is going to tip over and break her crown.

If Mamie hurt Angry in any way we both know she will not live through the night. Colored people are not allowed to put their hands on white people for any reason. They'll be dead before the cops show up, if they bother to show up at all.

I can tell by the look on her face that all Mamie wants to do is get back across the tracks where she might be safe. She knows if Normal tells Mommy that Mamie pushed her, even if it was to protect me, she would be in real trouble.

I walk over to her sittin' at the dining room table and I put my arms around her. I ask her how she feels. She is breathin' normally, and she wipes all of the sweat off her face with her starched-white apron. She looks at me with her big, round brown eyes and says, "I be alright."

But I think she's lyin'. I know she isn't sure if that is true or not.

I sit down beside her and tell her I need to tell her something. I begin by sayin' she doesn't have to worry about Normal tellin' Mommy about what happened.

She looks at me real confused and asks, "Why not?"

I know I have to tell her about The Sisters, but I don't know where to start. I have never told anyone about Angry before. I know Mamie has seen the changes Normal makes, but she probably assumes she's possessed by the devil, not possessed by other people. Or she just thinks she has a really bad temper.

I tell her Normal used to be a good sister, but deep inside her lives a person I call Angry. I try to explain to her that Normal doesn't know about Angry, but Angry knows about Normal. I tell her Normal can't tell Mommy what happened 'cause she doesn't know, and that Angry can't tell 'cause no one knows about her but me.

Mamie stares at me and says, "I knew the debil lived in this house, and I'm so sorry you have to live wid it. I'll stay till yo mama get home, but den I get back cross dem tracks as fast as I can go."

Hero switched with Angry that day and saved Mamie's life. I was so glad to see my guardian angel was there to protect Mamie and me.

At first I thought it was Normal, but the way she looked at me was just too kind, too gentle. It was almost like Hero could feel my pain and she wanted to take it all away. She didn't say anything to either of us; she just looked at me with such determined eyes. I felt safe by her just bein' there. It took me by surprise to see this other person standin' there beside me when I needed her the most. She saved me from Daddy, and now she saved both of us from Angry.

As soon as Mommy gets home, Mamie stands up and gives me a big hug. "God be wid you, chile." She picks up her purse and walks out the door.

I'm sad 'cause I don't think I will ever see her again.

7

The Paramount

A *day at the movies was different when I was child than it is today. First, I'd say the biggest difference is that we take kids to the movies these days, rather than sending small children off for an afternoon of a double-feature, cartoons, or maybe even a newsreel. As kids, the movie theatre was a relatively safe place to be. In fact, the movie theatre was the one place I felt any sense of security most of the time—until I found my way to a therapist office when I was in my twenties. There, I felt secure and in a safe place where I could finally release the anxiety and tension I'd carried all my young life.*

Angela and I would walk the fifteen blocks down Gallatin Street to Capitol Street to the Paramount Theatre. Our 25 cents each would buy us a Coke, one bag of popcorn and two Hershey bars. Then we were set for most of the day. Sometimes we would stay and watch both movies twice before making the long walk back home just before dark.

We went to the movies, no matter what was playing at the Paramount. It could be a western or my favorite, a Doris Day movie. Doris always lived in a pretty house and she smiled at her kids a lot. Even when they misbehaved it turned out okay. In Doris Day movies the children aren't afraid of Mommy or Daddy.

Although I often still had to deal with Angry, Sad, Normal, and all the rest, at least in the movie theatre I was safe from my father. That was true even after my parents separated and my father moved away. He had visitation rights, though, so we still saw him, whether we wanted to or not. The emotional rollercoaster of an afternoon at the movies was like the emotional ride of a visit to see my father: I would laugh and cringe and get scared, all in a single afternoon.

On our first visit to see him after my parents separated, I remember even now, almost sixty years later, how I curled up and went to sleep in my seat in the theatre in order to escape the terrifying monster in the 3-D movie, Creature from the Black Lagoon. *But then I laughed through a cartoon, worried with Doris Day when she had to find her kidnapped son in* The Man Who Knew Too Much, *and enjoyed listening to her sing "Que Sera, Sera," still one of my favorite songs today. But then I was scared all over again when I saw newsreels and my sister told me that David might have to go off to war.*

Later, the emotional ride continued as I happily ate ice cream in Daddy's kitchen until I saw him pour himself a large glass of whiskey. Normal was too nervous around our father to change out of her clothes and into pajamas. Not that her intuition about what he'd do ever protected her from him.

I learned early on it wasn't as easy to take a nap to escape the anxiety of being around my father as it was to avoid the monster in the movie. And until he died we had no permanent escape. As children, visitation rights meant just that. He had all the rights. We had no choice but to visit him.

* * * * *

The visits start when Mommy tells us Daddy is moving to Hazlehurst for a new job and won't be living with us anymore. He promised Mommy he would stop, but he is drinking again. Last night they had a big fight with lots of screamin'. I am hidin' under the covers with my fingers in my ears and I can still hear them. She told him he had to leave and to never come back. I've never seen her so mad, probably 'cause yesterday Daddy hurt Lola. I don't know what he did to her, but Stella said she left to stay with Aunt Lola for a few weeks. No one will tell me what happened, but I know it's bad 'cause Lola didn't even tell me goodbye. And Mommy kicked Daddy out of the house.

I ask Mommy why we're not movin' with Daddy. "Just bad timing," she said. "You can see him on the weekends at his new house whenever you want to."

Normal and I talk about it and decide we don't want to see him at his new house or anywhere else for that matter 'cause we don't want to be alone with him. We're both glad he's gone. For me, I wonder if maybe without him around Angry will go away for good.

It's been weeks since we've seen him, but one Friday afternoon he stops by to talk to Mommy about having us visit for the weekend. Mommy says we need to spend some time with him so we're going to his house for a few days. Normal goes crazy, but no matter how hard she cries to her or how big of a fit she pitches, Mommy insists we have to go.

Before Mommy agrees to let us go she asks Daddy what we'll do all day Saturday. Daddy says he'll be working in a restaurant on the square in downtown Hazlehurst and it's right next to the movie theatre. He tells her we can go to the movie, or Grandmother can pick us up for the day since she lives a half hour away. He tells her he will pick us up at the movie theatre or at Grandmother's house early in the afternoon when he gets off work. I don't think Mommy likes it, but she agrees to let us go anyway.

Daddy picks us up at nine o'clock on Saturday morning. Mommy asks Daddy if he has been drinking and Daddy says, "No, Rose, not at nine in the morning."

She tells him not to drink at all this weekend and he promises he won't. Normal is hidin' in her room and won't come out even though she knows we have to go. Earlier she told Mommy she's scared of Daddy when he is drinkin'. Mommy tells her that daddy is not going to drink this weekend and everything will be fine. She's sure we'll have a wonderful time, but we know better. It will be a nightmare for both of us once he gets us alone.

Normal laughs under her breath and says, "Daddy is the only one who's goin' to have a wonderful time." Then she jumps up and runs outside and climbs into the car without even sayin' goodbye to Mommy. She don't cry, but I know she's scared.

We get to Hazlehurst by ten o'clock. The restaurant doesn't open until eleven. We go to Daddy's apartment at the boarding house first and drop off our suitcase, and then Daddy takes us to get hot donuts. Then we go to the park before he has to go to work. I run and play on the swings and slides with all of the other kids while Normal sits on a bench under a big sycamore tree and sulks. After the park, we meet the people workin' in the restaurant. One waitress keeps makin' googly eyes at Daddy. She has bleached blonde hair, big red lips, and lots of makeup and mascara. My mommy doesn't have to wear makeup; she is pretty enough without it. This crazy lady tries to be friends with me, but I don't think I like her very much. I need to tell her my daddy is a married man. I smile at everyone else but ignore her.

Daddy sits us in a booth in the back of the room and asks us what we want to eat for lunch. I say, "Spaghetti and meatballs, please." Within a few minutes two pipin' hot plates are put in front of us, and as I'm scarfin' down my food I whisper to myself, "So far the weekend has gotten off to a good start."

Normal hears what I say. "Just wait," she says, "all of the nice stuff will be over soon." She looks down at her food, but she doesn't eat a bite. She says she isn't hungry and that she'll eat popcorn at the movie, but I think her stomach is doin' flip flops right about now.

After lunch, Daddy gives us a dollar each for admission to the movie and says we can buy anything we want with the rest of the money. Since it only cost a quarter for the double feature matinee we'll have seventy-five cents left for Cokes, candy and popcorn. That's a lot of money since everythin' else is only ten cents each.

When we get to the theatre, *The Creature from the Black Lagoon* is playin'. I stop at the door and don't want to go inside. But Normal won't leave. I slowly walk into the lobby, scared to death of the posters of the monster on the walls. I back up to the door and tell Normal I can't see this movie, but she punches me and tells me to shut up.

"We're goin' to the movie 'cause I don't want to go to Grandmother's house today."

I know for sure I'll be hidin' alone in my seat until the first movie is over.

We go to the counter and load up on goodies and then I find a seat in the balcony as far away from the screen as I can get. Normal says she's sittin' in the third row 'cause she doesn't want to miss anything, but I know she's hopin' to meet boys and I'm sure that's why she didn't want to go to Grandmother's today. I don't care. I just want to get as far away from her and the screen as possible.

I climb into the seat and eat popcorn, Junior Mints, Milk Duds and drink my Coke. Then I curl up on the seat and fall asleep. When I wake up, the movie is over and a cartoon is playin'. It's a really funny one about Steamboat Willie, and I laugh and laugh. The next movie is a Doris Day movie, and I love Doris Day. The movie is *The Man Who Knew Too Much* and Doris Day sings "Que Sera, Sera." I've seen it before but I like it anyway. I cry all the way through it 'cause I know her little boy gets kidnapped, but she rescues him. In the end they live happily ever after—something I wish for. After the movie, I watch newsreels about boys fightin' in a war.

Normal finds me in the balcony and tells me David could go to war and be killed just like the boys in the newsreel. I start to cry and she says, "I'm just kiddin'. There's no war right now, but if there is one he would have to go and fight just like everyone else."

I don't know anything about wars, and no matter what she says, I don't want David fightin' in one.

Normal wants to stay and watch the monster movie again but I tell her, "No, I'm goin' back to the restaurant to see Daddy."

She pushes me and says, "No, you'll stay here with me." It's dark inside the theatre, but I think I hear Hero when she says, "I will not let you be alone with Daddy for a minute, not even with other people around."

I tell her I am goin' back to the balcony, but I don't. Instead, I slip out the door and run down the street to the park to play with the other kids.

I see Daddy walkin' to the theatre. I run up behind him and tell him I've been waitin' for him outside. We go inside and find Normal talkin' to two boys. I can tell Daddy is mad when he says to her, "It's time to go home."

When we get into the car, I see he has a big box filled with fried chicken, green beans and mashed potatoes for supper. He tells me to make sure the bowls don't tip over in the box. At the house, he makes sweet tea and pours it into the glasses of ice cubes that he took out of the ice trays in the freezer. I look at Normal to see if she's watchin' Daddy fill his glass with a different pitcher. It is the same color as our tea, but we know better. He's pourin' whiskey into his glass. And he's fillin' it all the way to the top.

We don't say a word, we just try to finish eatin' supper. When we are done, Daddy takes ice cream out of the freezer and holds the box in front of us. He says, "Y'all want ice cream?" Then he fills bowls to the top for both of us and sets it on the table. It's cold, good and sugary. After we finish our dessert, Normal tells Daddy we're tired and need to get ready for bed.

Daddy tells us where the towels are, but Normal says, "Mommy doesn't make us take a bath on Saturday night." Then we quickly leave the room.

I get undressed and put on my pajamas, but Normal gets into bed with her clothes on. I ask her why she isn't gettin' undressed and she says she's cold. It's not cold to me, but I jump under the covers, turn over, and try to go to sleep.

After a while I think I hear someone stumblin' around, but I try not to wake up. I know it's Daddy and I know what he's doin' in our room.

Hero is always there to stop Daddy from takin' me, and tonight is no different. She sleeps on the side of the bed next to the door to protect me. When she hears him, she whispers to me to go to sleep. Then she slips out of bed and goes quietly with him out the door.

I lay awake, nervous as I wait for her to come back. I get up to find my doll and play with her for a very long time. After a while I finally fall asleep.

When I wake up in the morning, Sad is there and the bed is wet. I see drops of blood where she cut herself. I don't try to hide the sheets from Daddy. I would like to pee on all of his sheets so he will have all that stinkin' wash to do.

I smell awful from the wet bed so I get up to take a bath. I quietly sneak out of the bedroom 'cause Sad is still sleepin' and I know she needs to rest. I close and lock the doors on each side of the bathroom for safety. I try to be very quiet and not wake them up. Daddy is still asleep—I can hear him snorin' like a freight train.

After my bath, I get dressed and go sit on the front porch swing. It's a cool spring morning and there are tiny, pale green leaves startin' to pop out on all of the trees and bushes. God is makin' new life sprout everywhere, Mamie would say.

As I sit alone I wonder if other little girls in the world have daddies who can be so kind and nice one minute, and then become a monster you hate with all your heart the next.

8

It's a Sad Day

Back home, the next day I wake up I know Sad is here. Sad always wets the bed.

At first I think I am dreamin' of a warm bath. The warmth seeps in around me and makes me feel cozy, but then comes the icy cold chasin' me across the bed and surrounds me. I realize I'm soakin' wet with pee. Gross! I get up and get Sad out of bed so Mommy won't know she wet the bed again. Mommy gets mad and says Sad does it out of meanness. But Mommy doesn't know what mean is—she hasn't met Angry.

I pull the pee-soaked sheets off of the bed and stuff them in the closet. I lay towels on the wet mattress, so stained from other accidents it's now brown. I find clean sheets in the linen closet and put them on the bed. To hide our secret, I'll wash the wet ones tomorrow when Mommy goes to work. I find us clean pajamas in the dresser drawer and tell Sad to take off her wet ones and put on the clean, dry ones.

Sad sits on the bed like a zombie, not movin'. I dress myself and then help her get dressed.

After I get her into her pajamas, she says she wants a cup of warm milk to help her sleep. I know there's no use in arguin' with her. When she wants something she won't stop until she gets it. I sneak into the kitchen and turn on the burner. I pour enough milk for two cups and wait for it to warm, but not boil. I can't chance makin' it too hot or Angry will switch and beat the bejesus out of me if it burns her.

When it's ready, I take the cups to the bedroom but Sad is already asleep. I sit in bed and drink both cups of the soothin', warm milk. I put the cups on the nightstand, careful not to wake her up. I fall back on the pillows and try to go to sleep. I lie there hopin' I don't have to deal with Sad in the morning. It's just too exhaustin'. A day with Sad is almost as bad as a day with Angry.

As I'm fallin' asleep I pray, "Please God, help us. We don't need Sad to be any more sad than she already is."

When I wake up in the morning I turn over to look right into Sad's eyes. She is still here. She has the sweetest face of all of The Sisters, but she also has the saddest eyes. I have no idea why she cries all the time, but I hardly ever see her without tears in her eyes. When she is here, she's likely to stay in bed in our room all day long and she never eats or bosses me around. She just sits in the bed and draws in her art book, or finds ways to hurt herself.

Today she chooses razor blades. God how I hate razor blades. I try to keep them hidden during the day, but sometimes she finds one. I guess she just don't realize I'm the one who hides them, 'cause she never asks me where they are. I sneak them back into the bathroom right before everyone gets home so no one will know the things she does with them. My life would be a lot easier if no one had to shave.

When I walk back into the room she doesn't look up. She is slowly slicin' the skin at the top of her leg. She makes cuts that are about an inch long and about a half inch apart. She makes the cuts so red blood trickles down the side of her leg. She's sittin' on newspaper, bein' careful not to let any of the blood get on her clothes or on the bed. I want to throw up when I see the thin gaps in her skin. I look at her and wonder how she doesn't feel the pain? How can she do this to herself over and over? Why does she keep doin' it? I don't understand it.

I wish there was something I could do to help her, but I know if I distract her Angry could come out screamin' and beat the crap out of me. So I back out of the room and go into the kitchen to put on a pot of coffee. After what I have just witnessed, there will be no eatin' breakfast for me this morning.

I try to keep an eye on her the rest of the day to be sure she's not goin' to cut her wrists. The other cuts will heal. I know this 'cause she does it all the time. But if she cuts her wrist I know she could die. Lola said once there are lots of people that come to the emergency room with slit wrists, and a lot of them die from losin' too much blood.

Sad cuts herself on her body where no one else can see. Most of the time, she makes the cuts around the top of her legs, arms, and tummy. It's not any less scary, but at least it's not as dangerous as cuttin' her wrist.

Sad's cuttin' is a horrible thing to watch, so most of the time I run out of the room 'cause I don't know what else to do. I tried talkin' to her a couple of times but she just ignores me. I know I can't tell anyone about it 'cause I'm afraid of what she'll do to me if I do.

When Sad finishes cuttin' herself, she rolls up the newspapers and puts them in a grocery bag. She buries the bloody newspapers in the bottom of the trash so Mommy won't find out what she's been doin'. She puts iodine on her cuts which makes her shiver from the stingin', burnin' pain and then she smiles. It's weird, but cuttin' seems to make her feel better. Sad puts Band-Aids on her legs and then gets back into bed.

I know when she's done hurtin' herself she'll drink herself drunk like Daddy does. She keeps alcohol hidden under our mattress on her side of the bed or in her nightstand. She has bottles and bottles of all kinds of alcohol and pills. The pill bottles have other people's names on them, and they all say Valium. I know she steals some of them from our neighbors and relatives, but some of the bottles have names of people I don't know. I don't have any idea where—or how—she gets them, but I know she is stealin' from someone. Sad doesn't go anywhere but home and school, so I guess the boys at school that she has sex with give her the alcohol and the pills from their houses.

I see her drink a whole glass of whiskey without stoppin'. Then she takes a pill bottle out of her drawer and swallows two pills with more whiskey. She climbs into bed and covers her head with the sheet.

After she's asleep, I sit down on the floor and cry for a long time, feelin' sorry myself for havin' to watch something so awful and not bein' able to stop her. I get on my knees by the bed and pray to God. "Please help Sad get better before she kills herself." But I know in my heart it won't work. I have been prayin' for her most of my life and it hasn't helped yet.

9

Normal

It doesn't take long after The Sisters appear for Normal to start failin' in school. She cries a lot and begs Mommy not to let them hold her back, but Mommy knows she can't stop them if they want to. Mommy promises her we will try to help her keep up, but I think that's a pretty tall order for any of us to keep.

I call out her spelling words to her and try to help her with her reading. Her reading is awful and I don't see how she will ever catch up. She gets so frustrated when she tries to read. Lola helps her with her math and science, but none of us are makin' much progress with any of the subjects.

I don't think Normal has a chance at passin' this year 'cause Angry likes goin' to school in her place. Angry doesn't go to school to learn; she just wants to hang out with the boys at the back of the school yard where the smokers and bikers are.

Angry tries to act sexy, especially when she's around boys. She looks at them in weird ways that makes me uncomfortable. She tries to dress much older than she is and wears shorts two sizes too small for her that are so tight she can barely button them around her waist. Most of the tops she wears are too small, too, and she ties them up so her stomach shows.

I can't believe the way Angry pulls her long, brown hair on top of her head and leaves half of it hangin' down around her face. She has always loved playin' dress up, but this is a little over the top even for her. When she's at Mommy's dresser, where she spends a lot of time, she puts bright red lipstick on her full, pouty lips and lots of mascara on to make it look like she has long, thick eyelashes. Then she takes even more black eyeliner pencil to make dark circles around her eyes. It makes her look like a raccoon. When she's done, she looks into the mirror and smiles a sexy smile.

Whenever Normal looks at herself in the mirror after Angry has painted her face like a slut, she is mortified. I can see the change come over her. I try to talk to her, but she just runs into the bathroom and locks the door. Normal knows something is wrong with the way she is actin', but she can't wrap her head around what happens to her when the Other Sisters take over. When she comes out of the bathroom, she has changed clothes and washed her face until all of the makeup is gone. There isn't a trace of Angry left anywhere on her.

Later, when I go into the bedroom I find Normal sittin' on the bed. She is pretendin' to read a Nancy Drew mystery book like nothing happened. I ask her questions about Angry and tell her she switched to someone else. She looks terrified, and I think for a minute she's goin' to cry. She looks so small and innocent sittin' there. Then she jumps up and says, "Have you lost your stupid mind? What are you talkin' about? There is no one else. You are makin' things up and tryin' to scare me. You want me to think I'm goin' insane."

I'm feelin' pretty angry myself when I say to her, "Normal, you *are* the scary one. You can change into another person in a matter of seconds."

She just glares at me and turns her head away so I won't see her cryin'. I know this conversation is over.

The next day I walk in our room and see Sad drawin' an evil-lookin' creature on her body with a pen. It has a spiked head and a pointy tail like the devil. She draws him on her stomach and legs where no one can see him. I ask her why she is drawin' such evil things on her body.

"Lucifer is not evil, he is my friend," she says, lookin' at me like I'm the crazy one. "He is the only one I can trust."

Later I see Normal in the bathtub scrubbin' her skin raw, tryin' to remove all of the demons Sad drew. When I walk into the bathroom, she slides down under the water and hides her body. She pretends she's takin' a bubble bath. I guess she's hopin' I didn't see the awful drawings, but I did. I want to ask her about the drawings to see what she will say, but I know she has no idea who drew the pictures or how they got there.

It's hard for me to imagine how confusin' it must be for her. I wonder where she thinks she is when the Other Sisters take over her mind and her body. At least I see the changes and know they are happening. Does she not realize there are gaps in her life, or does she just choose to ignore the time she is missin'? These are questions I don't think anyone can answer for me, not even The Sisters.

10

Art Journals

Sad spends a lot of time alone in her room listenin' to the radio or drawin' pictures. She keeps her art books locked up in a drawer by her bed. I think she must steal the white composition books from school. I have never seen Mommy buy them for her.

I found a way to get inside her nightstand. I can get the back off by pullin' out the nails. The first time I had to use a hammer, but it's much easier now that I've done it a few times. I just use a screwdriver. I pull her stuff out the backside of the drawer and slip the back of the nightstand in place. I mash the nail a little bit until it holds the back on and I'm ready to put the books back. Ta-da!

I'm real careful when I go through the art books. I make sure I put them back in the drawer the same way she does so she won't know I've been lookin' at them. I do this a lot 'cause I need to know what crazy things are goin' on in their heads. And believe me, most of them are crazy and they all think way too much.

The Sisters draw demons, devils, and evil, dark beings in one book, fairies in another, and people in the third one. Sometimes the people are normal lookin' and other times they look all distorted.

I saw a book at the library with pictures like this once and asked my teacher about it. She told me that people who draw this stuff are disturbed or have some kinda mental illness. I don't think Normal is disturbed or mentally ill. I just think she is confused by the Other Sisters who are. Normal don't have a vicious streak like Angry even though she can be mean. She would never intentionally hurt me the way Angry does, even when she treats me like her slave. She mostly ignores me unless she wants something.

When I go through the books I notice a difference from page to page, especially with the scarier ones. I think Angry draws most of the demons 'cause they are so horrible, just like her. The people she draws are dead and torn apart with pieces of their bodies all over the pages. Their eyes are hollow or missin', and there is always lots of blood.

The animal-like creatures look like a cross between people, dragons, and other animals. There are question marks and words written at the top of some of the pages. What does this mean? and When did I draw this? or Am *I* goin' crazy? I think Normal is the one who draws red tear drops beside the ones she can't remember drawin'.

The fairy book is my favorite. I'm sure Normal draws all of these 'cause she shows them to me sometimes and tells me she wishes she lived there. The fairies have the most beautiful faces. I call them pixie faces 'cause they are small and delicate. Their skin color varies from light to dark tan and their eyes are big and almond-shaped, drawn in bright colors. She loves lavender eyes, but she also uses light green, light blue, and golden brown. All of the fairies have long flowin' hair that hangs below their waists and their bangs are wispy around their faces. The ones with lavender eyes have almost white hair, the light blue-eyed fairies have hair like spun gold, and the green-eyed ones have bright red hair. She's given the golden brown-eyed fairies hair the color of a Hershey bar, just like mine.

They all have silvery wings I know would glisten in the sun if they could fly away off the pages. And even on the pages it looks like they are flutterin' around each other, dancin'. None of them wear shoes, but they have ribbons tied around their feet and ankles that hang in long strands that flow in the wind. Their toenails are painted the same color as their eyes.

Diamonds and jewels dot their hair, and streams of jewels flow down their arms to their hands and fingers. Their tiny clothes are thin and gauzy with leaf-shaped tutus, with lots of gold and silver threads runnin' through them. They fly around on the pages in this magical place she has created. I wonder how she makes it look so real, but I guess that's what an artist is supposed to do.

I would love to take this book to school to show it to my art teacher. She would be as fascinated as I am lookin' at them, but I know Normal would miss it. God knows what would happen if I got caught.

The people book has a lot of drawings by Normal. I see pictures of everyone in our family, includin' me. She is a very good artist. It's a shame she doesn't show her drawings to anyone. No one else knows she can draw like this. Just me.

One book has FAMILY on the front. You would think the drawings of us were photographs, they're that perfect. And there are tons of them. Our hair is up, our hair is down. In some, we're wearin' hats, others we have ponytails. Our clothes vary from dresses to evening gowns. I am so happy when I look at these beautiful pictures I can't help but smile.

And then there's Stella dressed up in wedding gowns. When she and Stella are in her room, Stella always looks at magazines with wedding dresses in them. Sad has drawn Stella in at least ten different wedding dresses, but next to each one she draws a sad face. Stella and James spend a lot of time together, and I guess she feels like it's too much. And then there are the pictures of James. She draws him with horns and tail and forked tongues. She also shows him with arrows through his heart.

I turn the page and see lots of pictures of me in cute little shorts sets, bathing suits and pretty dresses. My hair is down with ribbons, under hats with big bows, and up on top of my head in Shirley Temple curls. All of my clothes are in different shades of pink, probably 'cause she knows that's my favorite color. And the backgrounds are all of places I love, like the park and school.

In some of the pictures, my hair is long and beautiful and my lips and cheeks are rosy. You would think they would be lovely, and they are, but she draws my face with such a sad look in my eyes. In all of the drawings I look like I am just about ready to cry. When I look at the pictures I think deep down Normal knows about Sad. I think Sad is gettin' through to her and she understands something is wrong, 'cause there is no question mark on this page. I am not happy when I look at this book.

Next come pages and pages of The Sisters. Those pages are harder for me to shuffle through. Angry is dressed in skimpy clothes with barbed wire jewelry around her neck and arms. She carries knives and guns, and she looks like she's tryin' to kill someone in every picture. The drawings remind me of a comic book character. She is fightin' something or someone in all of them. Her hair is a mess and her face looks mean and distorted. Normal has put a question mark by all of Angry's pictures.

Sad is dressed in black with the saddest face I have ever seen. There are blood-red tears runnin' out of big, black eyes with the tears runnin' down her face to her chin and off the page. She is stick-thin and her clothes are fallin' off her bony body. Her long, straight light-brown hair is too thin and it hangs loosely around her face.

In some of the drawings she is holdin' her arms out in front of her, bleedin' from her wrist where she has cut herself. The razor blades are floatin' around on the page. In others, she is bleedin' from cuts all over body and the blood is flowin' around her in swirls. There is nothing else in the background but blood, and she seems to be floatin', lost on the pages.

The pictures of her are so real and so sad I can hardly look at them. I know Sad feels the same way when she looks at the pictures. It makes me want to cry to know how miserable she is every day of her life. These pages have big black question marks all over them.

I can't find any pictures of Kind or Hero, but I'm not surprised. They have a smaller place in Normal's head and only show up when I need them. I don't think they can switch unless I'm in a lot of pain. I do know that they both know about Angry and Sad, 'cause that's who causes all of my pain and they always show up when I need them the most.

Lola and Mom don't understand or know about the kinda life Normal lives. They think she is strange and maybe even a little crazy. When they ask her questions and she doesn't answer them, they think she's ignorin' them. They don't know the scary place she lives in. And believe me, Normal has no idea what they are talkin' about most of the time 'cause she's not the one who's there. I wish I could tell them the truth so maybe they could help her, but I'm so afraid of what Angry would do to me if I said one word to anybody.

Sometimes I try to talk to Normal. I ask her if I can help her when she looks confused or lost, but she looks at me and says, "What are you talkin' about? Help with what?" But there is a look in her dark blue eyes that tells me she knows all is not well in her pretty little head.

Sometimes I think she knows about The Other Sisters, but who knows? Maybe I just want her to know about them so I'm not the only one who does. I would like to tell her where her time goes, but I don't think she is ready to hear it. All in good time, my sister, all in good time I think to myself. They can't stay hidden forever.

11

Why Do You Hate Me So Much?

Today has been a really hard day. It started out with Sad cryin' all night keepin' me awake followed by a wet bed. She has nightmares sometimes and rolls all over the bed, kickin' and fightin' the sheets. When I try to calm her down, she punches and kicks me and says I am tryin' to kill her.

I shake her and when she wakes up she has switched to Normal. Normal glares at me and asks what the hell I am tryin' to do to her, and why I peed all over her.

I pat her on the back and tell her she is havin' a bad dream, but everything is OK now. I get her up out of the wet bed, give her clean clothes, and put her on a blanket on the floor beside the bed. I put on clean pajamas and change the sheets. I am used to doin' this.

I have changed her clothes many times in the middle of the night. I know that if I'm not nice and quiet, Angry is sure to show up. I suppose Mommy might say that it wasn't so much I was being nice to her as I knew how to keep the peace.

I leave Normal on the floor and crawl into bed. The clean, crisp white sheets smell like fresh air and sunshine. I try to sleep, but I lie there until the first rays of sunlight creep through my bedroom window. I am so tired my body hurts, but I still can't sleep. Visions of my past nightmares of the witch woman in black invade my mind.

I crawl over to Normal's side and look over the edge of the bed. She is still on the floor sleepin' like a baby. Earlier I heard a lawn mower in the back yard. Our neighbor cuts our yard when he cuts his since we rent the house from him.

I drag myself out of bed and into the kitchen when I smell the percolator brewin'. I hope I can grab a cup of coffee before anyone catches me. I know I'm not supposed to have coffee, but sometimes I think I'm probably goin' to die young anyway, so what difference does it make?

I fix my usual: my cup half full of coffee and milk the rest of the way up. I add four teaspoons piled high with sugar and stir the cooled-down mixture with my finger. It's sweetened just the way I like it.

I sneak quietly down the hall past the bedrooms. I unlatch the screen door and walk out onto the back porch and sit in the old wooden rocking chair. The sun is shinin' and a slight breeze blows across the fresh cut green grass in the back yard. The trees are swayin' and in the distance I hear a train whistle blowin'. It smells like summer, and for a little while I get to enjoy a beautiful sunny morning. I wish my summers were fun and I didn't have to worry about what this day will bring. Torture and tears.

I grab the brown, soft knitted blanket off the chair next to me to cover my legs and I sit there drinkin' the sweet concoction, enjoyin' it to the last drop. I'd love another cup, but I'm too afraid to chance it. Instead, I hide my cup under the chair and walk back into the house to face the day.

When I get to the bedroom, Angry is sittin' in the middle of the bed and I think not today, not after such a long night.

Not a chance.

There she sits with pillows all around her, dressed like she is the Queen of Sheba. And I mean she is really dressed like the *Queen of Sheba*. She is wearin' Mommy's silky blue nightgown and robe. She has too much makeup on, her eyes are black from eyeliner and mascara. Her hair is pulled tight away from her face and her lips are painted bright red. She has even made herself a crown out of tinfoil.

She is smilin' at me and says, "Slave, fix me my breakfast."

I don't refuse. I ask her what she wants, and she throws a book at me and hits me in the face. "What do you think, asshole."

I know if I get this wrong she will beat the bejesus out of me. So I bow and say, "Pancakes and French toast with bacon on the side." Who eats pancakes and French toast together I think to myself, but I know that's what she wants.

Sure enough, she says, "Very good, slave, and bring me iced orange juice first."

I take her the juice and head back to the kitchen. I hope we have everything in the pantry I need to complete her feast. I always feel like her slave, so I should be used to all of her demands. But I still don't like bein' treated as a servant.

Mommy doesn't let me use the stove when she is home, but I've gotten pretty good at it when she's not here. I have learned I will not burn myself if I keep the gas flame down real low.

I fix Angry pancakes and French toast. I am careful to make them golden brown 'cause if they are too light or too dark she will throw them at me and make me start all over. I fry the bacon crisp just as she likes it and drain it on a brown paper bag. I know she will want to eat in bed, so I find the board on the back porch I use for a tray and put a pillowcase around it to make it look worthy of Her Highness.

I have to be careful and get this to her before the margarine melts on the pancakes or all hell will break loose. I put powdered sugar in a little bowl and I pour syrup into a small jar and heat it in a pan of warm water, 'cause I know she likes her syrup warm. She says, "Cold syrup means cold pancakes, stupid."

I take the tray to the bedroom and pray she doesn't throw it back at me. She must be hungry 'cause she didn't complain about anything I've cooked. I am shocked and thankful for her mood. It's not often she is so agreeable. I ask her if she needs anything else and she says, "No, slave, I will call you when I'm done."

I go back to the kitchen and clean up the mess I made cookin' all of the food. There is bacon grease everywhere and I spilled flour all over the floor while stirrin' the pancakes. I am not tall enough to reach the counter, so I have to move my chair around when I am cookin'. I have spread the flour all over the kitchen floor and there are tiny footprints everywhere.

I get the mop and a bucket and try to mop the floor. The mop is too big and my hands are too small to wring the water out. I finally give up and get down on my hands and knees to clean the floor with wash-rags.

I sense someone is standin' behind me. I freeze, waitin' for the blow to my back with her fist or a kick to my stomach. I slowly turn around and look up to see Kind wringin' out the mop into the mop bucket, costume and all. She doesn't say a word. She just mops and mops.

I don't look at her again. I walk over to the sink and start cleanin' the grease off of the counter tops and stove. When I'm finished, I look around and she is gone. The floor is clean, and the mop and mop bucket are sittin' in the corner of the pantry.

I fill a plate with all the food that was left after Angry's carefully prepared breakfast. I sit down at the kitchen table and eat the rest of the pancakes, French toast and bacon, and even though it's cold, it's still pretty good.

I hate bein' a slave, but I do love to cook. I try new recipes any chance I get, and with Angry around, I have to cook a lot. She wants her breakfast whenever she wakes up in the morning and her dinner at twelve o'clock noon when her soap operas start. And I know if I'm late, there will be beatings.

For her breakfast today, I added sugar and vanilla flavorin' to the pancake batter. Miss Hattie, Grandmother's maid, lets me help her in the kitchen when I'm visitin'. The last time I was there she told me it was the secret of her famous pancake batter—vanilla and sugar, not like Mamie who uses cornmeal for her secret ingredient. I was afraid at first to do it 'cause Angry doesn't like change, but thank goodness she did not seem to notice.

When Angry finishes eatin' she rings a bell. I didn't know she had a bell.

I guess it's goin' to be her new way to summon me!

When I walk into the room, she is smilin', if you can call it a smile. It's more like a half-smile, half-grimace. She tells me to take the tray; she is goin' to take a nap. Fine with me.

I walk down to the corner store to get a Coke and visit with Mr. Mike and Miss Edna. They are always glad to see me and make me feel right at home. Miss Edna is takin' a nap today, so I drink my Coke sittin' on the counter watchin' Mr. Mike cut the big red-rind round of hoop cheese into thick slices for sandwiches. We talk about what a lovely day it is and he tells me there is no rain in the forecast this week. I love talkin' to him 'cause he treats me like a grown up. I guess the Coke peps me up a little, 'cause after the Coke and the conversation I am wide awake. I jump off the counter wavin' goodbye as I go out the door and walk the two blocks home.

I don't know what possessed me to do it. I suppose the sugar and the caffeine didn't help any, but I feel brave today. When Angry wakes up from her nap, I walk into the room and I ask her, "Why do you hate me so much?"

She looks at me like I have lost my mind. "I hate you 'cause I think you are stupid and ugly. I hate you 'cause everyone else loves you so much. I hate you 'cause everyone says you are smart and prettier than me. But most of all, I hate you 'cause you were born!"

Then she sits up high in the bed and in a shrill voice screams, "Before you were born, I got all of the attention. Everyone loved me the most. I was the perfect one. Now you are the perfect one, and I hate you and wish you were dead."

Too late I start backin' out of the door.

She gets up, runs across the room, knocks me against the wall, and starts chokin' me. I can't breathe, and I think, *she is goin' to kill me!*

She presses harder on my neck and I see stars. I fall to the floor, and she jumps on top of me. I am frantic. I try to push her off, but she is too heavy. I can't move. She is straddlin' me and all of her weight is on my chest, her knees holdin' my arms down. She leans forward over me with her hands around my throat.

My head starts to swim and slowly the room goes dark. I think, *this is it, I am goin' to die.* And I pass out.

When I wake up, she is sittin' on the floor next to me starin' into my eyes, smilin'. "I just wanted to let you know I can kill you anytime I want to. Understood?"

I try not to cry as I nod yes.

She gets up and leaves the room in all her Queen of Sheeba glory. I just lie there on the floor for a while tryin' to decide if I would be better off if she had killed me, to finally get away from all of her torture! Where is Kind, and why didn't she help me? I needed her more now than when she was moppin' the floor.

I get up and stumble outside into what started out to be a lovely summer day. The sun is shinin' and the birds are singin' in the tall sycamore trees surrounding the house. The Kudzu vines are blowin' in the breeze at the end of the porch by the porch swing and I can smell Mommy's roses in her rose garden.

What a beautiful day it is. I lie down on the grass and look up at the clouds and think, *how wonderful it must be to live in Heaven!*

12

The Haven

*I*t's sometimes easy to fall into the trap of believing that the dysfunction dominating a child's life is everything— all there is. One long nightmare after another, rather than episodes, periodic flare-ups, or nightmarish moments etched in memory. However, it's difficult to describe my childhood using one type of language, that is, using only the language of mental illness, cruelty in the extreme, or the lack of understanding of the destruction going on with Angela that affected me so deeply.

Over my many years of therapy, my life changed—became truly my own—because of my willingness to delve deeply into the past. In therapy sessions I described in the same kind of stark terms I use in this book the trauma I suffered with Angela and the anxiety of never knowing what would make Hero disappear and Angry emerge.

When children live in the midst of this degree of inconsistency and cope with the unpredictable moods of those around them, they often develop low-grade anxiety. They're hyper-vigilant, watching for clues and signs that something is afoot. What will happen next? What will set off Daddy or what will make Mommy sad? Why is Angry beating me? Why does Hero save me from trouble? What do I need to do to keep Angry away?

Given the state of the unpredictability, it might logically follow that as a little child; I never had a good day and played or had fun like a normal child. But over the course of my *therapy, I had the chance to explore the good times, memories of kindness, and even the loving eccentricity of some of my relatives. In other words, in the midst of dysfunction and anxiety, I had grandmothers and aunts and cousins, each with a personality, each with a story. For me, summer visits offered breaks in the fearful, anxiety-filled atmosphere surrounding me. They each helped shape who I am today. In some ways, they're my slice of "normal".*

* * * * *

This week Normal and I are goin' to spend the week with our grandmother. Sometimes we visit on the weekends, but since Daddy moved to California we always spend a week with her during the summer.

Grandmother is my daddy's mother and she lives in Newhaven, Mississippi. The locals call it The Haven. It is a small, southern town about an hour away from Jackson, or that's what Mommy says, but it seems a lot longer when we're drivin' there.

Newhaven is a sleepy, little town where children are always playin' in the park and it has lots of big trees for shade. Grandmother takes us there in the afternoons when it's not a hundred degrees outside. After we finish playin', we get a banana split at the drug store soda fountain.

No matter when I pass the park, the benches are full of mothers watchin' their children play. Grandmother told me the mothers are there to gossip. She says, "Newhaven is a small town and the mothers have nothing better to do than sit around and talk about each other."

There is a water fountain in the park and it is only about a foot deep, but it's plenty big enough for kids smaller than me to cool off on a hot summer day. No one seems to care that most of the boys and girls are stripped down to their underwear, panties, and diapers. Grandmother thinks it's uncivilized to swim without a bathing suit, but I guess they don't ask her permission.

There is no public swimming pool in The Haven, so the fountain is the only place for the little kids to swim. Legion Lake is just outside of town, but the mothers think it's much safer for the little ones to play here in the park.

Mommy says Grandmother stays here 'cause she is "a big fish in a little pond". I think that means she is important here. My mommy says we have to call her Grandmother 'cause it makes her feel regal. I've always thought regal meant a queen or a princess, but she doesn't wear a tiara; she just carries herself like she's a queen.

We don't think she's rich, but Mommy says she isn't poor, either. All I know is she has a lot more money than we do since Mommy and Daddy got divorced.

Grandmother tries to make sure my daddy gets anything he wants. I think she feels guilty about his "mental state." Grandmother tells us, "He just hasn't been right since he came home from the Army."

But Mommy disagrees. She feels like Grandmother still treats him like a child and he has never had to grow up. That he uses the Army as an excuse to drink.

Daddy started drinkin' when he was in the Army. I know he was *overseas* for a couple of years before Mommy and Daddy got married. I'm not sure what overseas means, but I'm guessin' it's pretty bad since it made him an alcoholic. I have heard everyone in the family talk about all of the bad stuff he saw when he was over there. But Mommy says that's just his way of getting his way with her and everyone else in the family.

I don't know how many times I have heard Grandmother offer to help us "live a better life," but Mommy says she can make it on her own. She doesn't need to owe Grandmother anything. She says she expects too much in return for her kindness.

My grandmother's name is Alexandria. She insists everyone call her Alexandria, not Alex or any other short version of her name. She is a mystery to all of us. She has never told anyone exactly where she came from. Mommy thinks she is a Yankee and that Grandmother doesn't want to admit it, 'cause she would never be accepted into the inner circles of The Haven if she were. In the South, it is very important to know where your people come from and what their heritage is.

Grandmother is very pretty. She has long, dark brown hair she keeps up in a bun on top of her head and when she takes it down, it hangs down her back in ringlets. Before she goes to bed at night, she sits in front of the mirror at her dressing table and brushes it—one-hundred strokes every time.

She has mysterious blue-green eyes that look like the ocean, and Mommy says she has a perfect ski-slope shaped nose. Everyone agrees she is quite strikin' to look at and they are all amazed at her age. I have no idea how old she is, but I'm sure not goin' to ask. She still don't have any gray hair and she swears she don't use the bottle to keep it that way. (But her cousin is the only beautician in town she uses.) Her skin is porcelain white and she carries a parasol when she is outside in the sun. She tells me, "Patra, keep that sun off of your face and you will never age." But I don't listen to her 'cause I like to feel the warm sun on my face.

She's always dressed like she just stepped out of a band box—another one of my mother's expressions that means she is dressed fit to kill. I think Grandmother looks nice no matter what she wears. She's usually dressed in the morning long before I get up and she won't undress until just before bedtime, but she will let me come into her room at night and brush her hair for her. We talk about all the things I did that day and how much fun I have bein' in The Haven.

She wears soft, silky pastel colored gowns to sleep in and I wonder how she keeps from gettin' her legs tangled up in them while she sleeps. It must be really hard to be so perfect all of the time but she makes it seem so effortless.

Normal has always been a storyteller. Before The Sisters appeared, she would spin tales out of the air faster than a bedtime storybook. Even now when we are at Grandmother's house, before we go to sleep at night she sometimes crawls into the bed with me and tells me the story of how our Grandmother and Grandfather met. I've heard it so many times I know it by heart, but I always listen to her. She makes it sound so romantic, and it's one of the only times she's nice to me.

She starts by sayin', "The story goes, Grandfather fell in love with Alexandria the first day he met her. Everyone in town said it was love at first sight. She was standin' by the merry-go-round when he spotted her. She and her cousin, Julia, were eatin' strawberry ice cream cones and it was meltin' in the summer heat. Grandfather walked over, pulled out his hankie and wiped the drippin' ice cream off of her chin. She was startled and practically fell into his arms. Julia laughed and said, "Alexandria, this is David, and he is obviously a true southern gentleman." When he looked into her southern beauty queen face, the world ceased to exist for both of them."

Normal goes on with the story. Alexandria was visiting The Haven for the summer. Her cousin Julia James and her family had moved here ten years earlier. The James' said they wanted to get away from the cold and the city life up north, so they bought the only clothing store in town when the owners, the Masons, decided to retire. After ten years the James' are still considered outsiders. It takes a long time to be *from* The Haven. As Mommy says, "It's the snob capital of the world."

Even though she's an outsider, Julia was one of the most popular girls in twelfth grade that year. She was a tiny girl with short blonde hair and pale blue eyes. It was unusual to see a girl her age with hair as short as hers, but I guess it suited her. She had a full figure, which means she had really big boobies. She was the town sweetheart and all of the boys were in love with her.

David met Alexandria at the Strawberry Festival. The Strawberry Festival is the biggest event of the summer. It is held in one of the hayfields outside of town. The town people spend weeks cuttin' the hay, makin' sure there are no holes for people to fall into and break their legs. Kids could get cotton candy, strawberry snow cones and fresh, homemade strawberry ice cream. There are hot dogs, hamburgers and the best barbecue ever eaten. Everyone in the county brings their strawberry jams, strawberry pies and anything else you can think of to do with strawberries, to be judged. It is quite an honor to take home the blue ribbon. All the teenage girls are wearin' their best petal pushers, flats and a bright chiffon scarf tied around their necks.

Normal tells me David and Alexandria spent the entire summer together after that day at the festival. It didn't matter that the following spring he was supposed to marry Susan Wilson. He and Susan had been goin' steady since the ninth grade and both families assumed they would get married after they graduated from high school, but she didn't have a prayer competin' with Alexandria's beauty and charm. The whole town was in an uproar when Grandfather broke up with Susan, but he didn't care—he was madly in love with Alexandria. They eloped at the end of the summer and it was the talk of the county, along with Grandmother's hopes of the wedding of the decade.

I guess it's weird we know all of this stuff. She could be makin' it up since she does that sometimes. You don't ever know if she's lyin' or she really believes what she's sayin'. But I do know people talk in a small town, and she says she has heard this story a hundred times from a hundred different people.

"Gossip," Grandmother would call it.

13

Grandmother

Newhaven is still a small town and everyone said at one time my grandfather owned a lot of it. Grandmother still has a service station right outside of town and the local hamburger joint, The Hamburger House. Family members work for her since she is supposedly *retired*. But her retirement is a standing joke in the family.

Uncle Billy runs the service station and Grandmother says if he makes a go of it he will inherit it one day. He has three children: my cousins, little Billy and the twins, Lucy and Lily, and their mother is my Aunt Karena Reich. They live next door to Grandmother and Mommy says Karena has a heart of gold and gets along with Grandmother better than anyone else in the family.

Aunt Karena is from Germany. Her family is still behind something they call the iron curtain. She hasn't seen them in a very long time. She was at school in West Germany when the curtain went up. Her entire family lived in East Germany and was trapped behind that iron curtain and couldn't get out. I don't understand what an iron curtain is or why they put it up, but I know it has to be something really awful to separate people from their whole family and never let them see each other again. I imagine it must be this tall wall with big metal thorns stickin' out of it that will cut you to pieces if you try to climb over it. It is scary so no one will want to get near it.

Our teachers tell us we should be very afraid of the Germans and Russians 'cause they have bombs they can drop on us and kill us anytime they want to. We have drills at school where we have to hide under our desk in case there is an attack. Somehow I don't think bein' under my desk is goin' to save me from a bomb.

When Uncle Billy met my Aunt Karena she was sitting all alone by a fountain, crying. He asked her why she was so sad, and she told him she was all alone in the world without a family. He told her not to cry, he would take care of her, and he did. He married her and brought her back to Newhaven with him. Sometimes she is sad, but most of the time she is happy to be here and not in a communist country. That's what Grandmother says, anyway.

Cousin Margie owns the busiest beauty shop in town. Mommy says she drinks like a fish, cusses like a sailor and smokes like a train. But I love her. She is the sweetest and funniest person I have ever met. Her beauty shop is the only place to hear all of the gossip in town you haven't yet heard at the park. That's how Grandmother keeps up with what's goin' on in The Haven. Margie calls her every night to fill her in on the day's gossip. Grandmother says women will tell their hairdresser anything and believe that's as far as it goes. They say the only time gossip isn't flying in that place is when the preacher's wife is there. I know for a fact since I have heard her say firsthand, "this is not gossip, just passing on pertinent information but..." To me, it seems the preacher's wife likes gossip as much as the next person.

Great Uncle Durant is the nicest person in the family. He is my mommy's uncle and he is kinda old now and isn't able to work. He has a little house across the street from Uncle Billy's that's full of cats and dogs, and he even has a big red parrot that talks. The parrot's name is Buddy and he cusses a lot. Uncle Durant said he cussed long before he got him, but Mommy said Durant taught him to swear 'cause he thinks it's funny.

Buddy calls everyone who walks in the door "stupid shit" and he calls Normal "stupid bitch." She makes Uncle Durant put him in the bedroom when she is at his house, but from the other room you can still hear him sayin' "stupid, stupid, stupid". I love that parrot.

Most people in town say Uncle Durant isn't right in the head, but I think he is the smartest man I know. I like to spend time with him. Besides, spendin' time with him keeps me away from The Sisters.

Uncle Durant don't like most people and would rather be alone with his animals, but he seems to enjoy my company. He doesn't like Normal very much though, so she hardly ever visits him. I think he senses there is something bad wrong with her and he knows his animals are afraid of her. When Normal shows up, he whispers to me, "If animals don't like her, people should shy away from her." I agree. If a parrot flies to another room squawkin' "crazy bitch" you should probably stay clear of that person.

When I go visit Uncle Durant we bake my favorite sugar cookies and talk about the books he reads. It don't matter what kinda book I bring him, he will read it. He corrects my southern slang way of talkin' and says, "Knowledge is a very important part of life, Patra. Without it, you're an idiot." I know he is serious, but the way he says it makes me laugh. I promise him I will try to do better, but most of the time he makes me laugh as hard as I do at Buddy's cussin', and that's a lot of laughin'. I don't think he is amused.

I think I am so good at spelling 'cause Uncle Durant and I started reading together when I was really little. He would call out big words to me and tell me I could spell anything if I practice enough. To him, *enough* was one thousand times. He said I could do or learn anything in the world if I just do it one thousand times. I guess it works 'cause it wasn't long before I could spell any word he gave me, and I even enjoyed reading an encyclopedia.

And then there is my daddy, David Jr. He joined the Army against Grandmother's wishes and it almost killed her. She begged him not to go, but it was too late. He had already signed the papers. Grandmother wrote letters to everyone she knew but the President to keep him from shipping out, and she said she would have written him, too, if she thought it would help. Daddy told her he was an adventurer and he needed to see the world. Grandmother said he was a dreamer and he just wanted to get away from her.

He was gone for two years and Grandmother cried every day. When he returned he started hittin' the bottle pretty hard. Grandmother says it was 'cause of all of the horrible things he saw during the war, but Mommy says that's a bunch of bull.

My mother was young and attractive, barely eighteen when he met her. Daddy dated her older sister first, but after he met my mother he never asked Aunt Dot out again. It was a sore spot in their relationship for years.

When they first met, Daddy was a Chef at the Rotisserie Restaurant in Jackson, but he drove home on Saturday night to see Mommy. They were married the next year and moved to Jackson. Daddy told Grandmother they were moving closer to his work, but Grandmother said it was Mommy's plan to get Daddy away from her. My mommy said, "Exactly."

When my brother David drives us into town, we stop at my favorite cafe, The Hamburger House, for lunch. When I walk in, the smell overwhelms me. The place smells like onion rings, grilled onions and French fries all rolled into one. It's heavenly.

The cafe has stools that spin round and round at the counter and I can watch Willie cook the food right on the grill. The booths are black and white with a jukebox menu on each table to pick the songs you want to play. Pictures of Elvis Presley, Frank Sinatra and Jerry Lee Lewis hang over the tables, and someone is always playin' their music on the jukebox.

In the corner by the front door, there is a revolvin' refrigerated glass case that has the best pies and cakes you have ever eaten. My favorite is the Hershey bar pie with almonds, and the meringue they put on top makes it twelve inches tall. The chocolate filling is thick and creamy and has enough almonds that I get at least one or two almonds in every bite. The meringue is fluffy and toasted on the top and has just enough almond flavoring in it to make it feel like a party on my tongue. It's heavenly!

There's coconut pie, too, and lemon ice box pie, strawberry shortcake and banana pudding. The carrot cake, caramel cake and coconut cake all have seven layers with lots of icing between each layer. The dessert case makes me think of a fairy tale where I would like to live and be the Princess of Desserts.

I order the hamburger with lots of grilled onions and tomatoes, no lettuce. I tell my friend the cook, Willie, that I don't like lettuce. He always asks me why and I say 'cause I'm not a rabbit. He laughs every time. I stole that line from my brother, David, but Willie doesn't know that.

Even though they have the best French fries in the world, I don't order them 'cause I'm savin' room for chocolate pie. Normal orders a hamburger, plain, just meat and bread. She says she likes her food to be "uncomplicated." No mayonnaise, ketchup or mustard—just plain.

I order my chocolate pie and Normal orders chocolate ice cream. What an oddball she is. All of the desserts she can choose from and she orders ice cream. Her life seems so pointless to me sometimes. She never enjoys anything!

After lunch, we go to Grandmother's house. We drive down the long gravel driveway lined with tall, live oak trees. The house has a wraparound porch that covers the whole front of the house. There are rocking chairs on the front porch and a wooden swing at one end. The house is painted white with black shutters and a red door. Grandmother says a red door means welcome. Everyone knows they are always welcome at her house 'cause there is a welcome sign right by the knocker on the front door.

Flowers bloom all around the front yard and roses of every color grow in the rose garden. The wisteria is bloomin' and looks like huge bunches of grapes hangin' over the front porch. Their heavy scent in the summer air is glorious. It's so beautiful here that it looks like a picture-postcard.

Grandmother has lived alone in this house since Grandfather died long before I was born. She tells everyone she has no interest in leaving this house. She will live here until they wheel her out on a stretcher and take her to Wright and Ferguson Funeral Home.

Normal and I have our own rooms in her house decorated just for us. Actually, our rooms are decorated for all her granddaughters, but I pretend my room is just for me. My walls are wallpapered in light blue flowers and the bedspread and curtains are blue and white. I love everything about it. There are tall ceilings and lots of windows and a ceiling fan right over the bed. The bed is really old and has roses carved into the dark wood. A big dresser matches the bed and two chairs are covered in an embroidered design of flowers on the back with blue and green stripes on the seat. The bed has a thick feather mattress I can sink into and lots of handmade quilts to keep warm in the winter. It's like sleepin' on a cloud, and I hate gettin' up in the morning when I'm here.

Normal's room is beige and not quite as pretty as mine. She don't like lace and frills, and she wanted it black, but Grandmother almost had a heart attack when she suggested it. Grandmother said she would compromise and decorate it in solid colors. Normal agreed as long as there were no flowers or stripes anywhere in the room. They settled on beige walls with a plain chocolate-colored quilt. Grandmother had to have it made by the quilting club 'cause even the Sears & Roebuck catalog didn't have anything Normal liked. The whole room reeks of Normal's taste and I make it a point never to go in there. It's too sad.

14

Miss Hattie

Miss Hattie is waitin' for us when we get to Grandmother's house. I give her a big hug and tell her how much I've missed her, but Normal just heads straight to her room without a word. And I think, *how rude*. Miss Hattie just shakes her head and hugs me harder. I feel so special wrapped in her arms.

Miss Hattie has worked for Grandmother a very long time. I'm not sure how long but she has been here all of my life. She has a friendly face with big, sparkly eyes and a smile as big as Texas. She wears a navy blue house dress instead of a black one, and a white apron with a white cap on her head. Grandmother tells her she don't have to wear a uniform but Miss Hattie insists it would be disrespectful to wear street clothes when she is at work. She never ages; she looks the same year after year. She cooks and cleans and stays with Grandmother and takes good care of her, and I think they are very good friends.

Miss Hattie helps me unpack and tells me she knows I ain't hungry 'cause she smells the grilled onions from Hamburger House clingin' to my clothes. She says that she has a special surprise for me at afternoon tea time, and I know it's her apple dumplings 'cause the whole house smells like cinnamon.

Afternoon tea is a big deal at Grandmother's house. She calls it High Tea and expects us to be dressed and in the drawing room by two o'clock. We drink out of china tea cups and use dessert plates that have been in the family for generations. Grandmother says we have to be very careful not to break them.

"It's important to learn how to balance a tea cup on your knee while you eat your biscuits," Grandmother said.

You can put cream or lemon in your tea, but if you use both it becomes a science project. I know, 'cause the first time I tried usin' both, it curdled the cream. Grandmother laughed and said, "Cream or lemon please," and I had to start all over with a fresh cup of tea.

On the other hand, Normal hates hot tea and says the whole idea is stupid. She sits in the corner and pouts the whole hour.

Miss Hattie makes sugar biscuits with homemade blackberry jam, homemade butter she makes in a wooden churn and tiny sandwiches I have to eat with my fingers. They're soft and fresh, and she makes them with cucumbers, egg salad, and pimento cheese. Miss Hattie makes all these things in her kitchen. She even cuts the crust off the bread and makes them look like tiny triangles.

Mommy disapproves and says, "She's wasting perfectly good food cutting off those crusts."

But Miss Hattie says it is *tradition*. No one else in The Haven has High Tea every afternoon and most people say Grandmother is snobby 'cause she does. But it's my favorite time of the day and I enjoy it immensely.

I love it here and spend a lot of time in the kitchen with Miss Hattie. I feel safe in this big old house. The kitchen is huge with pots and pans hangin' everywhere. There is a table in the middle of the room where we eat breakfast and lunch. The Frigidaire is filled with fresh cow's milk, fresh-brewed ice tea and my favorite—bottles of Coca Cola. Miss Hattie always has homemade cakes and cookies on the counter by the stove and we can have anything we want anytime we get the least bit hungry.

The kitchen wallpaper has tiny red and yellow flowers on a light green background and spoons of all sizes hang on the wall. I think Miss Hattie has a thing for spoons 'cause she collects them and hangs them everywhere. She says it's her kitchen and she will put what she wants to on the walls in there. It's a big kitchen, but it still feels warm and cozy. And it always smells so yummy.

We can eat breakfast in our pajamas and eat lunch in our play clothes. But at supper we have to wear dresses, Sunday shoes and ribbons in our hair. My mommy says Grandmother is a stickler for etiquette and manners. Grandmother says she will teach us to grow up to be the Southern Belles we were meant to be, which is strange 'cause we all know she isn't from the South!

Some people think Grandmother is a hard person to get along with and they try to stay out of her way. She likes my mommy, but she don't understand why Mommy and Daddy got a divorce. It was a great big *embarrassment* to the family 'cause no one had ever gotten a divorce in the family before. She don't blame my mommy, but she said all men drink a little bit too much every once in a while. She doesn't have any idea what Daddy does when he is drinkin', and believe me when I say "*No one* will ever tell her."

I have lots of cousins to play with when I'm visitin' here. Uncle Billy, Aunt Karena, little Billy and the twins, Lucy and Lily live next door. The twins are one year younger than me and we love to play together. Lily and Lucy look just alike. When they were little I couldn't tell them apart, but now I can see their differences. They have long curly red hair. And I mean *really* bright red hair. I think it's beautiful. Their eyes are green and they have freckles across their noses. That's how I tell them apart, I count their freckles. Lily has more freckles on her nose than Lucy does.

They are the sweetest little girls in the world, and we can play all day without a fights as long as it's just the three of us. Little Billy is three years older and isn't around a lot. He likes baseball and is off practicin' with his buddies most of the time. But that's okay. Lily, Lucy and I love explorin' the back forty acres where all of the animals are kept. Luke, the farm hand, takes care of the animals and sometimes he lets us help feed them. The hens are kept in the hen house and chicken coops. The hens lay eggs every day, and we can gather them early in the morning when they're still warm. Mamma ducks and baby ducks live down by the pond, and the pond has bream and crappie swimmin' around the shallow edges. If we catch any fish, Miss Hattie cleans and cooks them for our lunch as long as we share with her. We love eatin' Miss Hattie's fried fish and hushpuppies. Her hushpuppies have corn, chopped onions and lots of hot peppers in them, and just thinkin' about poppin' one into my mouth makes my mouth water.

The mamma pig and baby pigs live in a pigsty. It's down behind the barn 'cause it smells too bad to be close to the house. We don't care how bad it smells; we still go down there all the time to play with the cute, pink baby pigs. They are so sweet when they are little and I don't want to know what happens to them when they grow up. All I know is they have baby pigs every year and when I come back all the babies are gone. Normal smirks at me and says "Bacon." But I try not to think about that.

The roosters roam all over the yard, peckin' at everything on the ground. We throw corn out for them, but I try to stay away from the roosters 'cause they will chase me. I don't like the idea of makin' friends with my food. When we have fried chicken for dinner Normal kicks me under the table. When I look up at her, she laughs at me and says it's one of the roosters I fed that day! She knows when she tells me that she will get both chicken legs, 'cause I can't stand the thought of eatin' something I have met face to face.

Miss Hattie says not to worry. "We only eat the roosters 'cause they are mostly useless since they can't lay eggs." Somehow I don't think that makes it okay to wring their necks and fry them up for dinner.

I wish my friend Mayze could visit The Haven with me. I know she would love it as much as I do. Her mamma, Mamie, would be amazed at the big kitchen and all of the fresh vegetables from the garden, and cows and pigs in the freezer. There is never a shortage of food at Grandmother's house, and she and Miss Hattie could gossip all day long about white folks. Even though I know it will never happen 'cause white people and colored people aren't allowed to visit one another, it doesn't stop me from wishin' anyway.

Early in the morning the next day, Normal and I go to the hen house to gather the eggs. The hens leave the nest in the morning to eat, so we take a big basket lined with soft linen dish cloths into the hen house and grab the eggs from the nest.

Sometimes they are different colors. Grandmother has hens that lay white eggs and hens that lay brown eggs and there's even hens that lay speckled eggs. They all taste the same to me, but they look pretty in the basket. With the different colors of cream and brown speckles they look like they could be dyed Easter eggs.

We are very careful not to crack the eggs before we get back to the kitchen or Miss Hattie will shake her finger at us and say, "I told you to be careful with dem eggs, little dahlin's." I'll giggle and run away, but Normal looks at Miss Hattie like she has lost her mind.

Normal is allowed to hang out with our older cousins down the street, but most of the time when she is not annoyin' me she stays in her room. Sometimes she will go to the creek with Lucy, Lily and me to swim. We'll have fun splashin' and playin' in the water. I won't go with her by myself 'cause I don't trust her not to try to drown me.

15

Mr. Owl

*C*hildren of my own someday? I once thought I never wanted any. I couldn't imagine how things could possibly turn out. I sure didn't have any good role models. But something started stirring within me, first when I was twenty-eight years old. I decided I wanted to open a kindergarten and day care center. I never have been able to sit still for long periods of time and I knew I couldn't sit long enough to work for someone else. I thought about it and decided I needed a business where I would be very active and have lots of fun. It wasn't easy in 1975 for two young women to start a business, especially two young women with no money. My best friend, Barbara McDaniel, and I talked a banker friend of ours into financing the business and a building we designed (back when no collateral was necessary!). I found that teaching and taking care of children from ages six weeks to twelve years was therapeutic for me. Barbara eventually got married and moved to Florida after a few years, but I continued to run the business and kept 125 children a day for eighteen years.

My work with other people's children began to shift my thinking about having my own children—with a nudge from Mother Nature. When I turned thirty, my gynecologist told me if I wanted children I needed to do it soon because my chances of getting pregnant after age thirty were not good.

My biological clock started ticking like a bomb after his

statement. That was in 1977 when I'd been dating Jim for five years. He was thirteen years older than me and he'd been trying to get me to marry him for years. I thought, What the heck? *and had my brother, David, now a Methodist minister, marry us in a small ceremony with only a few friends and no family present.*

The next morning I woke up to a completely new and different person than I had known for the past five years. Suddenly I became his possession. I wasn't allowed any phone calls to or from anyone, including my mother and my best friend and business partner, Barbara. Visits to friends or family stopped, and our social life inside and outside the home ceased immediately. I felt as though I were six years old again.

Even though Jim was never physically abusive, the mental abuse was astounding. His age difference, thirteen years, hadn't been an issue in our relationship before, but now it was. His jealousy and moodiness and refusal to let me see friends and my family became stifling. Fortunately, or unfortunately, I was pregnant within five days of getting off the pill and after being married only a couple of weeks. Nine months later, on July 24, 1978, Whitney K'hara Windham became the biggest blessing in my life.

I didn't want to raise Whitney in a broken home, after the embarrassment of being raised in one myself, so I remained with Jim. I knew how to live with crazy. I'd earned my PhD in that by the time I was ten years old.

But after two years with Jim I'd had enough. I didn't want that kind of tension and disruption in my life anymore. We divorced when Whitney was three, and I was single for the next nine years until I met the love of my life, my present husband, Bobby.

Eventually, I began to heal the hurts from my childhood and my life with Jim. I knew the kind of relationship I wanted and I found that with Bobby. We've been happily married for twenty-five years. I've also found loving relationships with relatives, especially my brother, David, and my sisters, Stella and Lola. My sister, Lola, passed away a few years ago and it was a devastating loss to me. Stella lives in Kansas and David still lives in Mississippi. I see him quite often.

When I was a child, being with them were always loving, bright spots in my life—as long as they were still living at home. When that changed, I was too often alone with The Sisters.

* * * * *

Today is Saturday and we are goin' home tomorrow—on Sunday. Luke is off today and Miss Hattie had to go check on a sick relative. Grandmother is goin' to the church this morning to help with Saturday dinner on the grounds and she will be gone for hours. She said there will be enough food for an army, and enough people there for the preacher to save at least a dozen lost souls at the service after lunch.

I was lazy this morning and didn't get up in time to go to the church with Grandmother, so I am stuck here with The Sisters. I know that could be a train wreck, so I get up to dress myself and think about how I will head downtown to the Hamburger House to see Willie, and maybe get a piece of Hershey bar pie.

I am almost finished dressin' when Angry walks into the room and I reckon it's too late now. I just wasn't fast enough gettin' out of the house.

Angry looks at me and says, "Let's go."

I asked her where and she says, "To the barn."

I'm so scared, but I follow her outside and down the path. I want to hightail it the other direction, but I know she can catch me. When we go into the barn she looks around like she expects someone to be there, but we are alone. I ask her what she's lookin' for and she says, "Shut up and listen."

I hear something above me and I look up into the rafters and see a barn owl lookin' down at us. His wings are shades of brown and cream, and he has the biggest eyes I have ever seen. He just stares at us without movin'. He looks like a statue. I am scared he will fly down on our heads, but he sits there on a rafter.

Angry starts throwin' corn cobs at him, but the owl just sits there and stares at us. I can tell she's gettin' mad, but he don't fly away. She goes into the supply room and finds a BB gun. I know she's goin' to kill him.

I scream at her to leave him alone. She hits me in the back with the butt of the gun and says, "Shut up, retard. He deserves to die."

"Why does *he* deserve to die?" I ask.

"'Cause I said so," she says.

She starts shootin' at him and I start bawlin'. I can't help it. She's so mean and it makes me sad to see her treatin' the owl this way. She pokes me in the stomach with the barrel of the gun, but keeps on shootin'. She has never killed anything in front of me before. I try to take the gun from her and she shoots me in the leg. It stings like fire, but the skin don't break.

I try to run away, but she trips me with her foot and I tumble to the ground. She puts the gun to my face and says, "I am goin' to shoot your eye out if you don't shut up."

I'm on the barn floor too scared to move. She looks up. The owl is still sittin' in the corner rafter of the barn. She starts to climb the ladder, but he flies to the other side of the barn.

She screams "Idiot" and then climbs down the ladder. She runs across the barn floor and I can tell she is really mad at the owl 'cause she can't keep up with him. When she is runnin' to the other side of the barn, she stubs her toe on a board that is stickin' up. It starts to bleed.

Now she is furious. I can see the fiery look in her eyes.

"Damned stupid bird," she yells. She shoots at him again. This time she hits him, but only a few feathers fly around and flutter to the ground. She shoots again but misses. She will not give up, though I pray she will.

The next time she shoots she hits the owl dead-on. He falls to the ground and his wings flop around when he tries to fly away.

I'm sittin' on the barn floor watchin' in horror. She walks over to me and says, "Pick it up."

"No, I can't," I answer.

She kicks me in the stomach so hard I can hardly breathe. She yells, "I said, pick it up." I'm thinkin', *have you lost your mind?* It is swelterin' hot and my face is grimy and sweaty and the hair is stickin' to the back of my neck.

I stand up and walk over to the owl. It's lyin' on the floor lookin' up at me with its big gold eyes. I try to pick it up as carefully as I can, but it's scared and it starts flappin' its wings as it tries to get away.

She tells me to go put the owl in the corn grinder, and I start to bawl again. She hits me in the face with her fist, but I still can't do it.

"You can beat me but I am not puttin' a live bird in that grinder," I yell back at her.

She snatches it out of my hand and turns around and starts across the barn. As she is walkin' away she says, "Don't move or I will kill you."

I close my eyes tight, but I still hear the crunchin' of the bird's bones as she cranks the wheel on the grinder.

Before she can turn around, I jump up and run as fast as I can out of the barn, through the woods down to the creek. I sit down on the soft grass feelin' like my soul has been sucked out of me and I cry uncontrollably. Big, belly wrenchin' cries. I just don't understand how anyone could be so cruel to something so beautiful.

I put my bare feet in the cool runnin' water and wish it was this easy to wash away what I had just seen. I sit there a long time tryin' to figure out why people are the way they are. I know I will not get that answer today. I realize when The Sisters are involved I may never figure it out.

Finally, I get up and walk the long way around the barn to the house. I pass the baby ducks, but I don't even look their way. I have to get back to the house 'cause church will start soon. I need to go pray for the owl and for myself. I don't know where Angry is, but I wish I didn't ever have to see her again.

When I walk into the house, Grandmother is waitin' for me so we can go to church. She takes one look at me, and even though she has on her Sunday hat and white gloves, she pulls me into her arms. I am dirty and bruised, my hair is a mess and there is a red mark on my face where she hit me. She asks me what happened and I tell her I fell out of a tree down by the creek. She looks at me like she half-believes that story. She says I must have a quick bath before we can go to the church. She helps me get cleaned up, braids my hair, and puts a big bow on the bottom of my braid.

She quickly changes her gloves and heads down the hallway to look for Normal. She finds her in her room in bed. She tells her we are already late for the church picnic, but Normal says she has a stomach ache and can't go. Grandmother is not happy about it, but she lets her stay home.

The picnic is fun. All of my cousins are here, but I'm too sad to play. I sit on a bench all alone and try hard to keep from cryin'. I can't eat a bite, and even the fresh made cookies and cakes don't tempt me.

I sneak into the sanctuary and drop to my knees on the red velvet-padded alter. I pray for the owl, I pray for myself, and I pray for all of the bad things Angry makes me do. After my prayers I just want to go home, go to bed, and go to sleep.

When we get back to the house, Grandmother fixes me a cup of warm milk and tucks me in bed. I'm tryin' to go to sleep, but the awful day keeps runnin' around in my head.

I hear my door open and someone walks in.

At first I'm afraid and pull the blankets tight around me. It's Hero, and she sits beside me on the bed. She leans over and kisses me on the forehead and says, "I'm so sorry." Then she gets up and walks out of the room, and I cry myself to sleep.

16

Icy Day

It's a cold, rainy November day and we are out of school for the Thanksgiving holiday. I will be alone here for the week with The Sisters. Mommy and Lola are working today, but they will both be home on Thanksgiving Day. That means I am on my own with The Sisters for the next three days.

I wake up on Monday and the dark clouds are hangin' in the sky like a huge canopy. It's sleetin' so hard I can hardly see the street in front of the house. As I sit lookin' out the front window at the sleet poundin' against the glass and landing on the front porch, I'm wishin' I was anywhere but here.

I feel so lonely. The entire house is dark and gray and cold. I always feel the same way when I'm alone with The Sisters, but today seems worse than usual. Today I just want to crawl into a corner and hide. Today I feel trapped with no way out.

I'm afraid to leave the living room for fear of wakin' her up. The longer I am quiet, the longer she will sleep. The longer she sleeps, the shorter my day with her will be. The hair stands up on the back of my neck every time I hear a sound comin' from our room, and the fear inside me grows with every passing minute.

Most days are not as scary as this, but Angry has been on a tear for weeks. She torments me every chance she gets. My heart pounds like it's goin' to jump out of my chest and I break out in a sweat when I'm in the room with her. I try my best to stay away from her, but it's impossible when I am alone in the house with her, especially with the weather outside today. I can't escape.

Her new pastime is trippin' me whenever I get close to her, or she kicks me in the back when I pass by. She kicks me so hard it takes my breath away. I don't know why this amuses her so much but she thinks it's hilarious when I hit the floor on my hands and knees, gaspin' for breath. She gets down in front of me and laughs and calls me a clumsy idiot.

All of a sudden I hear her runnin' down the hall, screamin' at the top of her lungs. I think, *oh my God, it's Angry,* and try to run away. She darts across the living room and catches me by the hair as I jump off of the chair I was sittin' in by the window. She drags me across the room by my ponytail, on my knees. I am fightin' to stay upright and crawlin', 'cause I know if I fall she will drag me across the room by my hair.

She opens the front door and throws me out on the front porch, and then slams the door behind me. I hear the lock click and I know she isn't goin' to let me back inside no matter how hard I cry or how loud I scream.

I'm numb and in shock tryin' to figure out what just happened, and why she threw me out of the house. The porch is covered with ice from the sleet, and it takes me a few minutes to realize I am soakin' wet and freezin' cold.

I am wearin' my pink bunny pajamas and my fluffy slippers Lola gave me for my birthday. My hair is hangin' down my back where she ripped the rubber band out of my hair. The knees of my new pajamas are wet, torn and dirty from the fall, and my bunny slippers are soggy from the rain.

Stunned, I sit and shiver on the front porch, not knowin' what to do next.

I get up and stumble over to the glider, but it's too close to the edge of the porch and is covered in ice. I try the chairs closer to the door, the cushions are still mostly dry. I grab the cushions and hover in the corner behind the chairs on the back of the porch. I take the bright-colored, flowered cushions and stack them all around me and on the floor to keep myself as warm as possible. I know Mommy will be mad at me for gettin' the new cushions wet and dirty, but her bein' mad isn't half as bad as how cold I am.

I try to tell myself Angry will come and let me back in the house when she realizes that it is freezin' outside. She has locked me out many times before, but never in the winter when it's rainin' and sleetin'. She thinks it's funny to lock me on the back porch, naked, during the summer when it's hot, but I keep a bathing suit hidden outside to wear until she decides to let me back in. But no warm clothes are hidden outside for me today.

I wait for what seems like hours, and she still doesn't open the door. I can tell the temperature is droppin' by the minute. The rain and sleet are comin' down in sheets. My feet and hands are frozen and my slippers are stuck in the ice. I'm so cold I can barely move. I know I'm goin' to have to do something soon or I'll freeze to death out here.

I try to stand up but I can't feel my feet or my hands. Slowly I crawl to the front steps and try to stand up. My legs are numb from sittin' on them, tryin' to keep warm. I crawl off of the front porch, down the steps, and on to the sidewalk and try to stand up again. But I fall down. It's slippery from the ice, but I keep tryin' to get to the grass. If I can just get to the back porch, maybe I can get into the house.

I go around the house and try to look into my bedroom window to see if, by chance, Normal has switched with Angry. I know she has no idea Angry has put me outside in this weather. If I can find her, she will open the door and let me in out of the freezin' cold.

The window is too far off the ground for me to see inside. I'll have to find something to climb up on to see whether she's in the bedroom or not. I go to the backyard, but the only thing I can find to climb on is an old lawn chair sittin' under the big China Berry tree beside the swing. I look around and the trees are covered with ice. The limbs from the bushes and trees are hangin' down to the ground and they are glistenin' like Christmas cards where the sun is tryin' to peek through the clouds. The whole backyard looks like a winter wonderland, and I think it would be beautiful if I was inside drinkin' hot chocolate where it is warm.

But I'm not inside, and if I don't get there soon I could freeze.

The rickety chair is frozen to the ground and it takes a few minutes to shake it loose from the ice with my numb fingers and drag it around the house to my bedroom window. I climb up as high as I can, but I still can't see inside. I knock the ice off of the arms of the chair with a stick I find on the ground, then climb back up and try to balance myself on the arms of the chair. It is very wobbly, especially with my wet bunny slippers. I'm afraid to take my slippers off of my feet 'cause my toes are already half frozen.

My fingers are too cold to hold onto the window, so I try to balance my feet on the arms of the chair. Finally I can grab the window sill. I can barely see inside the room, but as far as I can see the room is empty.

I start to climb down off the chair when Angry jumps up and beats on the window and screams, "Dumbass, I hope you freeze!"

My foot slips off of the arm of the chair, and I tumble to the ground and land on my right shoulder and right arm. When I hit the ground, I feel my arm pop right where my arm and shoulder meet. *God, please don't let it be broken,* I think. She will kill me if it's broken. She can hide the fact she tried to freeze me to death, but a broken arm is another story all together.

I try not to scream from the pain 'cause I know Angry won't come and help me anyway.

I roll over on the ground, my arm hangin' loosely by my side. I try to get up, but I fall down again on the icy grass. My arm doesn't look right and I start to cry, but I know it's useless to call for help.

I don't have a dry spot on my body. My hair is a frozen, tangled, dirty mess. I know I need to get to the back porch and out of the rain and cold as fast as I can, but my legs are barely movin' and my arm hurts so bad I can hardly breathe.

Somehow I make it to the back porch and slowly climb up the back steps. There are only five steps, but it feels like a mountain to me. I slowly walk up each step prayin' the screen door is unlatched. When I get to the top of the stairs I open the screen door as quietly as I can and slip inside. Relief floods my whole body. At least I'm out of the rain and ice. All I can think about is gettin' warm.

I try the backdoor, but it is locked. I feel like I'm at the end of my rope. I don't think I can last much longer. My arm throbs and my eyes blur as I look around the porch for something to dry off on. I just want to curl up and go to sleep, but I think if I do I will freeze to death. I find an old blanket in a box beside the chairs and pull it out with my one good arm.

I can't decide if I should take my wet clothes off or just roll up in the blanket and go to sleep. I know I need to get these wet clothes off before I do anything else, but that means bein' naked outside in the cold.

Finally I take off the slipper I still have on my left foot. I don't know where I lost the other one, but it's gone. I'm sure they are both ruined, but I set the one by the back door in case I can find the other one later. I laugh. I could die out here and I'm worried about my slippers.

I peel off my pajama bottoms and drop them on the porch. I try to take my top off over my head and down my right arm, but when I try to raise my arm I can't 'cause the pain is unbearable. I am so cold and my body hurts so bad. Then I collapse.

Just when I have given up and know it's over for me, the back door opens. Kind is standin' there. The warmth of the house hits me in the face and is overwhelming. I guess it's not my day to die.

I fall into Kind's arms, cryin' uncontrollably. She looks stunned when she sees the shape I'm in. I am half naked on the back porch, my hair frozen and stuck to my head; my entire body is blue from the cold. My pajama top is hangin' loosely on my body, and she's starin' at my right arm hangin' at a funny angle by my side.

As she drops to her knees and holds me in a tight hug, she says she felt something bad was happening to me. That she had been fightin' to get to me all morning, but Angry wouldn't let go. She says it took her and Hero both to make the switch with Angry so they could help me.

She's so distraught she can hardly pick me up and carry me inside to the kitchen. She sits me on a chair and tries to take my top off but I scream from the pain. She finds Mommy's sewin' box and pulls out the scissors and cuts my favorite pajama top off my body. I don't even care.

She runs to the bedroom and grabs a blanket to wrap me in.

I don't know if she is talkin' to herself or to Hero, but she's askin' if she should try to get warm milk in me or get me into a warm bath. At this point I just want to lie down and go to sleep. When I lay my head on the dining room table, the sound of runnin' water is the last thing I hear.

I feel someone pickin' me up and lowerin' me into a warm bath. My whole body seems to relax for the first time today as soon as I sink into the hot water. Even my arm feels better for a few seconds.

She lathers my waist-length hair with shampoo and scrubs it until all of the mud is gone. I can feel her fingers gettin' caught in the length, and it has so many tangles she can't get all of them out. She tries usin' a brush, but it doesn't work. She goes to Mommy's bathroom and finds her Suave conditioner. She pours a ton of the conditioner in her hands and slowly rubs it into my hair. She wraps a small towel around my head and holds it in place with a bobby pin.

Then she takes the bar of Ivory soap and washes my left arm and my body. She scrubs the blood and mud from my legs. I have deep cuts on both knees, but my left arm is unhurt. When she is finished scrubbin' me the water is brown from all of the mud.

She takes the towel off of my head and runs her fingers through my hair and the tangles seem to have disappeared. She uses a cup off of the sink to rinse my hair until the conditioner is gone. I know she is askin' me questions 'cause I see her lips movin', but I don't hear her words. I just stare at her. I can feel hot tears rollin' down my already wet cheeks.

She helps me get out of the bathtub and wraps a soft towel around me. The towel causes weight on my arm, and I cry out and drop it to the floor. I look at myself in the full-length mirror and don't recognize the little girl standin' in front of me.

I look like something out of a horror movie. My eyes look dark and hollow, not their normal bright blue. My hair is drippin' water and runnin' down my legs. My knees have started bleedin' again from the gashes, and the water from my hair causes streams of blood to run down my feet and form puddles on the floor. My right arm is hangin' loosely by my side—the pain is unbearable and is givin' my face a ghastly, distorted look. I try to get a grip on what happened, but it all seems so far away from me now. I just need to lie down. Then the room starts spinnin' and everything goes black.

Somewhere in my foggy brain I hear Kind sayin' she needs to get me dressed and into bed. I feel her wipin' away the blood on my knees. I look down and she has put a white cloth across my legs to keep me from bleedin' on the bed. She comes back into the room with a handful of bandages.

First she tells me she is goin' to put a small pillow under my arm to make it level with the rest of my body. She does it very slowly but it still hurts. I gasp, but I try not to cry out. She says she isn't goin' to put a pajama top on me 'cause she doesn't want to move me any more than she has to.

She sits down beside me on the bed and takes the towel off my legs. The bleedin' from my knees has almost stopped so she covers them in Vaseline and puts white gauze on them. She tapes them all the way around the back of my legs so I can't bend them and make them start bleedin' again. She tells me she called Mommy, and she'll be home as soon as she can. I know Mommy has to take the bus so it could take a while.

Kind carefully puts my pajama bottoms over my knees and up to my waist. My feet are still like ice so she puts thick socks on them. She lifts my head up and gives me two aspirin she has melted in a spoon. It chokes me and she puts a straw in my mouth and says, "Suck."

I do, and I feel the warm milk slide down my throat. I know I should be hungry, but all I want to do is sleep.

Before I fall asleep she asks me if I can tell her what happened. She asks me if Angry broke my arm. "No," I said, "but she threw me outside in the cold to die!"

She looks at me with all of the remorse she feels for bein' helpless when it comes to Angry hurtin' me and says, "Patra, I am so sorry I can't protect you from her. I try, but she is just too strong."

I know in my heart no one can help me. She will eventually kill me. She will find a way to do it so it's my fault or someone else is blamed, but no one will ever know she did it.

When I wake up, Mommy, Lola and Kind are there. I hear Lola say my arm is dislocated, but she don't think it is broken. Mommy says they can't take me to the hospital 'cause the bus lines have been shut down 'cause of the ice storm, but Lola called a friend from the hospital. He has a car, and he's pickin' us up in an hour and will take us to the emergency room.

Mommy keeps askin' me what happened, but I pretend I don't know. I will have to make up a story. I hurt too bad right now to think. I tell her Normal don't have any idea what I did to hurt myself, that she was watchin' the storm on the TV. I have to keep The Sisters out of this.

When we get to the emergency room, everyone there knows Lola since she works there as a candy-striper. The people there are very kind and gentle with me. First, they give me a shot of pain medicine. I am hurtin' so bad I don't even cry about it and I feel better immediately. It makes me feel like I am floatin' on clouds, and I laugh a lot. Wow, life is wonderful 'cause of a shot. I always thought they just caused pain.

Later, they wheel me to x-ray and I get a lot of attention from the nurses all the way down the hall. They tell me how pretty I am and how brave I am and I giggle all the way to x-ray.

The man dressed in green tells me he is the x-ray technician. He slides me onto a table and puts a huge machine over my arm. I am scared, but he holds my hand and tells me it is okay. He will take care of me.

After the x-rays, a nurse takes me back to a room with curtains around it. The curtains have yellow and blue ducks on them. Mommy and Lola are waitin' for me and we have to wait for the x-rays. Then we have to wait for the doctor to come by. It takes a while, but I don't mind the waitin'. Lola says it's 'cause of the medicine they gave me, but that I will change my tune as soon as it wears off.

The x-rays finally come back. The handsome doctor comes in and tells Lola and Mommy I was lucky it wasn't broken. He says Lola is right: it's dislocated. It hurts like the devil when they put my shoulder back into place. It takes two of them to do it, but it stops hurtin' as soon as it pops back in the socket. The doctor says I will have to wear a sling, but that it should be okay in a couple of days.

Next, a nurse comes in to look at my knees. She unwraps them and says whoever took care of them did a pretty good job. She says one knee has a bad gash on it and would need stitches. I ask if I will need another shot and she says, "Not in your hip."

When they come in with the second shot I'm not as agreeable as I had been for the first one. I tried really hard not to embarrass Lola around her friends, but a needle in my knee was not what I expected. I ask if Lola could give me the shot and they say she can hold my hand. She isn't a real nurse yet, so she can't give shots. The nurse says she'll let Lola stand really close and help if that makes me feel any better.

I know they won't hurt me if they don't have to, and it's over pretty fast. After my knee is numb, the doctor puts four stitches in it that will have to come out in a week. Then he says I'm almost ready to go home.

The doctor comes back a few minutes later with a clipboard and asks me what happened. He says, "It takes a pretty bad fall to dislocate a shoulder."

"I don't remember," I said.

He asks my mommy, and she tells him she and Lola were at work. I had been at home with my older sister. He says he needs an explanation for his report so I tell him, "I fell off of a chair."

He looks at me funny and asks if I'd hurt my knees from the fall off the chair.

I get scared and say I fell off the front porch 'cause it was covered with ice from the storm. He asks me if the chair was on the porch. I get confused and don't know what to say. I start cryin'.

He says it is okay, that it has been a long day.

And he's right. It has been a long day.

When we get home, Mommy fixes me Campbell's chicken noodle soup the way I like it with no water added. It is warm and salty and I don't realize how hungry I am until I taste the first bite. She crumbles up saltine crackers and they are floatin' on the top of the soup, and I think, *Mmm... Mmm good,* just like the TV commercial. I eat the whole bowl of soup, along with a glass of milk. (I want Coke, but Mommy says it is too late to be drinking a Coke.) As soon as my tummy is full I can't keep my eyes open.

The last thing I hear Mommy say is, "We'll talk about this in the morning, little girl."

After she leaves the room I try to think back to this morning. I know I didn't see Normal at all today. I only saw Angry and Kind. I didn't see Normal until we got home from the hospital. She was sittin' on the couch in the living room in the dark, wrapped up in her red blanket watchin' TV. She had an empty bowl of popcorn and half a bottle of Coke on the coffee table.

I knew she didn't have any idea where we'd been when we walked in the door. I know her well enough to know she'll wait until she has scoped out everything and everyone present before she says anything. She has learned to read the situation before she jumps in and volunteers any information. And she knows immediately this isn't a situation where she has any idea what is goin' on.

17

Thanksgiving

I'm so thankful the next day when Mommy stays home from work to take care of me. I won't be at home alone with The Sisters after what happened yesterday.

Aunt Lena says she will fill in for her at work since I am hurt and need tender loving care. She is such a great aunt. Besides, it's Thanksgiving Day and the restaurant is only open for supper since most people don't eat Italian for lunch today. Aunt Lena also says she will come by after lunch to check on me and bring me something special. I know it will be special 'cause my friend Bessie at Greco's will make sure of that.

Lola is bakin' pies, and Stella has been makin' fruit salad and homemade cranberry sauce since early this morning. I want to help cook, but Mommy thinks it's best if I rest until dinner is ready. That's OK with me. I know it's only a matter of time before Mommy starts askin' questions about my accident.

I heard her tell Lola she had found the chair by my window and saw where I had fallen off the chair and landed onto the ground in the mud. She said the arm of the lawn chair was bent and broken, and she guessed I had climbed up to look into the window. She also found my bloody, torn pajamas by the back door along with one slipper; she found the other slipper at the bottom of the stairs. She told Lola she didn't know why, but she felt sure I was lying about what happened. That I didn't fall off of the porch and was covering something up.

I know I have to come up with a story soon or Angry will beat me half to death. Just thinkin' about it puts me into a tailspin.

All of a sudden I feel like dark clouds are hangin' over my head again. I lie in the bed with my eyes closed. Sorrow and dread takes over my brain and overwhelms me. I feel like I will suffocate from the heavy air around me. All I want to do is crawl into the back of my closet, cover my head, and curl up in a tiny ball where I feel safe.

I try to breathe, but the air won't fill my lungs. I want to get out from under the covers, but my body feels stiff. I can't move, not even an inch. My body may not be workin', but my mind is and I'm terrified. Terrified I am losin' my mind. Terrified I am goin' to die. Terrified of everything.

I try again to roll over, but I still can't move. My mind thinks *run, run, run.* I feel the sweat pourin' off of me and my scalp is soakin' wet. I want this to be a nightmare, but I know it's real.

I've been havin' this feeling of hopelessness more and more often: the helpless feeling of not bein' in control of my own body or mind. Every day I wake up knowin' Angry controls whether I live or die. Not God, but another person, and I have no way to get away from her. I have to face her almost every day.

I don't know how long I can keep hidin' these feelings, and I don't know how long I can keep livin' through this turmoil.

Exhausted, I fall asleep.

When I wake up, I hear Normal comin' into the bedroom. I know she wants to ask me what happened. She needs to get her story to match mine.

She walks in, tiptoes over to the bed and leans over to see if I'm still sleepin'. I can tell she is as nervous as a cat. She reaches down and touches my arm lightly, but I don't move. She is anxious and turns to leave the room for the tenth time this morning.

I don't know what to say to her. It's sad, and I feel bad for her 'cause I'm sure she doesn't remember what happened yesterday. I know she wonders why I was locked outside in the rain and cold. She has to know she is missin' time in her life, sometimes hours or even days. I wonder how she can live her life never knowin' who or where she is?

Mommy comes in and asks me if I'm going to sleep all day. She is teasin' me, tryin' to make me smile. She says she will help me get up and get dressed. She takes my sling off my arm and is very careful not to move it too much when she puts on my softest pink pajama shirt. It is a button up, and it slides on easier than a pullover. I step into my pajama bottoms and try not to bend my knees so I don't break the stitches and make them bleed. My body is stiff and my knees throb.

She brushes my long, dark hair and gets all of the tangles out. Then she puts it in a ponytail and ties it up with a bright orange and brown ribbon.

I ask for a pair of socks 'cause I know my slippers are ruined.

Mommy walks over to my dresser drawer. She turns around and looks at me and says, "You know we have to talk about this, Patra."

I just nod my head yes.

Mommy sees I am upset, so she changes the subject and tells me dinner is ready and wants to know if I think I can sit up at the table. I ask her if I can eat in the living room on a TV tray.

"It's Thanksgiving, and you need to eat at the table with the rest of the family if you possibly can." Mommy is a stickler about dining etiquette just like Grandmother Alexandria and eatin' in the living room is hardly ever permitted, even if you are sick. I go with her. I'm starvin' anyway.

Mommy asks Stella to say grace and she blesses all of the food. And then she blesses everyone and everything else in the world, and I don't think she will ever finish her prayer. I missed breakfast this morning and my soup from last night is long gone.

Finally it's time to eat, which is not goin' to be easy since my right arm is in a sling. Mommy cuts everything up for me and she props me up beside her. She helps me guide my food to my mouth with my left hand. Everything is so good, and I thank Stella, Lola and Mommy for makin' Thanksgiving so nice for us.

After our early dinner, Mommy takes me to the living room. I grab a blanket off the back of the chair with my good arm and lie down on the couch. I turn on the TV to watch the end of the Macy's Thanksgiving Day Parade. Mommy tucks the blanket around me and walks back into the dining room and starts cleanin' off the dining room table. After the parade ends, I'm hopin' I can find something to watch, but it is Thursday and there is nothing on but soap operas. I don't really mind. I have been watchin' them with Mommy for as long as I can remember when she's at home from work during the day sometimes. She says you can miss them for months or even years, and still pick up right where you left off. Her favorite one is "As the World Turns," and she talks to them and thinks about them like they are part of our family.

It's not often that I get to lie around and do nothing while everyone else is cleanin' up the kitchen. I'm not sure that's a good thing, 'cause I know Angry is gettin' more jealous by the minute with all of the attention I'm gettin'. I tell myself to enjoy today and worry about her tomorrow, 'cause there is always going to be a tomorrow to worry about with Angry.

I see Mommy and Normal walk into the living room. I know it's time to face the music. I am still on the couch under the blanket watchin' TV, and I think, *this is it* and *it better be good*. I know Mommy is talkin' to both of us at the same time so we can't lie about what happened. She tries to start with Normal, but I say that none of this is her fault. Mommy looks at me, and I look her straight in the eyes and I lie.

It's not the first time I have lied to her, but before, I was never confident about my lies. This time I feel like I am not only protectin' myself, I am protectin' the Other Sisters and myself from Angry. It has taken a long time for me to realize I'm Hero, Sad and Kind's protector, and if that means lyin' to everyone about them, I have to be dang good at it.

I feel a little stronger now than I have in the past, and I feel confident that eventually I can overcome Angry's cruelty and come out on the other side.

I tell Mommy Normal was still asleep when I decided to go out and play on the ice on the front porch. I tell her I fell off the porch and hurt my knees and tore my pajamas.

I mumble, "I didn't realize the front door was locked until I tried to get back in, so I tried to climb up to the window to wake her up. I was just too short to reach the window and that's when I tried to climb up on the arm of the chair. The chair tipped over and I fell to the ground and hurt my arm."

Normal piped in and said, "I heard her scream and looked out the window and saw her on the ground. I ran out the back door, around the house and helped her get inside."

I went on and told Mommy when Normal got me into the house, she carefully undressed me and put me into the bathtub. She cleaned me up and got me into bed where I could be comfortable, even though she was wet and cold herself. She gave me aspirin and warm milk to warm me up. I told her that Normal did a good job of takin' care of me and it wasn't her fault I got hurt.

Beggin' Mommy, I said, "Please don't be mad at her. She did the very best she could to take care of me until you could get home."

After I finished the story I could see she thought I was tellin' her the truth. Mission accomplished! I can't say I felt good about how well I lied, but I know it was necessary. I grew up a little that day.

I guess I'm gettin' better at copin' with all of the crap I have to deal with at home. It doesn't mean I like lyin'; it just means I have decided Angry isn't always goin' to win. Maybe I do have a little bit of control, even if I do have to manipulate people to get it.

18

Battlefield Park

By Christmas, my arm was healed and I had put the whole incident behind me. I saw our neighbors had cleaned off a spot next to our house and sold Christmas trees. He painted them pink, blue and white. I really wanted a pink one, but Mommy said she would have no part of it. We would have a normal green Christmas tree just like every other year.

I made popcorn and fresh cranberry garland to decorate the tree, and Mommy bought packages of tinsel and colored lights. I got the doll I asked for in my letter to Santa and I named her Lula Bell.

Spring came and went, and before I knew it, it was summer.

I love the park, especially Battlefield Park. It is huge, with hundreds and hundreds of trees and lots of covered pavilions where people can have picnics even when it rains. It has a public swimming pool with life guards and it is the only place Mommy will let us go swimmin' by ourselves.

Some of the ditches have bridges with and without water runnin' under them. My favorite game to play under the bridges without water is Billy Goat Gruff. Normal and I take turns bein' Billy Goat Gruff. Mr. Gruff doesn't like anyone crossin' his bridge, and if he catches you, he will eat you. It sounds scary, but it's not. It's just a lot of laughin', runnin' and chasin' each other.

When we get up on this hot July day Normal decides we are goin' swimmin'. I ask her if she asked Mommy if we could go, and she said no, that it was none of her business. She tells me to skip cookin' breakfast; that we will stop at the store and get donuts and chocolate milk.

I run to the bathroom, wash my face and brush my teeth. I get dressed as fast as I can before Normal changes her mind about goin'.

We have to take two busses to get across town to the park. It's a one hour bus ride on two different buses and we have to walk a couple of blocks to get there. But I don't care. I am still so excited about goin' I could pee myself.

We pack our towels and swimsuits and sandwiches for a picnic, and off we go. After we eat our donuts and milk, we sit on the bench and wait for the bus. It is right on time. As we climb on, I ask Normal if I can sit by the window. She says she doesn't care where I sit 'cause she will not be sittin' with me. I look closer to be sure it's not Angry, but it's not; Normal is just bein' a jerk.

When we get to the park, Normal spots some of her friends and tells me to go swim by myself, that she wants to hang out for a while before she changes her clothes to swim. I know she thinks I am just a little kid and she doesn't want me around, so I head to the locker room and change into my swimsuit.

The last thing Normal says to me is, "Do not get in the deep end of the pool; you can't swim." She doesn't have to worry. I always stay in the shallow end of the pool close to the lifeguard. I hardly ever venture past the kiddie section.

I am mindin' my own business paddlin' around the steps, playin' with a paper cup when two boys come up behind me and start splashin' me. I turn around and ask them nicely not to put water in my face, but they just laugh and push me under. When my head pops out from under the water, they are on both sides of me. They start callin' me a stupid, little girl. I try to get out of the pool, but they block the steps and force me closer to the deep end of the pool. I guess they don't know I can't swim 'cause they keep pushin' me deeper and deeper.

I yell at them, but they don't stop pushin'. I am really scared and start to panic. I don't know what to do. I try to scream and my mouth fills up with water. I swallow the water and try to scream again, but one of the boys pulls me under by my legs.

I look up at the lifeguard through the water, but he is talkin' to a girl. He doesn't see I am about to drown. I close my eyes and try to get to the surface before I pass out, and that's when I feel someone grabbin' me tight around the waist and pullin' me out of the water.

When I feel the air fillin' my lungs, I open my eyes and look right into Hero's face. She pulls me to the side of the pool and gets me out of the water. She wraps her arms around me and she is sobbin'. "I thought you were dead; I will beat the devil out of those little punks."

She jumps back into the pool and punches one of the boys. Blood spurts out of his nose and turns the pool red. The lifeguard jumps in and pulls her by her arms and drags her out of the pool. Another lifeguard pulls both of the boys out on the other side of the pool and calls for first aid. I just sit there watchin', wonderin' how much trouble Hero is in.

The lifeguard tells her she has to leave the pool area and take me with her. She jumps up, gets in his face and tells him he should have been doin' his job watchin' the little kids instead of talkin' to girls.

He tells her he'll report her and make sure she can never swim here again. She says, fine, she didn't want me to swim around incompetent assholes anyway. That she would report him to park security as soon as she located one.

She walks over to me, picks me up and carries me to the locker room to change back into our clothes. She sits me on a bench and tells me she is so sorry she almost let me drown. I tell her not to worry, that I won't let two morons keep me from learnin' how to swim. That next time I will be able to swim away from them and get to the other side of the pool all by myself.

We walk over to a picnic table and spread our sandwiches and cookies on napkins and eat lunch. When we are finished eatin', Hero takes my hand and we walk across the park to the bus. On the ride home, she sits next to me. She puts my head in her lap and slowly massages my head. She tells me she will always be here to protect me from anyone who wants to hurt me.

I say thank you, even though I know she can't always protect me from all of the evil things that happen to me. But I'm growin' stronger every day and soon I will be able to protect myself.

19

Revelations

"*What is your nightmare about?*" my therapist asked.

"*My father's funeral,*" I said to him. "*Every year, the same time, the same nightmare about him since I was twelve.*"

"*Tell me a little more about your dream,*" he said gently, seeming to understand how upset I am just thinking about that nightmare.

"*My father is slowly rocking in a rocking chair, blocking the door and watching me sleep. In the dream I wake up. His eyes bore into mine and he calmly tells me that he knows I wish he'd die. He goes on to say that my wish has come true, and it's all my fault he's dead. He keeps on rocking. I'm terrified because the dream itself feels more like a visitation than a nightmare.*"

I was lucky to know Dr. Davis. He was the father of my best friend in junior high and high school, Donna. Back when we were in school together, she and her family lived in a house within the fenced grounds of Whitfield, the state mental institution near Jackson. Donna's dad was a psychiatrist there and I spent many weekends in their home at that facility. Donna and I would often sneak out and visit the women's dormitories and listen to the patients talk about their therapy—and about the boys they missed on the outside. Even at that young age, I soon realized mentally ill people weren't crazy all the time.

Far from it. They behaved normally most of the time—at least that was true for the women in these group dorms. This took on an importance for me, perhaps because the members of my family weren't crazy all the time, either. Not even my father.

But the specter of this dream terrified me so much I spent the month of March in dread, knowing the nightmare would return on the first night of April. While still in high school, I discussed this recurring nightmare with Dr. Davis and he didn't mince words. He was adamant I needed therapy. Although I'd never told him about Angela, he could see I had serious underlying problems and needed help.

He was kind and easy to talk to; he explained that therapy was helpful and nothing to be afraid of, that it did not mean I needed to be a patient at Whitfield. That meant the world to me, especially since back then psychiatrists and psychologists were spoken about only in whispers—it was shameful to need their help. So I was happy to learn that my treatment could be in the privacy of his office.

He explained that the dream and the visitation-like nightmare itself would be pivotal in helping me start a path to understanding and healing. And that was a big relief for me.

* * * * *

Angry found Mommy's family Bible in Mommy's room in a drawer. She took it and keeps it hidden under her side of the bed where no one can find it. When Mommy asks us where it is, Normal says, "I don't know, ask Patra."

Normal is tellin' the truth, 'cause Angry and I are the only ones who know where it is. And you can bet your bottom dollar I'm not about to snitch on Angry.

Angry only reads the Book of Revelations. She likes torturin' me by sittin' me in a chair and readin' it over and over again. Most of the creatures she draws in her books are pictures she has seen in the Book of Revelations. Our family Bible has pages of colored pictures of what Hell looks like, and Angry is obsessed with Hell. She will sit in the bed and recite passages from the Bible for hours. Most of the passages she reads say what a bad person I am and why I am goin' to Hell. And I believe almost everything she tells me.

We go to Sunday school and church every Sunday morning and again on Sunday night. Then we go to a prayer meeting on Wednesday night. My mommy is a very religious person and church is her favorite place in the world to be. She thinks you have to worship every time the church doors open, and believe me, we do.

I was taught readin' the Bible comforts you and prepares you for Heaven, but the things Angry reads to me in Revelations scares me to death.

On Sunday morning, I lie in bed and dread havin' to get up and go to Sunday school and church. I feel like behind all of the good people at church, there are demons and devils hidin', waitin' to take me away. Every Sunday since Angry started showin' me the pictures of demons, I hang on to Mommy's legs and refuse to go into my Sunday school class. She tells my teacher she is shocked, because I have been goin' to Sunday school since I was a baby.

The teacher peels me off of her legs. "It's just a phase. She will be fine once you are gone."

But I know better; the demons are there. Angry made sure I know that they are real.

During the week, Angry sits me in a chair and shows me pictures in the Bible of all of the horrible things that happen in Hell. She shows me where it is written in the Bible, so I know it has to be true. She reads the passages to me until I shake with fear, and then she laughs and says, "You better be scared, 'cause one day you are goin' to Hell. You are a bad person and you will have to pay for your sins, just like Daddy."

She tells me Daddy is an evil person and that he will have to die for his transgressions against her. She read that right out of the Bible, so it must be true.

The way she talks to me about Daddy she acts like he is my daddy but not hers. She says he is this horrible human bein' and does not deserve to exist in this world. That all he does is get drunk, smoke and do evil things to her. And through gritted teeth she says, "And one day he will die for his horrible sins against me."

In my mind I know she is right, but somewhere deep in the back of my head I still love him even though I hate him.

I start to believe that the devil lives in the church with God. They are both in the Bible and I can't seem to separate them from each other. I pray to God, and then I wonder—am I also prayin' to the devil—and which one of them will answer me?

I have nightmares about Daddy. He has horns and a tail like the demons in the pictures. He chases me around the church. I try to get out, but all of the doors are locked and there is no one here to help me.

I wake up in a cold sweat. I am so scared and bein' in the dark don't help none, either.

I stop prayin' to God in fear I am doin' something wrong. But then I'm afraid God will send me to Hell 'cause I stopped prayin'. I'm very confused. I don't have anyone I can trust, not even my mommy. I stop askin' for help 'cause I don't think I deserve it. How can I deserve the love of my family when Angry tells me I am such an awful person? Even if I need help, I don't ask. I try to do it myself 'cause I don't deserve help from anyone. It's a big lonely world I live in, and I feel like the Book of Revelations is makin' me crazy!

Sometimes my mommy calls me Little Miss Independent, or she will say, "When did you become so grown up?" And I think, *when I had to start tryin' to stay alive 'cause Angry says if I die, I am goin' to Hell.*

20

Teddy Long

Teddy Long has been with me as long as The Sisters have. They seem to have all appeared around the same time. I know I can trust him to be with me when I am sad. It's like he can *feel* when I am lonely and he comes to cheer me up. I can feel Teddy when he enters the room; he is like a ray of sunshine in my life. Like my pink bunny that I sleep with, he is comforting. And he talks to me. Sometimes he sounds just like a grown up, but when I look at him, he is still a little boy.

Teddy and I have spent many hours in the dark, in my closet, when Angry gets mad at me and locks me in there. He holds my hand and tells me that he is here with me and that I am safe. We talk about Santa Claus, the Easter Bunny, the Tooth Fairy and anything else he thinks will keep me calm. Sometimes I think the only reason I am able to stay locked in there so long is 'cause he is in there with me.

He is never around when any of The Sisters are in the room, or anyone else for that matter. He is my own personal friend. He is from up north, but he doesn't have any family left there. I don't know where they went. When I ask him, he just says, "They are gone." He tells me he knew I needed him so he came here on the train all by himself to be my friend.

He is smart, and he helps me with my vocabulary words, my grammar, which is still way off accordin' to Uncle Durant, and my geography, but he's not worth a hoot in math. Neither am I. We try to avoid math as much as possible.

We have tea parties with my tiny tea sets and he enjoys them as much as I do. I am obsessed with tea cups and keep them hidden from The Sisters. I hide them in the back of the closet in a Kotex box. I love that box 'cause it is as blue as the sky. I have no idea what a Kotex is, but it is written in big letters on the side of the box.

One day I asked Mommy if I could have the box, and she said, "No honey, I will find you another box." But I wanted the blue box, so I took it out of the trash and hid it in the closet.

I have three tea sets. One is white with red roses and gold around the edges. It has two cups and two saucers and a tea pot. The second one is solid blue and it has two cups, two saucers, a tea pot, and a sugar and creamer.

But the third one is the one I love the most. Cheyenne, Grand and Grandpa gave it to me for Christmas when I turned eight and it is my favorite color—pink. It has tiny, dark pink peonies and green leaves on every piece. There are four cups, four saucers, four plates and a tea pot with a sugar and creamer. It also has a bigger plate for cookies.

Teddy and I are afraid to use the pink and white set 'cause we might break it. I don't think I would ever forgive myself if we broke even one piece. It's kinda hard to have a tea party without plates, so we use both of the other sets. That way, we have saucers for our cups and saucers for our cookies.

Teddy Long is so cute. He has lots of honey colored, curly hair and big, brown eyes that sparkle when he smiles. And he smiles a lot. He always wears navy blue shorts and a white short sleeved shirt whether its summer or winter. I ask him if he ever gets cold and he just smiles and says, "Naa." He spends a lot of his time tryin' to make me laugh, and sometimes that's really hard to do but he never gives up.

We talk about The Sisters and he tries to help me understand all of the sadness they cause in my life. He doesn't seem to know any of them or why they are here, but he understands the pain they cause me every day.

When we are locked in the closet, I tell him things I don't tell anyone else. I tell him I think I am goin' to die soon, and I hope Heaven is all it's preached to be. I tell him how alone I feel and how I wish I could tell someone about The Sisters and that they would believe me.

Some days we don't even talk. I just put my head in his lap and he sings to me, and other days he wraps his arms around me like a warm blanket and I cry and cry.

He listens to everything I say and he never says anything mean to me. He doesn't blame me, and he never says I am bad or stupid or ugly. He never cusses at me or calls me bad words. And he would never, ever hit me.

He holds my hand when I cry and wipes my tears away. He never tells me not to cry; he just sits with me until I stop. Then he smiles at me with his big, brown eyes and says, "I will always be here for you, Patra. As long as you need me I will never leave you alone!"

When we are out of the closet we have so much fun. We play dress up and he doesn't mind anything I make him put on. We swing on the front porch and sing to the tops of our lungs. We play hopscotch on the sidewalk and jump rope. He will even climb trees with me. I love him so much. I don't know what I would do without him. I hope he is tellin' the truth and he never leaves me, 'cause I don't think I can survive without him.

21

Back to School

I am so happy summer is finally over and I can go back to school. The Sisters are in junior high school and I won't have to see them all day long. I will see Cheyenne every day and only be with The Sisters a few hours after school before Mommy gets home. I'll be a second grader, and I know I will love school this year as much as I did last year. There are four second grade classes in our school and we were surprised when Cheyenne and I ended up in the same class again this year. We were worried all summer long about bein' separated, but Mommy said if we were we'd adjust. Sometimes I think she doesn't know me at all.

George Elementary is in downtown Jackson on one of the busiest streets in town. We have to walk six blocks to school. Normal walks with us, but she always makes us walk a half a block behind her. Sometimes she stops to talk to friends or waits for them at the end of the street. We know to stop and not catch up with them, or she says there will be hell to pay. She makes it really clear what will happen if we get too close.

When it's really cold, Cheyenne and I wear our pajama bottoms under our dresses on the walk to school to keep our legs warm. We take them off a block before we get to school and hide them in the sleeves of our coats so no one will laugh at us. I have always wondered why girls can't wear pants to school when it's freezin' outside. It seems silly to me that only boys get to keep warm.

Cheyenne and I got the best teacher in the whole school. Her name is Ms. Naron and this is her first year teaching at George Elementary. She is kinda young but really pretty, and she has two children of her own. She is kind and patient and likes kids a lot. She told me on the first day of school that she loves art. So do I. I doodle on my pages all day long and she tells me I do a pretty good job, even if I'm not supposed to doodle in class so much.

Our classroom has lots of windows and is bright and colorful. Ms. Naron has decorated all of the walls with pictures of everything we will study this year. There is a math section; good luck with keepin' my interest there. There is a science section with a storybook of dinosaurs, volcanoes and outer space. The reading circle has different colored chairs with soft cushions she made for us to sit on, but the art section is the best. I could spend my whole day doin' art and readin' and nothing else at all. She makes learnin' fun and tries to keep us from bein' bored, which must be hard with a bunch of seven year olds.

I have a hard time sittin' still all day, but Ms. Naron said she understands how I feel. Her son has the same problem. My teacher last year didn't understand and stood me in the hall a lot because she said I disrupted her class when I wouldn't sit down and stop talking. I told Ms. Naron about what she did and she said, "You won't be standing in the hall this year because you have too much to learn in my classroom." She also said she could keep me busy enough and I could stand as long as I kept one leg on the seat of my chair and didn't bother the other children with my squirmin' around.

She makes sure I run and play outside at recess. I heard her tell one kid that she doesn't want to see any of us sitting around being lazy, that we should be running all over the playground getting a lot of exercise. I know she thinks she can wear me down so I won't have so much energy when I get back in the classroom. I hope she is right. I hate bein' so fidgety and don't want to disturb everyone else in class. But it's really hard sittin' still all day long.

Spelling has always been my favorite subject thanks to Uncle Durant. I am doin' very well in the spelling bee this year. I am first place in my class. I know it's 'cause Ms. Naron is so patient with me. She makes me feel smart and tells me I can go all the way to the finals if I want to. I haven't told anyone in my family how well I'm doin' 'cause I want it to be a surprise. Or maybe I'm just afraid what will happen if The Sisters find out. They get jealous of me anytime I'm good at anything.

Cheyenne and I help each other study on our way home and on the weekends. We play a game of spelling everything instead of talkin'; no matter what we are sayin' to each other we have to spell it out. We can only do it between the two of us 'cause everyone else gets irritated when we try to do it with them. Grand says she will pull our ears if we try it on her.

After a while it becomes easy to understand what we are spelling, and it's funny 'cause no one else can understand what we are sayin' to each other. It's kinda like we have our own language. We practice callin' out the words in our spelling books to each other over and over again. Ms. Naron and my uncle say practice makes perfect, and I think as much as we have practiced for this, we should be perfect.

Cheyenne is in second place in the spelling bee, but she says she doesn't mind me bein' in first 'cause she is better at math than I am. She says everyone needs to be first at something.

I want to win the spelling bee so bad I can hardly sleep at night. I stay awake goin' over and over the words in my head. I know Normal will be mad if I win, but I don't care. Like Cheyenne said, we all need to be first at something, and this is my something.

22

Spelling Bee

Finally the big day is here and I am as nervous as a cat on a hot tin roof. I know all the words, but I don't like the idea of standin' up in front of the whole school. We are in the auditorium waitin' on the stage and it's really big. All of the seats are full of teachers, students and parents. I don't see one empty seat in the whole room.

Mommy and Lola are here, but Normal said she would rather eat nails than watch me do something so stupid. I wanted Uncle Durant to be here, but Grandmother said it was not a good idea since he doesn't do well in crowds. I'm not happy that she didn't even give him the option but I guess she thinks she knows what's best for him.

Mommy told me this morning not to worry about being nervous, that I have studied enough and I know all of the words. She thinks I will do just fine. I sure hope so 'cause I don't want to disappoint Ms. Naron. She told me yesterday she was proud as a peacock to have me in her class this year.

The top ten students are standin' on the stage by nine o'clock. There are five from the third grade, four from the second grade and one from the first grade. They start with the third graders and work their way down to first grade. Thank goodness. So far Cheyenne and I are spelling all of the words right and we are still standin'.

The first grader and two of the third graders and two second graders are out by ten o'clock. Only five of us are left standin' by eleven o'clock. The words keep gettin' harder and harder.

Mrs. Pell, our principal, calls the five of us to the middle of the stage. I think I am goin' to pee my pants before I get there.

She introduces each one of us and gives our name, our age and our teacher's name. She tells everyone how proud she is of all of us for making it this far and wishes us the best of luck. I know she doesn't like me very much 'cause I spent so much time in her office last year. I heard her tellin' someone in the hall one day that she's not sure how I am still hanging in there. It makes me sad she feels that way, but I'm still goin' to do my best to win this bee.

Lola, Mommy and Cheyenne's mommy are sittin' in the front row with Cheyenne's grandparents. We are all goin' to Angelo's to celebrate when we finish the contest whether we win or not. Angelo's has the best steak baskets in town. If you like chicken fried steak fingers and French fries with gravy on the side, Angelo's is the only place to go. Cheyenne's mommy just got a new car and she is goin' to drive us. I just hope I will be able to eat with all of these butterflies in my stomach.

Cheyenne and I hold hands so tightly I'd think we are on a lifeboat, too scared to let go of each other. They call Cheyenne's name. She looks at me and smiles and walks out to the front of the stage. When they give her the word I can tell she is about to cry. I don't know if she knows how to spell the word they have given her, but I know we haven't practiced it. She misspells the word, turns, and walks off the stage without a tear in her eye. Before she leaves, she hugs me and says, "You will have to win for both of us."

Allen Davidson and I are the only two left in the competition. Allen is the smartest and the cutest boy in our class. He is the most popular kid in second grade and his daddy is a lawyer. I guess that's why he is so smart. His best friend is Jeff Jamison and they do everything together, just like me and Cheyenne. It makes me even more nervous 'cause everyone likes him so much and his daddy expects him to win.

Mrs. Pell calls Allen's name and he walks out on the stage lookin' confident. The word is "establishment," and I'm sure he knows this word. But he leaves out the S. He looks confused, like he just can't remember how to spell it. He turns and walks off the stage just like Cheyenne did. I feel sorry for him, 'cause unlike Cheyenne he starts to cry. I'm thinkin' to myself, we are just seven years old and sometimes we cry.

Now my word is "establishment". As I walk out on the stage I am confident that I know how to spell it. Before I spell the word I know I have won this year's spelling bee. "E-S-T-A-B-L-I-S-H-M-E-N-T establishment." I take a deep breath and wait to hear the principal say I have spelled it correctly. I did.

I won a blue ribbon and a silver dollar for first place. I know the blue ribbon is just for first through third grade, but it means the world to me. Cheyenne came in third place and got a red ribbon.

I can't wait to get off the stage to show the blue ribbon to Mommy 'cause I know she is so proud of me. I think she knows how hard I have worked for this, but I'm not sure she thought I would win. But I did!

At Angelo's, I didn't have any problem eatin' my entire steak basket including French fries and a chocolate malt. Cheyenne and I wore our ribbons and giggled the whole time. On days like this, I realize life isn't so bad. Sometimes it's just wonderful to be alive with the people you love.

23

Greco's

Greco's, Aunt Lena's Italian restaurant, is on Capitol Street on the other end of downtown Jackson kinda across the street from Capitol Street Methodist Church where we go to church. Aunt Lena named the restaurant Greco's after her family in Italy. Mommy has been managing the restaurant for Aunt Lena since the divorce. She and Aunt Lena are best friends, but that is not the only reason she hired her. She hired her 'cause Mommy is so nice and so beautiful and an *asset* to the business—whatever that means. When I'm in the kitchen, I hear Aunt Lena tell the cooks if she had more people working for her like Rose her life would be a lot easier.

Mommy is tall and willowy, and when she walks she glides like she's floatin' on air. Most of the customers stop and watch her when she walks by. She has long, dark auburn hair, porcelain white skin, gray eyes and a smile that could melt an ice cube.

She never meets a stranger. She's nice to everyone who walks in the door. Mommy will not gossip about anyone, no matter how juicy the gossip is. Aunt Lena tells her she is too good for her own good and that she is too trusting. Everyone knows she is as honest as the day is long. Aunt Lena says she lets people take advantage of her and one day it will get her in trouble.

Aunt Lena is married to my daddy's cousin, Uncle Johnny. I guess that makes them my cousins, but we all call them aunt and uncle anyway. She won't let Uncle Johnny work there. I overheard her say, "I don't need him hanging around screwing things up!"

Mommy says I shouldn't pay attention to a lot of what Aunt Lena says 'cause she has a potty mouth.

Uncle Johnny met Aunt Lena in Italy when he was stationed there with the Army. He had only known her for a few weeks when they fell madly in love, just like Uncle Bill and Aunt Karena. Mommy says half of Europe married American soldiers during the war and the girls are called war brides.

Aunt Lena is described as a firecracker. She told Uncle Johnny when she met him she was going to marry him and move to America. And that is exactly what she did. Uncle Johnny says Aunt Lena is a full-blooded Italian and that you really don't want to piss her off. Mommy says he's right. Aunt Lena rules the roost. She is very beautiful with black curly hair and dark brown eyes, and she speaks with a heavy Italian accent that I have heard Uncle Johnny tell her is sexy.

Before I started first grade, I spent some of my days in the kitchen at Greco's. I would beg Mommy to let me go to work with her so I could stay in the kitchen with my friend, Bessie—who's part of the kitchen help— 'cause I knew I would be treated like a princess.

The kitchen is a huge noisy room with lots of cooks, dishwashers and lots of food cookin' all day long. It always smells like garlic and tomato sauce. I love bein' here. I don't have to worry about bein' at home alone with Angry and bein' tortured.

I spend most of my time under the big round table in the back corner of the room. Bessie puts a fresh, white table cloth on the table and it hangs over the edge down to the floor. It's like my own private hideout where no one can find me. I keep a pillow and blanket for nappin', and I have books and pencils and paper for drawing. I call it my secret room.

Bessie is my favorite person in the kitchen and she is my second best friend. She works hard to keep everything spotless. All the workers in the kitchen know not to get in her way when she is cleanin' 'cause she will shake her finger at you and cluck like a chicken. She is soft and round, and she squishes me a lot. She smells like soap and fresh air. She wears a hair net to keep her fluffy hair out of the food and an all-white uniform that reminds me of an angel on a Christmas tree. When I tell her that, she says, "Patra, they ain't no such thang as a colored angel. But we don't know that for sure."

Bessie told me once she can't have children of her own. She says she would like to take me home with her but, "Black folks and white folks can't live together 'cause it agin the law."

I wish I could live with Bessie 'cause I know she would love me to death and take good care of me. She would never beat me the way Angry does.

My Aunt Lena calls me a nickname, Little Ugly. That used to hurt my feelings, but Bessie hugged me tight and said, "Little angel, she only say that 'cause you so purdy. Besides, she loves you almost as much as I do!"

Grandmother says I am the spitting image of my daddy, except Daddy and Mommy are both tall and I'm very tiny for my age. I have long, dark wavy hair that hangs below my waist. Daddy and I both have blue-green eyes like the ocean and everyone says my eyes are lovely. It makes Normal and Angry both mad when people stop my mommy and say, "What a beautiful child you have." When that happens, I have to watch my step 'cause Angry gets jealous. Then I know she's gonna punch me the first chance she gets.

Bessie makes sure I never go hungry, not even a little bit, fillin' me up with spaghetti and meatballs and tiny little pizzas and anything else I could possibly want. She sets up a little table for me to eat on made out of a wooden Coke carton that she covered with a red checkered table cloth and matching napkins. She uses a Coke bottle for a vase and puts live flowers in it she takes from off of one of the tables out front. Aunt Lena says it's OK as long as she don't leave a real vase empty on a table. My whole play area looks very Italian and it makes me feel special.

My favorite dessert is Spumoni ice cream. Bessie serves it in a fancy ice cream dish and puts it on a plate with a doily. They also make cannoli and homemade chocolate cake with fudge icing. Most of the time she fixes me a little plate with small pieces of all three desserts. You just gotta love Bessie!

When I see Bessie takin' her apron off, I get excited 'cause I know it's her lunch hour and we get to go to the park across the street from the restaurant. For as long as I can remember, Bessie has spent her lunch hour with me in the park.

As we walk outside into the summer sun I can feel the heaviness of the heat all around us. The sky is full of fluffy white clouds. There is not a rain cloud in the sky, and I smile in spite of the heat. We stop on the corner of the sidewalk and she takes my little hand into her large one. We step down off the curb and look both ways before we cross the busy street. We walk to the other side of the park where the slides are located. Bessie has just started to let me slide on the big slide. Before I would beg and beg, but she said the slide was too tall and I would fall off and break my neck. Even now when I slide down, she runs up and down beside the slide until the sweat is pourin' out of her big body.

I laugh and say, "Bessie, you are gonna drop dead if you don't stop runnin' around in this heat."

But she don't stop, and I know it's 'cause she would never forgive herself if she let me get hurt.

There are swings and seesaws and a sandbox. She will not let me play in the sandbox 'cause she says, "It ain't sanitary. Cats pee and do their bizness in there." Even though we have never seen a cat in the park.

After I am tired of slidin' and swingin', we take a walk. There is a dirt path with lots of trees and flowers and other fun stuff to look at, like green lizards and bugs. Bessie don't like the lizards and she makes me promise not to touch them. I try not to chase her with them, but it's hard not to 'cause she starts shakin' her head and puttin' her hands up in the air.

"Lawdy mercy, Miss Patra, don't touch me wif that thang."

I laugh until I cry before I drop the lizard on the ground and let it run away.

Bessie knows the names of every plant on the path. We are very careful not to walk through the poison ivy. We brushed up against some one day and we both blew up like a balloon. We touched our faces and arms with our hands and had blisters the size of quarters from head to toe within a couple of hours. Everyone at the restaurant laughed at us 'cause we had to wear calamine lotion for a week. They said we looked like pink ghosts.

Before we go back to the restaurant, we sit down on the park bench for a few minutes. She pulls me into her pillowy lap and squeezes me with her big, soft arms. I feel like maybe there is a God to protect me and he has sent Bessie as my guardian angel to let me know there are safe places in this world after all.

In the afternoons when the lunch crowd slows down, Aunt Lena and I sit out back under a shade tree at the picnic table where she smokes and drinks Italian wine she pours out of a bottle in a straw basket. We play checkers and jacks, and sometimes, we even play cards. I only know how to play Go Fish, but she says one day she will teach me to play poker for pennies.

Mommy says, "Don't think that will ever happen, little girl!"

I laugh and Aunt Lena says, "Oh Rose, don't be such a fuddy-duddy."

Aunt Lena loves to brush my long hair and put it in pigtails. She even keeps rubber bands and colored ribbons in a box in her office to make bows. She says my mommy is lucky to have four girls to dress up and fuss over, 'cause she only has my cousin, Alberto, and he's not very nice to her.

I think to myself, "I have a package of five sisters I will gladly give you." If only it was that easy to get rid of them.

24

Busy Street

I am sound asleep cozy in my bed, when Angry jerks back the sheet and drags me out of bed by my feet. My head bounces off the floor and I am stunned by the impact. When I look up, she is standin' over me with what looks like daggers shootin' out of her eyes. "Today you need to learn to cross a street by yourself."

We live on Gallatin Street. It is one of the busiest streets in Jackson. I know when she tells me, "You will learn a valuable lesson today," that it won't be easy 'cause she always makes everything hard for me.

She walks over to our closet and pulls out one of my Sunday dresses throwin' it on the floor beside me. Angry knows it is one of my favorites 'cause I got to pick it out all by myself.

A few weeks ago I spent the night with my Aunt Lena and the next day we went shoppin' at Sears & Roebuck. We both loved the white eyelet dress with a blue satin ribbon around the waist. She bought me the dress, a pair of blue, patent leather shoes and a pair of blue and white lacey socks to match the belt. She told me she wanted me to be the prettiest little girl in the Sunday school class, even if I'm not Catholic.

I knew when Angry pulled the dress out of the closet it was payback for me spendin' time with Aunt Lena without her. I pick the dress up off of the floor and slowly put it on. I walk over to the closet to get my shoes, but she screams, "No shoes or socks."

I just look at her and walk into the bathroom. I wash my face and take the time to put my hair in a haphazard ponytail before I follow her out of the room.

It's early in the morning, but it is already a miserable steamy day. I am sweatin' before we get to the corner. The sidewalk is hot and I'm hoppin' 'cause it's burnin' my feet. Angry don't care; she just keeps on walkin'.

We walk past the red light to the corner and then down to the middle of the next block. When she stops, I stand on the grass behind her to cool my red hot feet and she starts countin' cars as loud as she can. She turns to me and says, "Get over here."

I walk up next to her, afraid she is goin' to push me into the street. She counts one hundred cars, and I think, *why is she countin' one hundred cars before we cross the street?* But I know better than to ask that question.

When she finishes countin' the cars, she says, "We are goin' back to the house."

I'm confused, but I run off the sidewalk onto the grass and follow her home. When we get there, Angry flops down on the couch and turns on the TV. She tells me she is hungry and yells, "Go fix my lunch, you stupid idiot." I'm starvin' too, 'cause we didn't have time for breakfast this morning since she was in such a hurry to start my important lesson.

She demands a bacon and tomato sandwich (no lettuce or mayo) with cookies and a Coke. Pronto! When I have to walk in front of the TV to get to the kitchen, she kicks my legs out from under me and I fall backwards onto the floor. I catch myself with my elbows. When I look up, she is pretendin' to watch TV but I can tell she is holdin' in a giggle. I pick myself up off of the floor and limp to the kitchen.

After lunch she lies down on the couch and says, "I think I need a nap, but you are not goin' to move from the couch while I sleep." She knows how hard it is for me to sit still, but I know better than to move. She turns the TV off and makes sure there are no books or anything else close enough for me to reach. So I sit, not so patiently, for the next two hours without a thing to do just starin' at the walls, twiddlin' my thumbs.

When Angry wakes up, she is in a worse mood than when she went to sleep. She jumps up, pushes me into the chair, punches me in the stomach and says, "Loser, why didn't you clean the kitchen while I was asleep?"

She knew I didn't dare get up while she was sleepin', so I couldn't have cleaned the kitchen. I don't even look at her. I just pick up her plate and start walkin' across the room.

I thought maybe Normal would switch while I was cleanin' up, but boy, was I wrong. Angry started yellin' from the other room, "Get in here."

I went into the living room just as she is walkin' out the front door. Fear grips me. I want to run the other way, but I know she will catch me, so I follow her down the street to the same place we were this morning.

It is noon now and I am suffocatin' from the heat. She still won't let me wear my shoes and my feet feel like they are blisterin' on the sidewalk. When we stop at the same place we were this morning, she says again, "You better start countin' cars to see how many seconds you have between them before you cross the street."

I start countin'. Seven seconds, ten seconds, twelve seconds. I think I need at least ten seconds if I run as fast as I can, but I'm not sure. It's a busy street and there are lots of cars. There is a stoplight down the block and I figure I will have to watch only the cars comin' from one direction instead of both ways.

I am still countin' when she pushes me off the curb and says, "Run as fast as you can."

And I run!

I barely make it to the other side before she yells at me to run back to her. I turn around and run without even lookin' this time. She makes me run back and forth across the street two more times until I am tired and out of breath. The black asphalt is hotter than the sidewalk and I have to run even faster to stand the burnin' pain on the bottom of my feet. I'm so thirsty and my throat is dry. I ask if we can go home now, but she screams, "No, stupid, we cannot go home. You have not learned your lesson yet."

We stand there a few minutes until my breathing slows down. She looks at me and laughs and says, "Now the fun begins, little Miss Ugly."

I think it's more payback 'cause that is the nickname Aunt Lena uses for me. Angry says, "When I say go, you will crawl across the street on your hands and knees."

I am stunned. Fear grips me and I can't move. I know I won't make it. The street is too wide. The cars are goin' too fast. My knobby knees are shakin', so I sit down on the hot sidewalk and close my eyes, hopin' this is a nightmare and that I am goin' to wake up any minute.

But it's not a nightmare; it's real.

I stand up and walk the three steps to her and try not to cry. I beg her not to make me crawl across the busy street, but she just stands there smilin' at me with evil eyes. And I think this is it; I'm dead for sure this time.

I hear her countin' cars again and I know she is goin' to make me do it.

"You better crawl fast or you won't make it." She shoves me down on my hands and knees at the edge of the street, but she is holdin' me back by my ponytail. When she turns it loose and says, "Go" I start crawlin' as fast as I can.

My hands are burnin' and my knees are gettin' caught in my dress, but all I can think about is crawlin' faster before the next car hits me. I hear tires screechin' and I start to cry, but I keep on crawlin' as fast as I can to the other side of the street. I close my eyes 'cause I don't want to see the cars comin' at me.

I reach the other side of the street and I feel somebody pull me up off of the ground and hug me close to them. "Are you crazy? What were you thinking?"

I look up. It's Stella. I don't know where she came from, but I am glad she is here. I am hot and dirty and tears are streamin' down my face. My knees and hands are scraped and stingin'. My beautiful white dress is torn where my knees kept gettin' caught and it's black from the dirty street.

Stella looks at me with tears in her eyes. "Patra, you could have been killed. Why would you do such a stupid thing?"

My guess is I'm in a heepa trouble and I'm not about to say anything bad about Angry. But I think, I did such a thing 'cause your perfect sister made me do it. Of course Angry is nowhere to be found. I'm sure as soon as she saw Stella she ran to the house to make sure no one would know she was involved in this dangerous game she was makin' me play.

Stella carries me home, cleans me up and brushes my hair then carefully cleans the cuts on my hands and knees. She helps me change clothes and puts Band-Aids on my cuts and scrapes. When I'm all cleaned up I tell her I'm thirsty. We go into the kitchen, and she pours me a glass of cold milk and hands me a box of vanilla wafers. I don't really like milk so when she leaves I add a teaspoon of vanilla flavoring and a bunch of sugar to it so it will taste like melted ice cream.

While I am drinkin' my milk concoction and eatin' my cookies, Stella goes into the living room and pulls Normal off of the couch. She asks her, "Why was Patra crawling across the street in the middle of the day? You were supposed to be watching her!"

Normal says, "I guess she's just stupid. I've been sittin' here on the couch. I had no idea where she was and I certainly didn't know she was playin' in the street!"

I'm not at all surprised by her response. She never has a clue about what's goin' on in her life or mine. I'm just hopin' Stella doesn't tell Mommy. But I know she will, and I will be makin' up more lies to cover Angry's tracks.

25

Stella's Engagement

Today is Saturday and I love to sleep late, but I smell bacon fryin' and coffee brewin'. Mommy usually cooks breakfast on Sunday, but not on Saturday. When I stumble into the kitchen, Stella is standin' there makin' a big pan of biscuits. Lola is stirrin' bubblin' grits on the stove, adding butter and cream. Strawberry jam and honey are already on the dining room table and a cantaloupe is sliced, arranged in a circle on a plate to look like a flower.

Stella turns around grinnin' from ear to ear. She walks over and kisses me and Normal on the top of the head. This whole scene is strange, and then I see her boyfriend walkin' down the hall. He is never here this early in the morning. Something is going on.

She wraps her arms around him and says, "This is a breakfast celebration. We are here to tell you that James and I are getting married and we're moving to Chicago." She holds out her hand and giggles, showin' us the tiny diamond ring on her finger. My brain is screamin', *Where is Chicago and how far away is that?*

We all sit down to eat and Mommy looks at her sternly and says, "Not until you have graduated from high school and turn eighteen, little lady."

Normal looks mortified and says, "But that is only two months away." Then she jumps up, runs out of the room and slams the bedroom door.

I keep eatin' my biscuit and ask Stella, "Can I be in the wedding?"

Stella and James agree it will take at least two months to plan the wedding. James leaves for Chicago in two weeks to find a place for them to live. He will stay in Chicago to work at his new job with the railroad and he will not come back until a week before the wedding. That means we will have to make all of the wedding plans.

I keep eatin' my biscuit and ask again if I can be in the wedding. Stella says we will all be in the wedding and I can be her flower girl.

After breakfast we get dressed and go to Sears & Roebuck. I love Sears! It is the only store in Jackson that has moving stairs that remind me of the rides at the State Fair that comes in October. Mommy calls it escalators, but I still say, "I want to ride the moving stairs."

My second most favorite thing about Sears is the candy counter. There are rows and rows of candy behind glass and you can pick out how much you wanna buy. Today Stella buys me my favorite candy, Maple Nut Goodies. I love them so much I could eat the whole bag all at once, but I don't. I'm very good at hidin' them from Angry in my secret place in the closet and savin' them for later.

After we buy candy we ride the escalator to the second floor. When we get to the top, I run back down and try to get to the bottom so I can ride back up again. When I turn around and look at Mommy, she is tryin' real hard not to yell at me and I can tell by the look on her face I better hightail it back up the escalator. When I get to the top she takes my hand and dares me to let go. Normal looks at me and smiles, then she sticks her tongue out at me when Mommy turns her head.

First, we look at white dresses for Stella. She says she wants a short one 'cause it will be a summer wedding. She wants the rest of us to wear green 'cause it's her favorite color. I want to wear pink and she says that will be OK since there is only one flower girl. That makes me feel very special.

Next we go to JC Penney's. I hope we have better luck findin' Stella's dress at Penney's 'cause she didn't find anything she liked at Sears. We did find pretty green dresses with spaghetti straps and full skirts for Lola and the other bridesmaids though, so that's good. My mommy picked out a blue-green silk dress with colors that look like a waterfall. It is beautiful with her dark auburn hair and gray eyes.

In the children's department, we look for my dress. There are so many pink ones I can't decide. After an hour, everyone is ready to kill me so I pick a pink and green one. It has flowers and lace, a big pink bow on the back, a long, gathered skirt and puffy sleeves with lacey trim. It is so pretty; it looks like a doll dress. Mommy says she will buy me white patent leather shoes and pink lacy socks to match.

Still no dress for Stella. It is one o'clock and we are starvin' so we stop downtown at the Elite Cafe for lunch. I always have chicken and dumplings and their homemade rolls. Their homemade yeast rolls are pipin' hot right out of the oven and they give us little pats of butter to go with them. Mommy loves their chicken fried steak and Stella orders the shrimp salad with Comeback Dressing. Every restaurant in Jackson uses some version of my daddy's Comeback Dressing recipe. It has catsup, mayonnaise, lots of grated onions and some secret stuff in it. The Rotisserie where my daddy is the chef is famous for its Comeback Dressing. I'm not sure why, but I think it's called that cause you just have to come back for more.

Normal is still pouting 'cause Stella is gettin' married. She orders a Coke and no food. I think she's crazy, but Mommy says, "Let her pout. She will be hungry later and have to eat a butter sandwich when we get home." It's not every day we go out to lunch at the Elite and since it's a special occasion, Mommy says I can have strawberry shortcake with ice cream for dessert. I don't remember a more perfect day!

After eatin' as much as my stomach could possibly hold, we go to the fabric store to look at patterns and fabric. Mommy has a sewing machine and when she has time she makes us the most beautiful dresses. She always makes our Sunday dresses and she says she will find the time to make an extra special dress for Stella.

Stella finds lots of patterns for wedding dresses that she likes. She picks one that has lots of chiffon and lace with covered buttons that go all the way down the back of her dress. The under part material is white satin and the veil is made out of gauzy netting. She asks Mommy since she is making it, can it be long instead of short. Of course Mommy just smiles at her and says, "OK, honey, whatever you want."

I look at all of this material and stuff and wonder how in the world Mommy is goin' to get this done for the wedding. But I know Mommy will work her fingers to the bone to get it finished in time.

When we get home, Normal goes straight to our room and slams the door in my face. I decide I'm not goin' to change clothes 'cause I never know who is goin' to be on the other side of that door. I spend the rest of the day with Stella and Mommy plannin' the wedding and realize how much work it will be to pull this off—and how much fun it will be when they do.

That night after everyone leaves, I am scared to death to go to bed 'cause I can guess what a terrible mood Normal is in. I sneak in and undress in the dark and slip into bed, hopin' to avoid a confrontation with her. Then she reaches over and pinches the devil out of me. She rolls over and goes to sleep without another peep, knowin' she got the final jab.

I smile to myself thinkin' if that is the only punishment I get for such a wonderful day, it is well worth a bruise on my arm.

On Sunday we have a cookout for James and Stella to announce their engagement. Lots of their friends come by, along with relatives from both sides of the family. But Grandmother Alexandria does not come. She says, "I will have my own wedding announcement gala in The Haven."

David and James cook hamburgers, hotdogs and ribs. We have baked beans and potato salad, and Aunt Lena brings fresh Italian garlic bread. David gets out the ice cream freezer and we all take turns churnin' fresh peach ice cream. I smile. I know Normal will be furious 'cause she only eats chocolate ice cream, but it's not her party, is it?

James tells everyone about his new job with Illinois Central Railroad in Chicago. Stella says they are going to live in an apartment building in the city and people there call it The Concrete Jungle. James says there is no grass or trees in the city and it gets really cold with lots of snow in the winter. He also says there are thousands of people who live in the tall building with just a wall between them. I'm tryin' really hard to understand exactly what that means. How can that many people and children live in the same place without fightin' with each other? Especially when they can't go outside and play. Stella says we can come visit her, but I'm not sure I'm ready for Chicago living.

It's nine o'clock and the party is over. Mommy says it's time for me to go to bed, but after last night I wanna wait as long as I can. Before I go into our room, Mommy kisses me goodnight and says, "Good night and don't let the bed bugs bite." If only that was the worst that could happen.

I walk into our room and I don't see any one of The Sisters anywhere. The light is still on, but I am very quiet puttin' on my pajamas.

After I am dressed for bed, I sneak slowly across the room, knowin' she has to be somewhere in the room. When I get close to the bed, Angry comes out of nowhere and grabs me by the arm and twists it behind my back. She shoves me against the wall face first and says, "I think you had way too much fun today!" She ties my hands behind my back and shoves me into the closet and slams the door shut.

Through the door she calmly says, "Sleep tight and don't let the bed bugs bite."

26

Vicksburg

The next Sunday David asks Mommy if we can all go to Vicksburg after church for a picnic. He says he has some news he needs to tell us. Lola looks really suspicious and says she doesn't want to wait until tomorrow, that he should tell us now. But David can be just as stubborn as she can and he says, "No, you will have to wait until tomorrow."

When I tell Normal about the trip she says she is not goin' 'cause it must be bad news if he won't tell us about it today. After Angry made me spend the night in the closet Saturday night, I am glad Normal is not goin'. It means I will not have to ride for over an hour in the backseat of David's car with her shoved up against me (even if she wasn't the sister who put me there).

Stella and Mommy get up before church to make ham and cheese and tuna fish sandwiches for lunch. They chop coleslaw and bake sugar cookies with pink powdered sugar icing for dessert. Mommy stirs grape Kool-Aid in a Tupperware pitcher and looks for the Tupperware glasses and paper plates she keeps in the pantry. Lola stacks everything carefully in a cardboard box that she picked up at the Jitney Jungle yesterday while she and Mommy were shoppin'. She lines the box with a tablecloth and napkins she took out of the linen drawer in the dining room. During all of this time I stand there waitin' impatiently for the big adventure to begin.

Sunday school seemed to last forever and when it was time to go to church, I told Mommy I just couldn't sit still any longer. For the first time in my life she agrees we can skip church and head to Vicksburg. I am so excited about skippin' church I had to say a little halleluiah to keep from feelin' so guilty.

When we get to the Vicksburg National Park, we drive around until David finds a beautiful spot under a big oak tree overlooking the Mississippi River.

Lola is really picky about everything she does, so we let her spread out the picnic before we sit down to enjoy our lunch. I don't mind Lola takin' so long gettin' it organized 'cause it is so peaceful with none of The Sisters here to bother me.

After we finish eatin' Mommy and Lola want to enjoy the day in the breeze under the tree, but I wanna see everything in the park. David and I visit the soldier's graves. He says there are over five thousand confederate soldiers buried here, more than anywhere else in the United States. Then we visit the battlefields where all of the cannons and bunkers are, and where most of the soldiers died. It seems like such a beautiful place for so many boys to have been killed. David says that's what war is all about, killing people.

I tell David it is all too sad and I need to do something fun now. So we walk up at least a hundred steps to a huge monument, and then we roll back down the hill. I jump up and do it again. By the third time, I am hot and sweaty but happy. To me, this is a wonderful day 'cause I have David all to myself. I am enjoyin' every minute of it.

When we walk back by the graves, he stops and says, "There were a lot of Confederate and Yankee soldiers killed here during the Civil War and that's why there are cannons and bunkers everywhere." He tells me that the confederate soldiers would hide on top of the tall hills and shoot the cannons at the Yankees coming down the Mississippi River, but in the end there were just too many damn Yankees. He laughs and says, "The rumor in the South is that the war isn't over yet."

But that's not what my teacher says. She says, "The South lost the war a long time ago." Really!

After a full day of runnin' and playin' all over the park I am so tired that David has to carry me back to where we left Mommy and Lola. They are still relaxin' on the blanket where we left them. David sits down with us all in a circle and says he has joined the Air National Guard and will be leaving for basic training right after the wedding. We all look at him with blank faces. I don't think any of us believe him.

Mommy asks him why, and he says, "It's the best way to help support all of us."

Mommy looks into his eyes and knows there is no fighting him on this; that he is right. It is the best way for him to make a career for himself. Lola is too devastated to speak. I just hug him as tight as I can. Without a word, we all help clean up the picnic leftovers and pack the car for the long ride home. I am exhausted and fall asleep as soon as I lie down on the backseat with my head in Mommy's lap.

When we get home, David carries me into the house and puts me into bed. Dirt, clothes and all. I'm so tired I don't wake up until the next morning.

When I do wake up, I see my baby doll, Lula Belle lyin' next to me. Her eyes are missin' and her neck has been ripped open. I am so scared 'cause there is real blood all over her face and on my pajamas.

I turn over in the bed and see Kind lyin' next to me. She looks at Lula Belle's torn body and shakes her head. "We have got to do something about her before she kills you!"

27

Smoking

Normal started smokin' when she was twelve years old. I know how much she hates bein' outside, so I thought it was strange when she started spendin' so much time in the back yard. I watch her out of the kitchen window and see her disappear behind the bushes in the very back of the yard. I know she is up to something.

Maybe I'm just too curious, but I need to know what she's doin' out there. This morning after she goes outside I slowly open the screen door, just a crack so it won't squeak, and slip out. I'm not sure which sister it is, but if it's Angry and she catches me, I know there will be heck to pay.

I slip down the steps and around to the end of the porch, but I can't see her. I crawl across the yard to the far side of the bushes and try to see what she's doin'. I hear her strike a match. I still can't see her, but I can smell cigarette smoke. You could have knocked me over with a feather. She is smokin' a cigarette. I saw her smoke one of Daddy's once, but she almost choked to death so I had no idea she was still smokin'.

I sit on the grass thinkin', *she is just twelve years old.* Why is she smokin'? I had to believe it was Angry 'cause I can't imagine Normal bein' brave enough to smoke. And then I thought, *where in the world is she gettin' cigarettes?*

I crawl back to the house. I run around to the front door and go inside to my bedroom and shut the door. I have never seen a child smoke before and it looked so wrong. I know my cousin Billy smokes, but he's fifteen years old and his mother and daddy know he smokes. I know Mommy does not know Angry is smokin'!

I start watchin' her to see where she is gettin' the cigarettes. After a few days, I see her stealin' them from David's shirt pockets. She took two from the pack and then hid them in a cigar box under her side of the bed. I can't believe I haven't found them before now. I'm pretty nosy, and I usually know everything that goes on in our room. I guess I need to pay better attention to what's goin' on around me 'cause it's the only way I stay alive.

Now I know that when I hear the backdoor slam she is headed to her secret smoking place. I have already checked out her little living room in the bushes, after I caught her in the act the first time. I was surprised, but she had made herself a pretty nice hideout in the back yard just for smokin'. She cleaned out a space way back under the trees and bushes where no one could see her. Even I wouldn't have found it if I hadn't followed her. She had an old green metal chair to sit on and a wooden box she was usin' for a table. She even had the clear glass ashtray she told Mommy she had broken while cleanin' sittin' on the table for her cigarette butts.

After a few days, I got brave enough to ask Normal if she was smokin'. She looks at me with the same blank face she always does when I question her about things Angry or Sad does. And without hesitation she says, "No stupid, I don't smoke. I'm just twelve years old. Why would you ask me such a dumb question?"

I shrugged my shoulders and said, "I don't know."

Strike one. Now I will ask Sad. If it isn't her I will know it is Angry.

It takes about a week until Sad switches, and when she does, she is in a terrible mood. She locks the bedroom door and won't come out all day. I know there will be blood when she comes out, and I am right, there is. I'm not sure what she did to herself this time, but she carries the bloody newspapers she used to catch the blood to the outside trashcan in the back yard. She takes the lid off the can, stuffs the newspapers in, picks up enough trash to hide them, puts the lid back on and comes back in the back door.

She walks straight through the house, out the front door to the front porch and sits in the swing. The swing seems to calm her down, so she spends a lot of time there.

I walk out and sit down beside her. "How are you doin'?" I ask.

"Not too bad today," she said.

I get up my nerve and ask my important question. "Can I ask you a question and you won't get mad?"

She looks at me and says, "Sure, why not?"

I ask her if she smokes. She simply says, "No."

Strike two!

Now that I know it is Angry doin' the smokin', I stay as far away from her secret smoking spot as possible. I just hope she don't get the Other Sisters caught up in her smoking habit.

I guess I should have known it wouldn't be long before Angry got me involved in her new hobby. I'm in the bathroom when she comes in and says, "Get dressed, we're goin' to the store."

I'm confused, 'cause she normally sends me to the corner store by myself when she wants something. It's a nice day and it's early, so it's not too hot yet. We walk down the block past the store and I ask her where we're goin'. She's careful not to hit me when we are outside where people can see, so she pinches my arm and says, "Shut up and walk." We walk down streets I don't know and I'm completely lost.

It seems like we've been walkin' for hours when she stops outside a Tote-Sum-Store. She looks in the window and walks back over to me and says, "Sit down."

I sit on the curb and she sits down beside me. She looks at me with her crazy eyes and says, "You are goin' to steal two packs of cigarettes today. One pack of Cool Menthol and one pack of Lucky Strike's."

I start to cry. I have never stolen anything in my life but an empty blue Kotex box from the garbage.

She grabs me by the shoulder, shakes me until my head rattles and says, "You will do it or I will beat the crap out of you. Understand?"

I feel tears in my eyes and slowly shake my head yes.

She tells me when we get inside the store that she will ask the lady at the cash register for help with something in the back of the store. She tells me I'm gonna run behind the counter and steal the cigarettes off the shelf and walk out the door. Then she says that if I get caught, she's gonna say she knew nothing about it, and I will go to jail all by myself. Dang, dang, dang, I don't want to do this. I am so scared I will get caught.

When we get inside, Angry walks up to the lady, smilin' at her and tells her she can't find the marshmallows. Angry has already checked to be sure there ain't no marshmallows on the shelf so she won't be expected to buy them. The big lady is kinda grumpy about havin' to get up off of her stool and mumbles under her breath all the way to the back of the store.

As soon as they turn the corner, I shoot behind the counter and reach up, but I am too short and I can't reach the cigarette shelf. I panic, and then I see the stool. I grab it and climb up and get the two packs of cigarettes and jump down.

Just as I come around the counter, the woman is walkin' back to the front of the store. My legs are shakin' and my heart is beatin' a hundred miles an hour. I hide behind a pile of boxes until she passes me, and then I walk out of the store and run down the street. I'm shakin' so hard I almost drop the cigarettes. All I want to do is go home, but I don't know how to get there. So I sit down on the grass by the sidewalk and wait for Angry to come out of the store.

She walks up behind me and yanks me up off of the grass by my ponytail. She asks me if I got the cigarettes. I pull them out of my pocket and hand them to her.

She laughs and says, "I knew you could do it."

She pushes me back down and leaves me sittin' there, and walks away down the street. I don't want to be around her, but I have to follow her 'cause I don't know my way home. And she knows it. The sky is still blue and the grass is still green, but I feel so gray and so sad. I feel like a monster after what I have just done and I whisper one of her favorite sayings, asshole.

I trudge along a couple of blocks behind her. I don't wanna be near her right now. I need time to think. I know I can go to Hell for stealin' and cussin' 'cause that's what it says in the Bible, but maybe if I pray for forgiveness it would be okay just this once.

When we get in front of our house, Angry stops me. She tells me it is my job to get her two packs of cigarettes a week. She tells me she doesn't care if I steal them or buy them, but I will get them! I don't know if anyone will sell cigarettes to children, but you can bet your bottom dollar I will try buyin' them before I steal any more.

When I get home, I go and sit in my closet alone for a while. I talk to Teddy Long about what she made me do and how awful I feel about it. Teddy Long is the nicest friend in the world. He always understands what I am feelin'. He's sorry I feel so bad, but he is sure God understands I didn't *want* to steal the cigarettes. He says, "God has a big heart and he loves you and will forgive you no matter what you do." Teddy Long is a good friend to have when I feel all alone in the world.

28

Alligators

Sad wakes up screamin' about alligators crawlin' around the room on the floor. I try to wake up from a dead sleep to see what she's screamin' about. I reach over and realize she wet the bed again last night. She smells like pee, but at least it didn't reach my side of the bed this time. I am still dry.

I sit up and when I look at her, her eyes are wild; she is frantic. Her hands are tremblin' as she points at the clothes that are strewn all over the floor. She's screamin' that alligators are crawlin' toward the bed and that they are goin' to eat us.

She grabs me by the arm and drags me to the head of the bed. She jumps up onto the bookshelf on top of the headboard and drags me up next to her. The headboard isn't very wide, my feet barely fit on the shelf and my toes are hangin' off the edge. It's hard to keep my feet balanced without fallin'. Sad is cryin' hysterically that the alligators are climbin' on the bed and up the walls. She keeps sayin' they have big teeth, red eyes and are gonna rip us apart with their big mouths.

The longer we sit here, the harder it is to stay balanced and not fall off the headboard. My feet are crampin' and my toes are white from grippin' the edge. At first I think she is havin' another crazy episode, but the longer I stand there, the more I believe her.

And then *I* start to see alligators crawlin' toward us!

I'm scared and start to cry, and she is cryin' with me. We're both hysterical and can't stop shakin'.

I finally stop cryin' and calm down. I'm not sure how long I've been hangin' on the edge by my toes but I know it's been a long, long time. I wanna jump down and run out of the room, but she won't let me. She is holdin' me so tight I can't move.

After what seems like hours, I realize she is crazy. Nothing is movin' on the floor. It's just my imagination gettin' the best of me.

I tell her I gotta go to the bathroom, but she says no. When I can't wait any longer, I pull myself away from her. I jump off the bed, run to the bathroom, shut the door and sit down on the toilet just before I pee myself. I'm finally free of her. I don't know whether to laugh or cry, but I know I'm not gonna get back on that headboard.

I hear her yellin' for me not to come out of the bathroom 'cause the alligators are still there. I wait until she is quiet before I slowly open the bathroom door a crack. I peek out lookin' around the room. I don't see her on the bed. I don't know where she is, but she's gone. I make a run for it and try to get out of the bedroom to the kitchen before she comes back. Before I manage my escape, my hair feels as though it's bein' pulled out of my head; someone's yankin' me to the floor.

It's Angry. Where did *she* come from?

Angry jumps on top of me and starts beatin' me in the stomach with her fists. When I try to get up and run, she trips me. I fall to the floor face first and she starts beatin' me on the back with her fists, pullin' my head back by my ponytail. Somehow she stands up and puts her knee on my back so I can't move. With her other foot, she kicks me in the head. I see stars. The room starts to spin and I pass out.

When I wake up, I'm in our room alone lyin' on the floor with all of the alligator/clothes facin' in a circle around me. I don't know who put the *alligators* on the floor to start with, but I'm sure it wasn't Sad. It was all so real to her and she was petrified during the whole ordeal.

I try to get up off the floor, but I am dizzy. My head feels like it is splittin' wide open. I go into the bathroom and take two aspirin before I get back into bed. I know I have to fix lunch, but I need to stop my head from poundin' and stop this dizziness before I can do anything else. Instead of gettin' up, I crawl under the covers and pull the sheet over my head and pray Angry will leave me alone.

I don't think Sad would ever hurt me, but she's not goin' to try to help me, either. She's too beaten down by her sadness to help anyone, even herself. Most of the time she lives in her own little world and don't know or care that I exist. I can't say she is a good sister or a bad sister. Only that she is a sad sister.

Sad tries to push Angry deep inside her head, but Angry is way too strong for any of The Other Sisters to control. Angry tries to keep Sad inside their head and not let her switch 'cause she knows how dangerous Sad is to her and to The Other Sisters. All Sad wants to do is die and that would mean she'd kill all of them!

I'm still in the bed and my mind moves to a dark place. I am all alone. I can't tell if this is a nightmare or not, but there is tape across my mouth and ropes wrapped tightly around my body. I am trapped, sittin' in the bottom of a birdcage. There is no door, and layers and layers of dark, gauzy cloth are draped over the cage. I hear people askin' where I am and I can hear someone lookin' around for me, but no one sees me. It's like I don't exist.

I wanna scream, but with the tape over my mouth I can't say a word. No one is goin' to help me or save me. If I am gonna make it, I will have to be strong. I will have to be brave cause there is no one else I can trust.

I sit up in the bed and think, *was I dreamin'?* I am very confused, so I get up and go into the closet where I feel safest. I close the door and curl up in a ball goin' to sleep, forgettin' all about the alligators.

29

Wedding Day

Today is Stella's wedding day. The wedding is at Capitol Street Methodist Church. I have been goin' to church there since the day I was born. It's big and old and beautiful. It has pipe organs at the front of the church that go from the top of the ceiling to the floor behind the front of the altar. The ceilings must be one hundred feet tall. The brass pipes are shorter on the sides and get taller as they get closer to the middle. It feels like we are drownin' in music when someone plays the organ. Most people say it sounds majestic, but to me it just sounds loud.

The walls are covered in dark wood; the front doors have stained glass windows of Jesus on them. The rest of the windows in the balcony are stained glass Bible stories, runnin' ceiling to floor all the way around the sanctuary. It is the most peaceful place I have ever been in my whole life. During church, my family sits in the third row of the balcony, but for the wedding we will sit on the front row with all of our family and friends.

There are white ribbons, waxy green magnolia leaves and big, white creamy magnolia blooms on every pew from the back of the church to the front alter. The arch Stella and James will stand under at the front of the church is also covered with magnolia blooms.

My grandmother had the only magnolia tree on her property cut down this morning. She said her first granddaughter was getting married today and she would have the most beautiful wedding ever, even if she had to cut down her favorite tree. Grandmother said magnolia blooms are very delicate and turn brown soon after they are cut. In order to keep the blooms fresh, the decorators have to decorate the church as close to the wedding as possible. They finish their decoratin' just before the wedding begins. The white blooms look lovely.

David is walkin' Stella down the aisle 'cause Daddy called and said he couldn't make it back from California for the wedding. At first Stella was upset he wasn't comin', but Lola said David was the man of the family now and he deserved to be the one to give her away. Grandmother almost had a heart attack when we told her Daddy was too busy to come. She frowned and said she would have a word with him about that. Obviously that didn't matter 'cause Daddy still didn't come.

When the pianist starts playin' I walk down the aisle first. My dress is pink and green perfection. Or that's what Grandmother said when she saw me at dress rehearsal. My long, dark hair has baby's breath and ribbons woven through my tiny braids. Mommy even let me wear pink lipstick. I have a basket full of pink and white rose petals I picked this morning out of Mommy's rose garden. As I walk down the aisle, I feel like I am floatin'. I drop the petals on the floor and think how beautiful this must be to everyone watchin'. The wedding must look like the fairy tale pictures Normal draws in her art books.

When I get to the front of the church, I walk to the side like we practiced and stand on the first step. I thought I would be nervous standin' in front of all of the people alone, but then I see Lola, Beatrice and Angela walk down the aisle one by one. Their green dresses and green shoes are perfectly matched and they're carryin' bouquets of white roses with green and white ribbons. As they walk down the aisle, they are all smilin' at James. Even Normal looks happy.

We hear the "Wedding March," and David and Stella start to walk down the aisle. They look like movie stars, they are so beautiful. Stella's wedding dress takes my breath away. She looks like an angel. I try not to cry, but when David gives Stella's hand to James and walks away I have to bite my lip to hold back the tears.

They stand there lookin' at each other while they repeat their vows and I just stay there in a trance watchin' them. James put the ring on Stella's finger and I can see both of their hands tremblin'.

Then the minister says, "I pronounce you husband and wife. James, you may kiss the bride."

And James does.

The next thing I know they are runnin' down the aisle and out of the church. The rest of us walk slowly down the aisle to the front door of the church and down the steps. As soon as we are outside, we start laughin' and cryin' and huggin' each other. James and Stella are standin' on the sidewalk kissin,' and we almost knock them down with our hugs.

When everyone comes out of the church, the single girls gather on the front lawn and Stella throws her bouquet. My old maid cousin, Elsie, catches it and she is smilin' from ear to ear.

"I'm sure," I said, "she is hopin' one day she will have a beautiful wedding just like Stella."

Angela says, "Fat chance of that ever happening."

We go around to the back of the church to the recreation hall for the reception. The room is decorated just like the sanctuary, with magnolia blooms on all of the tables and green and white ribbons on the back of the chairs. Music is playin' and a spinnin' light hangs from the ceiling makin' the room look like it is filled with stars.

Oh, and the wedding cake. I have never seen anything like it. Solid white with pale green leaves, four tiers with pillars between each layer and it's almost as tall as I am. The bottom layer has magnolia blooms, the second tier has tiny high-heeled shoes and the third tier has tiny doves, all made of crystal white sugar. A bride and groom were set on top of the cake and around them are magnolias blooms, tiny shoes and tiny doves. I don't know how anyone could possibly make anything so perfect.

This is the first wedding I have ever been to and I had no idea it would be so much fun. The music is playin' loud and everyone is laughin' and dancin'. I see more food than we can possibly eat, and then there's the punch. It's the best punch I have ever tasted—pineapple juice, Ginger Ale with lime sherbet floatin' on top. I could drink the whole bowl.

We dance for hours until I think I will fall over, and then we dance some more. At ten o'clock Mommy says it's time for the bride and groom to leave for their honeymoon. Uncle Johnny let them borrow his 1956 Thunderbird convertible and everyone says it is the coolest car ever.

We all go outside and throw rice as they get into the car. David tied tin cans on strings to the bumper and wrote, "JUST MARRIED" on the back of the car in white shoe polish. We can hear the cans clangin' all the way down the street until they are out of sight.

After Stella and James are gone, we go back inside and I look around the room. I am so glad Mommy has a cleaning committee from the church comin' in after the wedding. It has been the most fun and the longest day of my life. But right now I just want to go home and fall into my bed and go to sleep.

The next morning everyone is really quiet. We slept in and didn't go to church this morning 'cause we are all so tired from the late night last night. No one mentions Stella, but we are all sad she is gone. She will be back in a week to pack up her things for the move to Chicago and she will never live here again.

Normal spent most of Sunday in our room and she hasn't eaten anything since the wedding. Mommy says she will come around in a few days, but I'm not sure she will. She just sits there on the bed and cries.

I try to talk to her, but she just points at the door and says, "Leave." And that's exactly what I do. I'm sad, too, but I don't tell her how much I will miss Stella.

30

Train Tracks

I wake up Monday morning and I can't find Normal. When I went to bed last night she was in the living room watchin' "The Tonight Show" with Johnny Carson on TV. But it's almost noon now and I can't find her. Normal said last night before she went to bed that we were goin' to the store this morning to do *God knows what*, so I was up and dressed by nine o'clock.

I walk out to the front yard and call her, but she does not answer. I walk up and down the street, but I still can't find her. I knock on the neighbor's door and ask if they have seen her, but they say they haven't seen her for several days. I go around the house to the back yard thinkin' she may be hangin' out in her secret smoking place, but she's not there either. It's not like her to disappear for an entire morning.

Then I see her sittin' on the railroad tracks behind the house. I yell her name, but she doesn't even look at me. I start to run toward the tracks as fast as I can. I try to jump across the ditch between the back yard and the railroad tracks, but I fall on a huge rock at the bottom of the ditch and scrape both of my legs. I half climb/half crawl out of the ditch. At the top, I pull myself to my feet and start runnin' toward her. There are a lot of tracks to cross 'cause this is a railroad yard and they park a lot of trains here. My mommy told us we are never to go near the tracks 'cause they are dangerous. Lots of hobos hang out around railroad cars and the railroad tracks.

I look around. I do see blankets and a burned-out place where the hobos made a fire to keep warm, but I don't see anyone here today. I keep runnin' toward Normal even though my legs are hurtin' and I am almost out of breath.

I know there are only a few tracks that have runnin' trains on them. By the time I get to her, I see that it is Sad lyin' across one of them. I know she knows this track has live trains runnin' on it 'cause it's shiny where the trains have been passin'; the other tracks are dull from not bein' used.

I run up to her and scream, "What are you doin'?"

Sad glares at me and looks away.

There is silence. I touch her arm, and she shakes her head back and forth and stares blankly at me as if she can't tell who I am. I do my best to calm down. I keep repeatin' to myself, "We are safe and everything is fine," though I know everything is *not* fine. My sister is lyin' on a railroad track and I am here with her. We can both be run over by a train any minute. Mommy will kill me if she finds out I'm anywhere near the tracks.

I try to pull her off the tracks, but she won't budge. I kneel down beside her and plead with her to get up, but she won't move. It's like she doesn't hear me. I don't know what to do.

I look dead into her eyes and ask, "Do you know who I am?"

Sad just looks right through me like I'm not even there. I don't know who this is. I think it is Sad, but she is too lost to know who she is or what she is doin'.

I think the trains run every few hours. I sometimes sit on the back porch and watch them, but I don't have any idea when the last one came through which means I have no idea how long we have before the next one comes flyin' down the tracks and kills her.

I start to bawl. What if I can't get her up when the train comes? I can't watch her get run over by a train. I can't.

I see a man walkin' down the tracks lookin' at the rails. He must work for the railroad 'cause he's not dressed like a hobo. I run down the tracks until he sees me, and I lie. I tell him my sister has fallen and hit her head on the tracks and I can't get her up. He follows me, and we run as fast as we can back to her.

When we get there, she is lyin' motionless with her eyes closed as if she is asleep. As soon as we touch her, she starts screamin', "I want to die, please let me die!"

The man backs away and says we may need to get some help. I beg him to help me get her up. He looks at my terrified face and nods his head. It takes both of us to pull her off the tracks.

She starts screamin' again and the man looks at me like he doesn't know what to do. I tell him she must be crazy from the hit to her head when she fell. Then she jumps up and takes off runnin'. She falls into the ditch, but she crawls out and stumbles across the back yard. I see her disappear around the side of the house.

The man asks me my name and where I live. I don't wanna tell him 'cause I will be in trouble if Mommy finds out about him or the train tracks. I tell him we live a few houses down the street, but that I can make it across the ditch and back to my house by myself. I thank him for his help and walk away.

I am careful not to let the man see me go to my house. I don't want him to know which house we live in, so I start walkin' around the house to the front door. When I turn the corner I look back, he is standin' there watchin' me. After I thanked him I promised him I would call my mother as soon as I got home, but I won't.

When I walk up to the front porch, Sad is sittin' there still in a daze. I try to talk to her, but she looks straight ahead with a stone face and says, "Why didn't you let me die?"

I sit beside her and try to get Normal or Kind to switch with her, but it won't work. I pull her up off of the steps and lead her inside the house. I take her to the bedroom, put her in bed and cover her up. She falls asleep.

I walk into the living room, sit on the couch and cry my eyes out.

After my pity party—that's what my mommy called it when she told us to get over something—our pity party—I quietly slip into the bathroom to find some bandages. I clean my knees with soap and water and put iodine and Band-Aids on my cuts. I find a bottle of aspirin and take two for the pain. I'm not sure if that is too many, but Mommy always takes two for her headaches and my knees hurt really bad.

I am so tired I crawl into a place I feel safe—my mommy's bed. The smell of Mommy's perfume lingers on her pillow and it smells like roses and Jergens lotion. I wish Mommy was here with me right now. As I fall asleep I think, *I am just a little girl and right now I need my mommy.*

Normal wakes up around two o'clock like nothing happened. "What's for lunch?"

I look at her and think, are you crazy? Am I really livin' in a nightmare and could any of this possibly be happening?

I go to the kitchen and fry some bacon. I toast some bread and carefully slice a fresh tomato. I make the bacon and tomato sandwiches and put them on a plate. I take two Cokes out of the refrigerator and pour them over ice. Balancin' everything on a tray, I take it into the living room where Normal is waitin' for her lunch. We watch "American Bandstand" while we eat and Normal never says a word. I take the dishes back to the kitchen and clean up the mess I made fixin' lunch.

I try to pretend everything is fine, but inside I am a big mess. I've had diarrhea four times in the last hour and threw up my lunch. I find a bottle of Pepto Bismol in Mommy's bathroom and drink it to settle my stomach.

When I go back into the living room, Normal asks, "What is wrong with you, and what happened to your legs?"

I don't bother to answer her 'cause I know she doesn't care anyway.

That night I have nightmares. I have been havin' these same dreams forever. Someone is chasin' me. I can't see who it is cause they're too far behind me, but I can feel their eyes on my back. I run and run until I can't run anymore. I fall down, turn around, and then I see her. An old woman dressed in black with a long nose and nasty hair tryin' to coax me under the bed. She is slowly motionin' with her long, dirty finger for me to come to her. I am so scared I can't move an inch. I try over and over to scream, but I can't make a sound.

Thank God I wake up. I roll over to one side of the bed and open my eyes. I know I am safe in my room 'cause I can see the picture of the baby kittens on my wall. Under it is a picture I found in a magazine of palm trees on a beach. My mommy says it is a picture of Hawaii and I love to look at it and pretend I am there. On my nightstand is my clock radio that David gave me for my birthday last year, and also there's the glass full of water I keep by my bed every night.

The light that comes through the window is pale and makes the room look eerie. I know it's almost morning by the glow of the room. I hope today will be a better day than yesterday. I get up and get in the bed with Mommy in case the dreams come back. Mommy is warm and soft and she pulls me close to her and holds my hand. I feel like a little girl when I'm in bed with her and not a grownup tryin' to survive. Why can't I always feel this safe?

The next few weeks after Sad's train track incident I see only Normal and Sad. I have a hard time tellin' them apart 'cause both Normal and Sad can't accept the fact that Stella is gone. They cry and stay in bed most of the day and won't have anything to do with the rest of the family.

I waver between feelin' sorry for them and wishin' they would just grow up and get over it. I miss Stella, too, but I'm not actin' like a two-year-old cryin' all the time. And I'm certainly not goin' to starve myself to death.

This morning Mommy told Sad she is gonna have to take her to the doctor if she doesn't start eatin'. Angry is stayin' out of this mess and hasn't switched since before the wedding. I keep hopin' she is gone forever, but I don't think I could be that lucky.

Mommy stops by my favorite bakery on the way home from work and buys a German chocolate cake, hopin' to cheer Normal up. The only time anyone gets German chocolate cake around here is for a birthday, so I know Mommy must really be worried since it's not Normal's birthday. Lola says to leave her alone, that she is not going to starve to death and that she is just being stubborn and wants attention. She also tells Mommy, "Don't worry; she is not getting any attention from me."

When Normal won't eat any of the cake, Mommy calls Stella and tells her what a hard time Normal is having dealing with her moving so far away. Stella tells Mommy that if she will let Normal ride the train to Chicago by herself, she will send her a ticket so Normal can come for a visit until school starts.

When Mommy tells Normal she is going to ride the train to Chicago to see Stella, she smiles for the first time since the wedding. I know I should be happy she will be gone the rest of the summer, but I'm jealous. Then I think, *maybe I should stop eatin' and I will get to go to Chicago, too.* The only problem with that is Angry would not have a problem gettin' rid of me by throwin' me off the train.

31

North Jackson

*B*esides movies, traveling is my passion. I've been all over the world. I'm not sure if it's an escape, or if I just have wanderlust. In China, I walked The Great Wall and spent a fun day in the Forbidden City. In Chengdu, I fulfilled a dream and held a baby panda. I took a boat up the river through the Gumdrop Mountains in Guilin and drank snake wine out of a jug full of snakes and lizards. And in Xian, I visited the world-famous TERRA COTTA WARRIORS, one of the most fascinating things I've ever seen.

I spent three weeks in Australia where I snorkeled the Great Barrier Reef in Canes and stayed in a treehouse in the rainforest where I could feed the animals and exotic birds right out of my hands! I watched New Year's Eve fireworks from the top of the Intercontinental Hotel in Sydney overlooking the Coat Hanger Bridge and the Opera House, and roamed through the wine country outside Melbourne.

I have visited Venice, Rome, Florence, Sienna and Lake Como and made numerous trips to Paris, London, Amsterdam, Prague and Brussels. And in Austria, I visited St. Peters Cemetery and Lepoldskron Palace where The Sound of Music was filmed. It was so nostalgic. I closed my eyes and imagined the children running through the garden to escape the Germans.

In 2005, Phoenix Big Cinemas Management opened one of our largest theatres in Kansas City, "The Legends." For *the opening gala, we invited legends in the movie industry to attend to help us celebrate. Since we were in Kansas, naturally we thought of* The Wizard of Oz. *We contacted Jerry Maren, the only surviving dwarf from the iconic movie. He played the green garbed lollipop kid—the one in the center— who handed Dorothy a lollipop from the lollipop guild. We also invited Tippi Hedren, the star of* Alfred Hitchcock's The Birds, *and George Kennedy, who was best known for his role in* Cool Hand Luke.

Never in my wildest dreams would I have imagined as a child that I would live such a magical life. Bobby and I also own a business in Canada, and we've traveled every major city there more than once. We never visit a country that we don't tack on a week of vacation after our business obligations are completed. We love traveling with each other; our lives are truly blessed. When we retire we hope to take a one year trip around the world. My travels are a testimony to how life can go on in spite of hardships and seemingly unbeatable odds. I marvel at all my travels, because when I was eight years old I felt my life was over when my mother decided we needed to move from our home in Jackson. She and my sister, Lola, spent weeks looking for the right place. I could hear them talking about bedrooms and bathrooms and kitchens, but I wasn't too upset—at first. We'd already moved three times over the past three years, but never so far away that I had to go to a new school. As long as I was close to Cheyenne, I didn't care where we lived.

But all that changed and tore my life apart all over again.

* * * * *

Mommy and Lola have been lookin' for a new place to move. They say we need something bigger, that this house is old and smelly. I don't know why 'cause this house is perfectly fine with me. Mommy likes to move once a year. She says it keeps things from piling up. I wonder why we don't just clean out the place we have instead of movin' year after year! Stella tells Mommy and Lola they are just antsy-pantsy and like to move around like a band of gypsies.

My grandmother, Mommy's mother and Aunt Lola moved to California after my grandfather died and the two of them lived all over California before they passed away. I'm guessin' that's where Mommy gets her movin' around from.

When my mommy was eighteen, she met my daddy at Grandmother Alexandra's cafe, The Hamburger House. After a whirlwind courtship, they were married in the Methodist church on New Year's Day. Grandmother

Alexandra wasn't happy, but she couldn't say anything 'cause she had done the same thing when she met my grandfather years before.

Mommy's older brother and sister stayed in California after Mommy's mother's death. They said the small southern town was way too hillbilly for their liking. They still live there. Mommy hasn't seen my Uncle Christian or my Aunt Lola for years. My sister, Lola, went out to California and spent the summer with Aunt Lola last year, but they had a hard time gettin' along 'cause my Aunt Lola is so ornery, or so Mommy says. Mommy's other sister, my Aunt Dottie, married my Uncle Joe and moved to Baton Rouge soon after Mommy and Daddy got married. So that's why we are the only ones in Mommy's family besides Uncle Durant left in Mississippi.

Lola likes to move as much as Mommy does. She can talk Mommy into doin' anything she wants her to do. She tries to do the same thing with David, but I can tell he just pretends to agree with her about everything she wants.

One Saturday afternoon Lola came into the house all excited. Mommy and me are sittin' in the living room watchin' TV when she runs across the room and stands right in front of the show we were watchin'. I stand up to walk across the room to the kitchen. Lola says she found a big house closer to downtown that we will all love, that the bedrooms are big enough for Normal and me to have our own twin-size bed and our own closet. I don't need that much room for my stuff, but a dry bed would be nice every night.

I turn around and ask Lola where it is and she says, "North Jackson."

I can't breathe. My knees go out from under me and I have to grab onto the chair. They both run over to me askin' what the heck is wrong with me.

"I can't move to North Jackson, Mommy, that's the other side of town." They look at me like I am crazy and ask why?

I look at the both of them like they have lost their minds and say, "I can't leave Cheyenne, Grand and Grandpa. They need me and they love me!"

Lola looks at me and says, "Don't worry. You'll make new friends in no time."

Suddenly time stands still. I can see Lola's lips movin', but I can't hear a word she's sayin'. I am bein' ignored as if what I have to say isn't important. And I know, no matter what I say, I am movin' away from the only best friend I have in the world.

The next few weeks are a nightmare. They say we're gonna move as soon as school is out, but that's only two weeks away. How can I possibly prepare myself for this disaster in two weeks? I feel like I'm dead inside; I can't eat or sleep. Even Angry can't get any satisfaction out of torturin' me 'cause I'm so miserable.

My teacher can't understand why in the last two weeks of school I miss every assignment and fail every test I take. She asks me if I am sick, but I shake my head no.

Cheyenne and I are both in shock. Cheyenne is holdin' it together better than I am. She is not losin' her whole family. She is just losin' me.

I don't know how I am gonna survive without the security she and her family give me. I will be all the way across town, in a house with Angry... all day long...every day...by myself. I have never had to endure Angry's cruelty for so many hours in a day. I spend a lot of my time at Cheyenne's house in a soft blanket of love and care from her family.

That night in bed I lie stiff as a board. It's hard to breathe. I can feel a mountain of weight on my chest and I feel like I am gonna suffocate. No matter how hard I try I can't move. There are no tears and my eyes are wide open. I get cramps in my legs from holdin' them so straight, but they still won't move. I lie there tryin' to figure a way out, but no answer comes to me. I am doomed...

* * * * *

I have been dreadin' this day for two weeks, and now it's here. Moving day. But now I gotta go to Cheyenne's house to tell them goodbye. They try to make me feel better by tellin' me they will see me soon. I know it won't happen. Once I am gone they will forget all about me. I can't live without them. My days will be filled with pain and sorrow.

For the last three years I have had Cheyenne's house to go to for a little while every day to get away from Angry. After I cook Normal's breakfast and clean the house she could care less what I do the rest of the day, and I spend as much time as I can away from home.

Angry is happy we are movin' 'cause I will be with her all day long, every day. She laughs and says, "You will clean the house, fix all of my food and do anything else I tell you to do." She says she plans to make my life a livin' hell and then adds, "You will smile and say yes ma'am while I make your life miserable."

As Grand hugs me goodbye, she says, "I will miss watching you grow up, little one; it has been one of my life's joys for the past three years having you in my house."

When I pull back away from her, she looks into my eyes. "Don't change, precious girl, I want you to always stay as sweet as you are now."

Grandpa is sittin' in his wheelchair on the front porch. He holds me in his lap for a long time, huggin' me so hard I can barely breathe. He says in his gruff voice, "Honeybee, I don't know how I will get along without you. I love you so much. You have filled my days with such joy."

Holdin' back my tears, I say, "You are the only grandfather I have ever known and I will always love you more than you will ever know."

He looks at me and says, "I don't have long left in this world, but you have been a blessing to me. I will never forget your kindness to this old man." He reluctantly lets me go, and I slowly walk away and over to Cheyenne.

I can't say a word. With tears in my eyes, I hug her tight.

Then I turn to walk down the nineteen steps to the busy street below. I know they are watchin' me walk away, but I can't turn around and see the sadness in their faces or let them see the tears flowin' down mine.

When I get to the bottom of the steps, I feel Cheyenne touch my arm. She turns me around to face her. In her hands she holds her gold heart necklace her mother gave her for her birthday. Without a word, she puts it around my neck and fastens the chain.

Neither one of us says a word.

Then she leans over and kisses me on the cheek. "This will keep you safe. And no matter what she does to you, remember I will always be with you."

I nod to her, but can't speak. Walkin' away from her is the hardest thing I have ever done in my life. Ever.

I trudge the two blocks to my house, unable to pick my feet high enough off of the sidewalk. I stumble and fall. I don't have the strength to get up, so I just sit there on the side of the street on the hot sidewalk and belly cry until I get the hiccups. What am I goin' to do without Cheyenne?

After a while, I pick myself up off of the sidewalk and wipe the blood off of my scraped legs with the tail of my dress. I put my chin up, turn my face toward the sky and know the world isn't comin' to an end today, even if I want it to.

I walk the rest of the way home without any tears in my eyes. If I have learned one thing today, it's that I'm alone in this big, old world. I can depend only on myself; I can't rely on anyone else. I feel a hard shell formin' around my mind and my heart. I think, *trust no one and don't ask anyone for anything ever again. I feel like my own family is the enemy.*

When I walk into the empty house, I try to swallow and wonder if I am goin' to have this lump in my throat for the rest of my life. Will the hollow hole where my heart should be stay in my chest forever? I want to run, but I have nowhere to go. I'm too little.

My footsteps sound loud in the front hallway. The rooms are big and empty, and the walls look naked, caught without any clothes on. My small bedroom looks huge without any furniture. The nails where all of my pictures have been hangin' on the walls are still there, and I want to pull them out and jab them in my body to make the pain go away.

I stop in my tracks and grab the gold heart around my neck and think, *thank you, Cheyenne, for bein' here with me,* 'cause I know stabbin' myself with nails is something that Sad would do!

Mommy is in the dining room packin' the last of her best glassware. Her mother gave it to her along with her dishes as a wedding present. We only use them at Christmas and Thanksgiving time, and Mommy insists on washin' and dryin' them by herself.

I look at the dishes and want to smash them on the floor to hurt her the way she is hurtin' me. But then I remember the last thing Grand said to me about staying the same and never changing into someone else.

Mommy turns and looks at me and says, "Holding my mother's things makes me feel closer to her even though she is gone." She puts each glass in the box with great tenderness, givin' them a pat. Only a bomb could break her treasures the way she packs them. And after seein' her sad face I know I could never hurt her with my selfishness.

About that time, Lola walks in the front door. "We better get going." She climbs into the pick-up truck she borrowed from her friend, Ronnie to make the move.

I scramble into the truck next to her, tryin' to hold back the tears and I pray that God will give me the strength to do this without dyin' from the pain. I know it will be a long time before I will see my best friend again, if ever. The six or seven miles across town isn't far if you're a grownup, but I am only eight years old. I might as well be movin' to China.

32

The Homecoming

The whole house smells like fried chicken. Mommy is runnin' around the big old-fashioned kitchen like it's Christmas morning. Normal is sittin' at the dining room table, foldin' our best linen napkins, the ones we gave Mommy for Mother's Day last year. They are the prettiest shade of yellow, just like the fresh-churned butter Miss Hattie makes at my grandmother's house in Newhaven. They are covered with light blue and dark yellow tulips with green leaves. We use them only for very special occasions, along with Mommy's best dishes.

Lola is rollin' out her famous biscuits; she makes the fluffiest homemade biscuits ever. Mommy taught her just how much baking powder to use to make them rise a full three inches. She melts a stick of butter in a skillet and turns them to make sure they are drippin' in butter on both sides before she puts them back in the iron skillet. The extra butter makes them brown just right so they will be nice and crispy on the top and bottom.

When I walk into the kitchen, I see a cherry pie on the top of the counter. I know there is a chocolate pie in the refrigerator, 'cause that's David's favorite. I tell Mommy I'm hungry and Lola says, "Hold your horses, Miss Priss, dinner will not be ready for another thirty minutes."

Mommy walks over to the Frigidaire, opens the door and pulls out a bottle of cold milk. I can see the cream has risen to the top and I remember how many times I have used a straw to suck the heavy cream right off the top of the bottle. Mommy shakes it up and pours me a glass of milk. She sits the glass down in front of me and says, "That should hold you until dinnertime."

I sigh loudly and think, so much for scorin' a slice of that cherry pie.

Mommy just looks at me and smiles. "All in due time, Pitty Pat." This is the nickname the entire family has given me and I don't like it one bit. It sound like something you would call a cat.

David called yesterday from the base in Biloxi and said he will be home on leave for two weeks; that he should be home around one o'clock in the afternoon.

At twelve forty-five, the chicken is fried and the whole house smells like Mommy's home cookin'. The fresh-cut corn and butter beans are bubblin' on the stove. The mashed potatoes and gravy are pipin' hot. Lola just put the juicy, sliced tomatoes and crispy bread-and-butter pickles on the table, along with tall glasses of sweet iced tea. Mom takes the golden brown biscuits out of the oven just about the same time the front door opens.

I try to get to him first, but Lola beats me to the door. David hugs her and puts his arm around her waist as he walks her into the kitchen. He picks me up and gives me big kisses all over my face and neck, which gives me goosebumps up and down my skinny legs. He puts me down and walks over to Mommy and gives her the biggest hug ever, and I can see tears formin' in her beautiful gray eyes.

Normal never moves from the dining table. Her rigid body sat still when David entered the room. Her eyes are starin' straight ahead like she's in a trance and she acts as if she isn't aware it's a special day for all of us. No one else understands what her life is like. They just think she is a difficult child, and that she enjoys makin' everyone else's life miserable. They have no idea what a confusin' life she lives.

David walks over to the table, leans over and kisses her on the top of the head. He looks down at her motionless face and says, "Are you not happy to see me, or are you just pouting about something as usual?"

She jumps up and runs to the bedroom and slams the door. David looks at Mommy and shrugs his shoulders. "There's something wrong with that girl," he says.

If he only knew the half of it.

I go into the bedroom and ask Normal what is wrong and why she ran out on David.

She says, "Nobody even told me he was comin' home."

I didn't bother to tell her that she was sittin' in the living room last night when he called, or that she had helped set the table for lunch. Why would I? She wasn't there; someone else was.

Lunch was delicious, even if Normal refused to come out of her bedroom. I went back into the room two different times to try and coax her out, but she was too embarrassed by that time to show her face.

The next morning she is actin' like herself and you wouldn't know she had acted so crazy the day before. David suggests Mommy take her to the doctor about her memory lapses, and she promises him she will check into it next week. A lot of good that will do. I have watched Angry pretend she is normal forever, and no one has ever caught on to her shenanigans. Even a crazy person doctor can't figure their mess out. Angry has too much control over all of them.

The next day after church we go to the Krystal and pick up hamburgers and French fries for lunch. Mommy says she cooked a feast yesterday and there would be no cooking today. We all love Krystal burgers and can't wait to get home. The whole car smells like grilled onions and mustard. The buns are so soft they melt in my mouth and I have to be careful not to drip hamburger juice down my chin. We buy twenty-five burgers and I know there will be zero left when we are done.

After lunch, David tells us he is getting married and he will not be living with us when he gets back from summer camp. He spends two weeks in Biloxi, Mississippi every summer for training and we always spend time on the beach while he is there. It's sorta our vacation. No one knows what to say. We don't know whether to laugh or cry. He has been the head of the family since the divorce, and he has taken care of us over the past few years. I can see the sadness in Mommy's eyes. She is torn between bein' happy for him and hidin' the fact that she can't endure him not livin' in the house with us every day. Lola looks horrified and tears well up in her eyes. Normal just sits there stone-faced. I try to smile and say, "At least he's not movin' to Chicago."

I look around at my sad family and think, please Lord, don't let my family get any smaller and don't let me throw up my Krystals on David's lap.

33

Mad Dog

One Saturday morning in the middle of the summer I beg Mommy to let me go play outside all by myself. I promise her I won't leave the yard or go near the street.

I need to get outside by myself cause my neighbor's cat just had kittens. I heard them meowin' under their house yesterday, but I didn't have time to find them before it got dark. I'm not gonna tell anyone about them 'cause the last time Mamma cat had kittens, I heard Mr. Tommy say he put them in a paper sack and threw them over the bridge into the Pearl River. He did it on his way to work. Today I am gonna try and move them under our house before he finds them. It's the only way I can save them.

After I begged her for an hour, Mommy finally says I can go outside. I fly down the steps and around the house to the back yard. It's early, so I don't think anyone is up yet. I find a small opening to crawl through on the side of Mr. Tommy's place. I sneak in under his house and crawl toward the space under the porch. It's dark under here, but I need to get to these kittens. I didn't think about what to wear when I got dressed this morning and my dress keeps gettin' caught up under my knees. I'm gettin' sick to my stomach from the awful moldy smells, too, but I keep goin'.

When I get underneath the porch, I see them—two white ones, one that's black and white, and one that's gray. The kittens are so cute I can hardly stand it. They're on a pile of paper in the corner and meowin' their heads off, but Mamma cat is nowhere to be found. I pick them up and try to keep them quiet. I know if Mr. Tommy hears them they'll be takin' a swim.

Finally Mamma cat returns. I put the kittens in a flour sack I brought with me and I crawl back to the opening. I see Mamma cat when I stand up and she follows me like I knew she would. I put the kittens under our house where I know they'll be safe.

Then I make them a nice bed with the flour sack and a towel left at the back door earlier this morning. I hold them and play with them until I hear Mommy callin' me. I kiss each one and tell them I will be back to check on them later.

I run into the house to see what Mommy wants and she says she has to go to the grocery store. She said Lola and Angela were still sleeping and I could stay home with them, but I must stay inside the house. Normally I'd want to go with her so I can coax her into buyin' junk for me to eat, but today I'm needed here.

I go to the front porch and watch Mommy get on the bus down at the end of the street. When she's out of sight, I run into the kitchen and find an old cracked bowl in the pantry. After I pour some milk in a mason jar, I put the top back on so I won't spill it. I crawl back under the house and pour Mamma cat some breakfast, and she laps it up like she is starvin'. I figure I need to feed her so she won't leave the babies alone.

I pick up the kittens one by one and rub them on my face. They are so soft and so cute. I've never seen anything this tiny. Their little pink tongues hang out of their mouths when they cry, and when I put them down they crawl around and around in circles lookin' for their mommy. I sit and play with them for a very long time and Mamma cat doesn't even mind. I name the two white ones Kippie and Snowball. The gray one I name Stormy, and the black and white one I name Boots, 'cause he has three white paws.

I know Mommy will be back soon so I crawl out from under the house and walk around the back of the house to the back door. When I turn the corner I stop in my tracks and my hair stands up on the back of my neck. A brown and white stray dog stands in front of me, growlin'. He has foam comin' out of his mouth and his eyes look funny. His front legs are wide apart and he looks like he is gonna jump right on top of me.

I back away, but he moves with me. I don't have anywhere to run but to the back steps, but the dog is blocking the way. He never takes his eyes off of me.

I scream so loud my throat hurts. Then I hear the back door open behind me and Normal comes out to stand on the porch. She freezes, and looks at me with terror in her eyes.

A few days ago our neighbor, Mr. Tommy, told us there were some rabid dogs caught and killed in Jackson. He says we are supposed to be on the lookout for any strange dogs in our neighborhood and to watch out for dogs with foam coming out of their mouths.

And this dog is foamin' at the mouth.

I start to run toward the steps, but the dog chases me. When I turn around to see where he is he runs straight for me. I try to push him away, but he sinks his teeth in my right hand and then shakes his head. I feel my skin tear and hear someone scream. I don't know if the screamin' is comin' from me or Normal.

I hit the dog on the head with my left hand and he lets go of my right hand. He grabs my left hand in his mouth and shakes his head again and blood spurts everywhere.

I stumble toward the steps. He still has my left hand in his mouth, shakin' it, but then someone behind me picks me up. I look up and I see it's Hero. She kicks the dog hard in the side; he yelps and lets go of my hand. He grabs her shoe in his mouth and shakes it. Her shoe comes off and we fall on the back porch. My head hits the floor and I hear a loud bang.

When we sit up I see Mr. Tommy standin' over the dog with a gun in his hand. I look around and Hero is still holdin' me in her arms, rockin' me back and forth in her lap. I look at my hands and they are covered in blood, but I don't feel any pain.

Mr. Tommy asks us where Mommy is and Hero says she's gone to the store.

"We have to get Patra to a hospital as soon as possible," he says, "to get her the rabies vaccine."

He picks me up and carries me into the house. He tells Hero to get some clean towels.

She runs to the bathroom and pulls Mommy's favorite hand towels off the towel rack and hands them to him. He wraps my hands in the towels and tells her not to let me take them off.

He goes to the phone and calls an ambulance. Then he calls the police and tells them he just shot a rabid dog in his neighbor's back yard, and that the dog had attacked a child. He gives them our address and tells them he would be waiting for them out front.

About that time, Mommy walks through the front door. When she sees all of the blood on the towels, I think she is goin' to faint.

"What have you done to her?" she screams at Hero as she runs to me.

In the middle of all the chaos, Lola walks into the room. But she runs to me and unwraps the towels from my hands. I look down and see deep gapping bite marks on both hands. I throw up all over Lola, Mommy and the floor.

I hear the sirens gettin' closer, so loud it hurts my ears. The front door opens and two men run inside the living room. They take one look at my hands and start wrappin' them up in white gauze. They pick me up and carry me out to the ambulance.

Mommy gets inside the ambulance with me, but they won't let Lola or Hero go. Mr. Tommy tells them he will change from his work clothes and drive them to the hospital. Lola and Hero are standin' in the street when the ambulance takes me away.

* * * * *

By the time we get to the Baptist Hospital my hands are hurtin' and I'm cryin' really loud. They wheel me into the emergency room on a stretcher and put me behind a curtain. I tell Mommy my hands are hurtin' so bad I can hardly stand it. The nurses tell me the doctor will give me some medicine as soon as he arrives, but I don't think I can wait much longer. Mommy sits beside me holdin' my gauze-wrapped hands in hers. I see concern on her face and she looks really scared.

I've had stitches before, so I know what's comin'. Big needles and shots. I beg Mommy not to let them stick the needles in my bites, but she tells me that's not her decision to make. She keeps tellin' me as soon as they put the medicine in it will stop hurting and I won't feel a thing.

It's not long before the doctor walks in. The name on his white coat is Dr. Jerry Riley, MD. He walks over to me and pretends to shake my hand, but pulls his hand back. "Do you have paws or hands?" he asks.

I would laugh if I didn't hurt so bad.

He's gentle when he takes off the bandages the ambulance people put on my hands. He takes the gauze off slowly, makin' sure he doesn't hurt me. As he unwraps the gauze, he smiles and asks me what happened.

I look at him, but I don't smile back. I don't know where to start. Do I tell him about the kittens or do I start when I first saw the dog? If I tell him about the kittens, they might die, so I don't know what to say.

Mommy can tell I'm confused, so she tells Dr. Riley that my hands were chewed up by a rabid dog.

He has a very strange look on his face, but he finishes takin' off the bandages. When he sees my hands, he asks if she's sure the dog had rabies. She told him our neighbor shot the dog because it was foaming at the mouth and that it had gone crazy and attacked me.

Then Dr. Riley turns around and tells everyone else in the room to put on gloves. He takes the bloody rags from my hands and throws them in the trash. He warns the nurses not to get my blood on their hands if they have a cut. The nurses who were takin' care of me look scared and put gloves on before they come close to me again. Now I feel like everyone is afraid of me and that makes me wonder if I'm goin' to die.

Dr. Riley asks Mommy if he could talk to her in the hall, but I yell, "No, Mommy, don't leave me here by myself!"

The way Mommy looks at me then I think maybe she's afraid, too, that I am goin' to die.

A nice nurse comes over to me. "I won't leave you alone, honey. I'll stay with you until your Mommy comes back."

Mommy and the doctor are only gone a few minutes. When they come back the doctor tells me they're giving me a shot in my hip to stop the pain. He has to clean my bites really well since the dog might be rabid.

Another nurse brings in a huge needle and I start to cry. I ask them where my Mommy is and they all say she'll be back soon. I ask them to wait for her before givin' me the shot. The doctor nods his head.

They roll me over and poke the needle in my booty. I try not to scream, but I am scared and my hands still hurt. Mommy is at the side of the bed, runnin' her hands through my hair. "Everything is going to be okay," she says.

It doesn't take long before I have the feelin' that I am floatin' above the bed. I feel almost happy, and I'm not afraid anymore. I think I had this shot before when I hurt my arm. I smile at Mommy and she smiles back. I know it's goin' to be all right.

The people helpin' the doctor put a big pan on my stomach and put my hands over the pan. Then they start pourin' something over my hands and the doctor keeps tellin' them to "flush" all of the blood out of the wounds.

I feel rubbin', but I don't feel any pain. I ask about the shots in my hands, but the nurse says they have already numbed them so I shouldn't hurt anymore.

She was right. I didn't feel any pain. I was floatin' around the room feelin' happy. After a while, I feel the people around me pullin' on my hand, but it don't hurt. Then I fall asleep.

When I wake up, both of my hands are bandaged and I can't move my fingers. I have to go to the bathroom, but I'm alone in the room. When I start to get up a man comes into the room. I don't know who he is, but he's wearin' hospital clothes. He gently pushes me back down on the bed, but I tell him I'm goin' to pee in my pants. He says he'll help me get to the bathroom. That scares me and I panic. Who's goin' to pull down my panties? I don't want him to touch me. I start to cry, and he says he'll find my mother.

A few minutes later Mommy and Lola walk into the room, but it's too late. I've already wet my pants. Now I am really upset. I feel like such a big baby. I haven't wet my pants in a very long time. Lola tells me it' okay, that she'll look for some clean ones. Mommy stays with me until the hospital papers are ready and I can go home.

When Dr. Riley comes back he tells us we need to come back in a week to have the stitches taken out.

The shot has worn off and my hands hurt again. I'm not happy about comin' back here for anything. It sounds like takin' out stitches hurts. But I don't say anything 'cause I want go home.

Lola couldn't find me any panties, but Mommy says we're going straight home and I can wear the hospital gown until we get there. Mr. Tommy is waitin' outside for us in his truck, and he takes us back to the house. When we get home he carries me inside, puts me in bed and covers me up. He tells Mommy he will be back shortly to talk to her about what happened to the dog.

"How could anyone so nice throw baby kittens off of a bridge in a paper bag?" I mumble.

After my nap, Mommy makes me a bed on the couch and asks me if I want to eat in the living room and watch TV. It's too early for me to go to sleep. "It's only five o'clock, and if you go to bed now you'll wake up in the middle of the night."

Mommy fixes me a grilled cheese sandwich and a cup of Campbell's Tomato soup and feeds it to me 'cause I can't use my hands. She crumbles my crackers into my soup just the way I like it. When I ask if I can have a Coke, she says yes and Lola gets it for me. They are bein' so nice. I don't think I've ever had this much attention before. I don't ask, but I wonder if I am goin' to die.

At six o'clock Mr. Tommy comes back over to the house. He sits in the chair across the room from me. He looks very serious. The police and the dog catcher came and took the dog away, he says, and the dog catcher is almost positive the dog was rabid, but to be sure they have to examine his brain. That means it will take at least a week before we know if it had rabies. We still need to keep a watchout for any other animals that could be infected. He says his dog and cat had to be quarantined for two weeks to be sure they were ok.

I shoot up off the couch and ask where Mamma cat is right now. He says they took her and the dog with them.

I cry hysterically. Mommy can't understand what I'm sayin'. I ask Mr. Tommy if he knows Mamma cat had kittens last night.

Mr. Tommy looks shocked. No, he says, he hasn't seen any kittens. I tell him where I hid them 'cause I was afraid he would drown them. He looks very sad. He tells me he'll get the kittens and take them to their mother as soon as he can.

Mr. Tommy crawls under our house and finds the babies all alone. He brings them inside and asks Mommy if she would give them some milk. Mommy opens a can of Carnation evaporated milk and warms it in a pot. She finds an eye-dropper in the bathroom and cleans it in hot soap and water.

I can't help feed them 'cause of my bandages, but Mommy, Lola and Hero take turns feeding the kittens. I sit next to each of them to make sure they give them enough milk. The kittens don't like the dropper at first, but I guess they are hungry 'cause they drink all the milk. I want to hold them so bad, but Mommy won't let me 'cause I need to keep my bandages clean.

The next morning Mr. Tommy comes over and tells us he has taken the kittens to the pound. The people there said if Mamma cat has rabies the kittens might be infected, too. He promises that if they're okay after two weeks he will bring them all home.

I look at him and wonder if I can believe him.

He sits down beside me and says, "If your Mommy says it is okay, then after they come home you can have the pick of the litter."

I look at Mommy and she nods. All I have to do now is make a really hard decision. Which one?

34

Dragnet

On Monday morning, two men dressed in black suits are standin' on our front porch. I'm on the couch watchin' TV. It's still hard for me to sleep with my hands hurtin' so bad. Mommy opens the door, and they ask if they can come in. They look like the men from the TV show "Dragnet". I slink down under the blanket and wonder if they're here to take me to jail.

Lookin' at me, they ask if I'm the victim. Since I have no idea what *that* is, I shake my head.

But Mommy says yes. "This is my daughter, Patra, and she was attacked by the dog on Saturday."

The men tell Mommy they're from the Health Department and hand her a piece of paper with their names on it. I'm so scared I can't remember what they even say their names are. All I remember is mister something and mister something else.

"Why are you here?" she asks.

"To make sure she gets the rabies vaccine," one of the misters says.

They ask Mommy to get me dressed, then they'll take us downtown to the Health Department. The tall mister says a doctor there will explain everything to us.

I don't understand. Why does a doctor have to explain? We're goin' back in a week to see Dr. Riley to get my stitches taken out. Hasn't anyone ever been bitten by a rabid dog before?

Mamma starts dressin' me in my room. She looks worried and that makes me afraid to go with them. "Are you goin' with me?" I ask.

She squats down in front of me. "No one is taking you anywhere without me, sweetie pie." She looks so sad.

I try to hug her, but my hands won't fit around her back. I lean over and kiss her on the cheek. "Don't be sad, Mommy. It'll be all right."

We're in the backseat of the big, black car. Mommy can't drive, so we usually take a bus to get to the Health Department downtown.

It is so hot I can hardly breathe, but I am afraid to ask the men to open the window. I just pray we get there before I throw up in their car. I look out the window and watch all the big houses as we pass them by. We are drivin' down North State Street and it's pretty in this part of town with all of the big fancy mansions. Soon we see nothing but tall buildings and sidewalks. I know where the Health Department is 'cause Mommy takes us there to get shots. I don't like it there. It's an unfriendly place.

The two men walk us into the building and lead us down a long hallway. One of them opens a door to a small room and tells us to take a seat. I look around the room, but there is nothing to look at—it's bare except for the two chairs, a little table and an empty garbage can in the corner.

We wait a long time and I tell Mommy I am really sleepy. She puts me in her lap and tells me I can take a nap. But before I fall asleep, a woman in a starched white uniform with a funny looking hat opens the door. She tells us to follow her. We walk down more halls and seem to go deeper and deeper into the building.

We go through swinging doors into a big room with walls of medicine and lots of other stuff. The lights are so bright I can hardly see. Two doctors and two nurses are in there and I'm gettin' really scared about these people 'cause they're lookin' at me strangely.

They ask us to sit down, and one of the doctors sits in a chair in front of us. He don't smile. In fact, I don't think any of them know how to smile.

One doctor talks to Mommy. "This is very serious. Your child probably has the rabies virus." He explains that the initial test confirms rabies, but it will take about two weeks to be one hundred percent sure. "If we wait two weeks for the final confirmation and the dog is rabid, it will be too late for treatment for Patra."

My treatments will start today, he says, but he don't even look at me, only Mommy. I hear the part about twenty-one injections and start to cry. Then I stop cryin' long enough to ask, "What are injections?"

"Shots, honey," Mommy says.

My whole body stiffens. How can I stand twenty-one shots? I'm sure that would kill me. But the doctor tells Mommy she has to bring me to that building every day for the next twenty-one days.

"The injections are painful," he says, "and we'll give them in her stomach and back to minimize swelling. She'll probably be sick to her stomach and have muscle cramps, but the shots are necessary to keep her from contracting the disease and spreading it to other people." *Oh dear God, help me!*

I try hard to understand the part about dyin' without the shots, if the dog was rabid. Suddenly I feel like I'm freezin'. My body starts shakin' and Mommy holds me tighter.

He's sayin' all this to Mommy. It sounds like he's talkin' about a cat or a dog, not about a little girl. Not about me.

Without sayin' goodbye, the doctor stands up and leaves the room. I think Grandmother would have a fit at his lack of manners.

* * * * *

Two weeks later Mommy tries to drag me out of the house, but I hang on to the door with my scarred hands. She tries to unwrap my tiny fingers from the screen door, but I'm determined not to go with her. As she pulls me loose I scream at the top of my lungs, "Please Mommy, I don't want to go."

I wrap myself around her legs as tight as I can. Tears stream down my face. I beg her again. "Mommy, please don't make me go!"

Mommy peels me off of her legs and picks me up into her arms, holdin' me so tight I can hardly breathe. She sits down on the steps and rocks me back and forth to try to calm me down. She's cryin', too. I can tell it is hurtin' her to do this to me.

It's the fourteenth day of my rabies shots. After today, I still have seven shots and seven trips to the Health Department left. I have a calendar on the wall in the kitchen and every day when we get home I cross another day off. I do the same thing at Christmas, and like Christmas, I can't wait for the last day to be crossed out.

Mommy picks me up and carries me the two blocks to the bus stop. When she walks down the aisle I hide my face in her shoulder so no one can see my swollen eyes from cryin' so much. It takes over an hour of riding on the bus to get to the Health Department. The bus stops and starts about a hundred times, rollin' across town closer and closer to the monsters that say they are helping me.

Finally I'm standin' in front of the huge gray building where people will hold me down and torture me again today. I look up at the building and feel like I'm in a scene from one of the horror movies Normal takes me to on Saturday mornings.

My stomach is red and swollen from the shots and the muscles in my legs hurt so bad I can hardly walk into the building. I have headaches, too, and sometimes I throw up. Yesterday, I heard someone tell Mommy they'd start giving me the shots in my back today 'cause of the severe reaction the drug was causing to my stomach.

"She is just too small and the medication is taking its toll on her body," the nurse said.

I start cryin' again as soon as Mommy opens the door. "Patra, please don't make me drag you down the hall today. I will take you to Woolworths for the biggest banana split you have ever had when this is over."

There isn't a big enough banana split in the world to keep me from fightin' them.

When we get to the room of torture I try really hard to be brave, but when they take my shirt off and put me on the cold metal table, I lose it. I start fightin' and screamin', but it doesn't matter. Four people hold me down and one jabs me with the needle. Today it is in my back just like they said. My stomach is sore and swollen and it hurts to lie on it. They don't care. They stretch me out and hold me flat anyways. I scream.

They keep tellin' me to be still, but it just hurts something awful. My stomach, my back and my mind hurt. And then it's over. For today!

I can't sleep that night. I lay awake thinkin' about the way that dog looked before he attacked me and started rippin' my hands apart. I can see the foam drippin' out of his mouth and drippin' to the ground. His eyes are wild and I remember how scared I was that he was gonna kill me. I know if Hero hadn't been there to save me I *would be* dead.

Lyin' in bed, I rub my big swollen tummy. It's really hot and it aches and throbs. I have trouble rollin' over and gettin' up by myself to go to the bathroom. Mommy puts Normal in her room in her bed. She pushes our twin beds together so she can sleep with me, but not touch me. She holds my hand with one of her hands and slowly winds my hair around her fingers with the other 'cause she knows this makes me calm down. I cling to her to make sure she won't leave me alone.

I know I keep her awake all night with my moanin' and wigglin' around, but I can't help it, I can't be still. I'm sorry she's not gettin' any sleep 'cause we have to be on the bus early again the next morning.

Even Angry hasn't switched for the past three weeks. I'm guessin' she thinks I'm in enough pain and she don't need to punish me even more right now. The difference is that with Angry I never know when she's gonna torture me. But at the same time every day I know four big men in white uniforms will hold me down while a mean nurse shoves a huge needle into my stomach or back and shoots what looks like a gallon of yellow stuff into my body.

Angry threatens me with Hell, but I have been livin' in Hell here at the Health Department every day for the last twenty-one days.

35

Running away

*W*hen I turned eighteen, I started confiding in the minister at my church. Reverend Pace led me to a counselor from the church that helped me a great deal, but my problems proved to be a little out of his league. I needed a professional. When I was twenty-three, I started seeing a psychologist and spent several years in intense therapy before I felt like my life was finally on track. Later in life, I went to Al-anon and became a facilitator for alcoholics and pedophiles in a therapeutic setting. Over the years, I continued to see a therapist for different reasons. I also took my daughter, starting when she was about age three. I wanted her to be able to deal with my divorce from her father. It's possible she's a therapist today because of the number of years she spent in therapy for problems she had with her father, and simply being a teenager.

I believe these caring individuals trained to help me made it possible for me to find such joy in my marriage to Bobby. I owe my success to his help as well. When I met my husband in 1989 he was the General Manager for a 50 year-old company that installed stage equipment for acting stages, schools, college auditoriums and movie theatres. Both of the owners died within a year of each other of unrelated illnesses, and within weeks, customers were calling Bobby to ask if he could still do their work. My daughter had just gone off to college and I wanted a new start different from the day care facilities

I owned. Eighteen years was long enough in one profession. I sold the day care center, and in 1990, a year after we were married, Bobby and I started Franklin Designs.

Today, Bobby runs the construction side of the business and I run operations for the company, which is a consulting and design business for theatre chains in the industry. As I said before, given the role movies have played in my life, it's no wonder I found my way into the movie business industry.

We work together well. I guess I know how to get along with just about anybody. The General Manager of Franklin Designs, Diane Melohn, tells people I am just as comfortable with paupers as I am with queens, and she is right. Even as a child, people like Mayze and Mamie were drawn to my pleasing smile and down-to-earth personality. Some people would call it manipulation, but I call it survival. That doesn't mean I'm not sincere, because I am. And I'm loyal, too. That's why I had to see Cheyenne and Grand again.

* * * * *

For weeks, I've been plannin' to run away today. As soon as my birthday money from Aunt Lola came in the mail, I knew exactly what my birthday present would be used for. I'd take the seven mile trip across town alone so I could see Cheyenne.

Mommy has been tellin' me all summer that she'd call Cheyenne's mother and set up a time for us to get together. We moved from South Jackson to North Jackson the end of May and I haven't seen her since. It is now July fifteenth and we still haven't made plans. Everyone is so busy with their lives, they have forgotten about how devastated Cheyenne and I were about the move.

Cheyenne and I met on the first day of school in the first grade. We became best friends the minute we set eyes on each other and we were together every day for three years. We both think six weeks is a little too long to wait to see each other, so we made plans by ourselves.

I know eight is young to be takin' a trip all the way across town by myself, but I have been very careful in plannin' how to get there. I have been livin' in Jackson my whole life, so I kinda know my way around. Plus, I've been ridin' the buses in this town my whole life. How hard can it be?

I spent the entire day yesterday plannin' my escape. Normal sleeps half the day, Lola is away for the week and Mommy leaves for work at eight o'clock. It's Wednesday, so I know Mommy is gonna pull double shift at the restaurant and will not be home until around eight o'clock tonight. That gives me twelve hours for my adventure.

My plan is to catch the bus at the top of the hill at nine o'clock in the morning. Normal and I ride the bus downtown to go to the movie on Saturdays when Mommy is workin' so I know the bus I need to take is Number 12, Capitol Street. Yesterday when Normal was sleepin', I went to the store by myself to make sure I have the correct change for the bus.

The correct change is important 'cause if I have to talk to the bus driver to get change he might ask where my mommy or sisters are. This way I can go with the crowd and pretend I am someone else's kid. Even when Normal is with me, I drop my own money into the machine so I don't think anyone will notice I'm alone.

I pick out what I am gonna wear and hide my clothes under the bed. I spent a lot of time pickin' out my clothes cause I want to look nice for my visit. It was a hard decision, but I finally decided on white shorts and my favorite blue top that buttons down the front. The buttons are dark blue rhinestones and the collar is made out of white lace. The shirt is white and has lots of tiny blue flowers that match the color of my eyes.

My Easter dress was pink and blue this year and Mommy bought me a pair of pink and blue sandals with lacy blue socks to wear to church. They're not the most comfortable shoes for walkin', but they sure are cute.

Normal wanted to know why I was ironing my own clothes yesterday, so I told her Mamie forgot to iron some of my clothes when she was here last Friday. She never looked up from the soap opera she was watchin' when she said, "She is such an idiot."

Sometimes I think Angry is rubbin' off on Normal more and more every day.

I make sure I put all of my stuff in the front bathroom before I go to bed and that includes my shoes, socks and a clean pair of panties. I put a brush and a rubber band for my hair in the drawer by the sink and I find my blue hair ribbon in a drawer in my bedside table and add it to the pile. My hair is really long now and I have a hard time puttin' it up in a ponytail by myself. Normal puts it up for me in the morning, but I'll have to do it myself tomorrow. It's gonna to be hot, and I need to keep my hair up off of my neck and back so I won't be sweaty when I get to Cheyenne's house.

I have my Sunday purse filled with everything I need. My money is hidden in a side pocket and I put in Band-Aids in case I get blisters on my feet. I have ChapStick, gum and a handkerchief with the letter P embroidered on it. When I'm convinced I have everything I need, I climb into bed. But I'm way too excited to sleep.

Finally, my big day has come. I hear Mommy leave right on time at eight o'clock. I get up and sneak to the bathroom. The house is so quiet I'm afraid to make a sound. If I wake Normal up, my plan is shot and I could spend the day with Angry. If Angry figures out my plan, she'll beat me and put me in the closet for the rest of the day. That will mean twelve hours in the dark without food or water, not to mention no adventure.

My hands shake. I'm so nervous I can hardly get dressed. I do everything in slow motion to be sure I don't make any noise. If I knock one thing over

I know I'm done. I put my hair in a ponytail and tie the freshly ironed ribbon around the rubber band.

When I finish dressin', I go into Mommy's room and look at myself in the full-length mirror to be sure everything I planned is in place. I did a pretty good job with my hair, and my clothes are ironed to perfection. My sun-tanned skin makes me look healthy and happy and my blue eyes have a sparkle that's been missin' for a long time. I smile at myself in the mirror and then my journey begins.

I tiptoe slowly down the hall to the front door. *God, please don't let the door squeak when I open it.* I slowly open the door and slip out of the smallest crack I can get through. I shut the door as gently as I opened it.

And then I run.

I don't stop runnin' until I get to the end of the street. When I turn the corner, I feel free for the first time in as long as I can remember. My day has begun!

I planned to have at least half an hour to make it to the bus stop. This gives me enough time to stop at the corner grocery to buy Twinkies and a Coke for breakfast. I'm breakin' all the rules today.

They are just opening up the store when I get there and Mr. Mike, the store owner, says, "My, you are all dressed up early this morning."

At first I panic, but he doesn't act like it's a big deal.

I smile and say, "Yep, Angela decided she wants Twinkies this morning for breakfast before we head downtown to a movie."

"What about your Twinkies?" he asks.

Mr. Mike knows how much I love Twinkies, but I don't want to buy two packages. "I already had breakfast with Mommy this morning. I'm just having a Coke."

Mr. Mike is a nice, old man. He's had this store for at least a hundred years. It sits at the bottom of the hill on Lorraine Street and is next to the railroad tracks. He has a huge cheese slicer and a big hoop of fresh, red rind cheddar cheese sittin' on the counter. He also has ham and thick-sliced bologna in the refrigerator he keeps in the back of the store, and there is a barrel of homemade dill pickles sittin' on the floor by the cash register.

The railroad workers line up at lunch time to buy his mayonnaise, bologna-and-cheese, or mustard, ham-and-cheese sandwiches. He also sells pickled eggs and pickled pig feet. He tells me he has a hard time keeping them in stock because the workers around here love them so much.

The store has creaky wooden floors and every kinda sign you can imagine on the walls. He has old screen doors at the front and back of the store that lets a little breeze pass by if you're standin' at the cash register. He collects anything he can find around town and calls these things his treasures. He and his wife, Miss Edna, live above the store, but she's way too sick to come downstairs to the store anymore. Their only son was killed when he was a teenager in a car wreck years ago and they've been alone ever since.

Sometimes I go up and sit with her and read books to her. She's a nice, old lady and keeps chocolate milk and cookies for me when I come read to her. I can tell she's lonely 'cause she loves it when I sit close to her on the big, overstuffed couch.

Mr. Mike opens my Coke for me and says, "Have a nice day and come back anytime."

I turn and walk out the door smilin' as I go up to the top of the hill to catch the bus. I open my Twinkies and fill my mouth with the creamy goodness of the filling and the light sponge cake. I eat both of them without stoppin' and then wish I had bought the second pack. No saving the second Twinkie for me.

It is a beautiful summer morning. The dew is still on the grass and the birds are singin'. I watch worms crawlin' across the sidewalk and think, *You better hurry up. Haven't you guys ever heard that the early bird gets the worm?*

I think about helpin' them to the grass, but I don't want to touch them with my bare hands. I pick up a stick off of the ground and flip them off the sidewalk into the dirt. Then I keep walkin' up the hill, thinkin' I have done my good deed for the day!

The sky is blue with big, white fluffy clouds. Jefferson Street is one of the busiest streets in Jackson, but there's hardly any traffic this time of day. The trees lining the street are a deep green and the yards are filled with flowers. Walkin' along by myself, I notice things I'd never noticed before. I guess not havin' to worry about Angry poppin' me every few minutes helps me be a little calmer and to focus on the scenery.

At nine o'clock I get on the bus. No one even looks at me. Never in my life have I been on a public bus alone before. I pick a window seat toward the back of the bus, just before the colored section. The colored section is full of the maids on their way to work. They have on black dresses with starched white aprons and they act like they all know each other. They laugh and talk about how hard their jobs are, about their kids, and how mean or how no count their husbands are.

I feel safer in the back of the bus 'cause there are only women in the back. The front is full of men who look like they don't have a job at all. No one says anything to me and I keep my mouth shut. I don't want to draw attention to myself.

I stare out the bus window watchin' the houses go by, careful not to miss my stop. I'm not scared. I thought I would be, but I'm not. The bus is really high up off of the ground and sets me above the street. The bus bumps along stoppin' and startin' over and over again. It seems like a long time before we get to my stop.

I get off the bus on Capitol Street. Capitol Street runs from one end of town to the other through colored downtown to the train station. Downtown is about twelve blocks long, give or take a few blocks. My church, Capitol Street Methodist Church, is on the other end of Capitol Street, but it's not in the downtown part.

Colored town has only one street and it's called Farrish Street. It's where all of the colored people have to go to shop. They're not allowed to shop or eat in our stores and restaurants. I'm not sure why it's not allowed, but Mommy says it's the law.

When I stand at the train station, I can see all the way up Capitol Street to the Old State Capitol building. It's a big, beautiful building that I can walk through and see all of the history of Mississippi. They built a new Capitol building over on the corner of High Street and North President and the new one is even prettier than the old one.

Normal and I walk past the new Capitol building to get to school, and sometimes in the afternoon we stop and play on the steps. It's so big it takes us forever to walk all the way around to the other side. We see people who spend all day every day workin' on the grounds. We see them early in the morning and again in the afternoon. They do a good job keepin' it lookin' nice; the flowers are always perfect. If I look up, I can see where a golden eagle sits on the very top of the building with its wings spread as wide as it can reach.

When we lived on the other side of Jackson Normal and I would walk down Farrish Street on our way to the movies. We'd see the old colored man, Otis, who roasted the best peanuts in town. He'd sell us a big bag for a nickel and we'd take it into the movie with us.

On Saturdays, Normal and I walked the ten blocks from Gallatin Street to the Paramount Theatre to watch a double feature. Mommy gave us a dollar for the movies and lunch, but we never used our money for lunch. We ate popcorn and candy all day long!

Most of the time, we watched both movies and the cartoon twice before we walked home. On Saturdays, the movies would run from ten in the morning until late in the afternoon. We would spend the whole day sittin' in a cool theatre eatin' popcorn, peanuts and candy. We would buy four or five Cokes and have to run to the bathroom every hour. I knew Mommy would be mad about all of the Cokes, but Normal said, "What Mom doesn't know won't hurt her, so keep your stupid mouth shut."

I'm not one to argue with any of The Sisters but I thought it was strange that Angry never showed up when we were in a movie. And I was glad for that.

When I step off of the bus at the corner of State Street and Capitol, I smell the fumes from the bus and the smell of the hot pavement rising from the streets in the morning sun. I have a tiny feeling of fear and a whole lot of anticipation.

I know I should feel scared about bein' on the Main Street of my city alone with all of the hustle and bustle, but I'm not. There are people comin' and goin' all around me. The cars and trucks whizz by on their way to God knows where and all the noises just excite me more. Instead of bein' scared, I imagine this must be what it feels like to be grown up.

I know I'll have to walk all the way down Capitol Street, twelve blocks to Gallatin Street. Then it is another ten blocks to Cheyenne's house. I can't catch another bus, 'cause I have no idea which bus to take from here. I don't mind the walkin', but I think wearin' the Sunday shoes might have been a mistake.

About three blocks down Capitol Street I decide to stop at the Krystal to get a hamburger. It's hard to pass a Krystal and not have at least one hamburger. The smell is unbelievable and I can hardly wait to sink my teeth into the soft bun. I walk in and hope no one notices I'm alone. I walk up to the counter and a nice lady asks me what I would like. I tell her two Krystals and a Coke, please. She asks if I want fries, and I shake my head no.

"Is your Mommy with you?" she asks.

I almost run out the door, but I stand as tall as I can. "She is next door shoppin'. I was hungry."

The lady takes my money and doesn't ask any more questions.

I sit at the counter by the window and slowly eat my hamburgers, enjoyin' every bite while I look out of the huge window watchin' the cars go by.

Then I continue down the street, walkin' in and out of shops lookin' at everything that interests me. It's hot and it feels nice to walk into the air-conditioned stores to cool off.

Woolworths is about halfway down the street. It's the best store in the world. It has everything anybody could possibly want or need. Normal and I spend hours in there on Saturdays when we go downtown.

I go to the toy department first so I can look at the dolls. I love to play with dolls. They have big ones and tiny ones I can hold in the palm of my hand. There are blond ones, red-headed ones, and brown-headed ones. They have baby dolls and grownup dolls to dress in fancy dresses. Sometimes, Mommy makes my dolls' dresses to match mine. She uses scraps she has left over when she's making Sunday dresses for Normal and me. She adds buttons and bows and ribbons to make them beautiful.

I stay long enough to pick out which doll I will ask Santa to bring me for Christmas, and then I head to the jewelry counter. I know the diamonds and the rings aren't real, but they are so sparkly. I love tryin' them on. I try on ear bobs and bracelets and necklaces, too. I find a rack of hats and try all of them on. When I get tired of dressing up, I head to the candy counter.

I pick out Cheyenne's favorite: grape Tootsie Roll pops. The cherry ones are my favorite. I buy us both a Slo Poke and a box of animal crackers, and on the way to the cash register I pick up a pack of Juicy Fruit gum.

At the register I see Margie. Most of the time, Margie checks me and Normal out when we come in together. I know her name is Margie 'cause she wears a name tag on her shirt and it has flowers around her name.

She sees me standin' there alone with my money and asks where Normal is? I tell her she had to go to the bathroom and she is meeting me outside.

Margie smiles. "Don't get a bellyache from all of this candy."

"Don't worry," I say, "I'm not eatin' it all today. I'm savin' some for tomorrow." This is a total lie. I do plan to eat all of it today, and there is no one here to stop me!

I walk out of the store and down the street. I pull the red wrapper off a cherry Tootsie Roll pop and stick it in my mouth. *What could be better than this?* I have the whole day all by myself to do anything I want to do. I'm all alone with no one to beat me or lock me up or tell me what to do. I can go anywhere I want to go and no one will stop me. I don't even mind the stifling summer heat. When I finish my Tootsie Roll pop I eat the whole box of animal crackers.

When I get to the end of the street, I turn on Farrish Street to go buy some roasted peanuts from old Otis. Suddenly, I run smack dab into Mamie and Mayze. Mamie sees me and looks around to see if I'm with Mommy or Normal. She knows Normal and I come downtown to shop and go to the movies sometimes, so she is not surprised to see me.

I can tell by the look on her face she doesn't want to run into Normal today. I tell her I'm alone and then I think, darn, if she ever tells Mommy she saw me downtown by myself I'm in trouble for sure.

She narrows her eyes at me and says, "Chile, what yo doin' down her by yo sef?"

I have to think fast, so I say Normal is in the movie and she sent me out here to get some peanuts from Otis. Mamie isn't surprised that Normal has me runnin' around fetchin' stuff for her, and I know she won't go near the theatre in fear of runnin' into Angry. Besides, colored people can't go to our movie theatre. They have to go to the Alamo theatre around the corner.

Mamie, Mayze and I walk down to Otis's and buy our bags of peanuts. She said they had finished shoppin' and were about to catch the bus back across town.

I give her and Mayze a big hug and say, "I'll see y'all soon. If you see Mommy don't tell her Angela sent me out on the street by myself."

Mamie shakes her head. "Okay. That girl be crazy as a Betsy bug, but you be careful."

I look at the clock in the train station and see it's twelve o'clock. I told Cheyenne I would be at her house at twelve-thirty and I still have ten blocks to go. She'll worry if I'm late, but I'm beginning to feel blisters on my feet so I can't walk any faster. I guess I was havin' too much fun shoppin' and eatin' and forgot the time.

I sit down on a bench in front of the train station to put Band-Aids on my heels where the back straps of my sandals are rubbin' a blister through my socks. The walking part of this trip is much farther than I remember, probably 'cause David always carries me when he's with us.

I sit here for a few minutes and watch the trains go by. It's loud and smelly where I'm sittin' and the tracks are high above the street. The cars and trucks fly by under the bridge to the other side of the tracks. From down here, the trains look so big. The train cars are full of people and I wonder where they could all be going. What would happen if I just got on one of them and disappeared?

I turn on to Gallatin Street and trudge my way toward Cheyenne's house. It seems like her house gets farther and farther away instead of closer. It seems to take forever.

When I get to the Hub Cafe where daddy used to work, I am so thirsty I stop to buy a Coke. It's cool inside and I crawl up on a stool at the counter and pull a napkin out of the holder. I wipe my sweaty face. "Can I please have a Coke?" I ask the waitress.

She asks if I'm all right, and I'm so tired I almost start cryin'. But I don't. "Yes ma'am," I say. "I've just been playin' too hard with my friends."

She puts a bottle of Coke in front of me and asks if I want a piece of pie on the house?

"I don't know what that means," I say.

"Darlin', that means I will give it to you for free," she said.

I remember Aunt Lena does that sometimes so I thought it must be okay. I smile at her and say thank you 'cause my Krystals are long gone. I see the clock on the wall behind the counter says it is 12:30. I know I gotta hurry up and get to Cheyenne's.

The big piece of apple pie is warm and has a big scoop of vanilla ice cream on it. She says she fixed it just like her little girl likes it. I eat the whole piece, crust and all, in less than five minutes. She gives me a glass of milk instead of a Coke and I drink every drop.

She comes around the counter with a brush and takes my ponytail down. I guess I didn't get the rubber band tight enough this morning and my hair is fallin' down around my face.

As she is re-doing my hair she says, "You are such a pretty little girl. Do you live around here?"

"No, ma'am," I say, "I'm visiting my friend down the street."

She looks at me funny. "You look a lot like Rose's youngest girl, but I haven't seen her around here for a while 'cause they moved to the other side of town."

"Nope," I say, "I'm just visiting."

I know Cheyenne is worryin' her head off by now, so I slide off of the stool and head toward the door. The lady calls to me as I am leavin'. "Come back to see me soon."

I keep walkin' and wave as I walk out the door. As nice as she is, I think, *there isn't a chance in the world that's gonna happen.*

Cheyenne and I decided we better meet in one of the apartments before we tell anyone I'm here. Our plan is to tell her grandma that David dropped me off to spend some time with them today.

Cheyenne is so happy to see me she's not even mad at me for bein' late. I don't look as fresh as I did when I got dressed this morning, but she doesn't care. We hug and hug, and it seems like years since we saw each other last.

She asks me if I'm hungry, and I tell her about stoppin' for pie at the cafe. She said that was Miss Ella. She hasn't worked there very long and is a nosy mosey. I tell her what she asked me and she says she isn't surprised. She likes to know everything about everybody that walks in the door.

The old house looks the same. Cheyenne takes me around and shows me the new stuff Grand had bought for the apartments. Cheyenne said she even put TVs in most of them to entice new renters.

We go through the back door and Grand gives me the biggest hug I've had in a long time. She kisses me on the head and tells me she has missed me mountains. She takes me by the hand and pulls me into the living room to see Grandpa and says, "Look what the cat's drug in."

He's still sittin' in his wheelchair in front of the TV just like he was the last time I saw him, with his green plaid blanket draped over his legs. He has a big smile on his face and his eyes sparkle like Christmas lights when he recognizes me. I run over and give him a big hug. "I've missed you so much."

Grandpa hugs me back. "It's been too long, little one. "Fury" hasn't been the same without you."

Cheyenne and I would spend hours with Grandpa watchin' TV, especially on Saturday morning. I'd be at her house by nine o'clock to watch "Mighty Mouse" and then Grandpa would wheel himself in from the bathroom at nine-thirty to watch "Fury" and "Spin & Marty". Grand was always busy with the apartments, and Grandpa had to sit by himself most of the day. Cheyenne and I loved bein' with him so much that we'd spend all morning with him watchin' anything on TV he wanted.

Grand would fix us a big plate of melt-in-your-mouth biscuits with lots of butter drippin' down the sides. She would fry at least a pound of bacon and warm a pitcher of cane syrup for us to pour all over the butter-logged biscuits. There were huge glasses of fresh-squeezed orange juice for us and a glass of buttermilk for Grandpa. I never got hungry at Grand's house!

Grand puts it all on a tray and brings it into the living room for us to eat in front of the TV. Most adults won't let you eat in the living room, but Grandpa's living room is special. It's where he lives 'cause it's his living room and his bedroom. It's bright and sunny with wood around the bottom half of the room and yellow wallpaper on the top. He has pictures of hunting dogs and fishing stuff everywhere. The curtains have pictures of trees with rivers runnin' through them and fish jumpin' out of the streams. And it feels like home.

Cheyenne's Grandpa spends most of his time in the wheelchair, but he has a big chair where he can take a nap. Cheyenne and I can sit in two big, comfortable chairs, but most of the time we lay on the big rug on the floor in front of the TV. A hospital bed sits in the far side of the room, but Grandpa keeps it covered up during the day and refuses to use it except at night. "My legs don't work," he says, "but I ain't no invalid."

When Grand leaves the room, she says, "Y'all take care of Grandpa while I go check on the apartments."

Checking on the apartments could mean anything from goin' to the grocery store to workin' in the flower garden. She knew we would attend to his every need until she returned and we'd find her if there was a problem. She was always back by twelve o'clock to fix lunch anyway. We would roll Grandpa out on the front porch and have sandwiches, cookies and iced tea on the veranda. The house was way above the street and the veranda overlooked the flower garden. We'd watch the cars passin' below on the street and pretend we were stayin' in a hotel, like we were big shots on vacation.

Over the past three years we spent a lot of time on that porch listenin' to Grandpa tell us stories about when he was a young boy in the late 1890s. It seems like a long time ago to me, but his stories keep us glued to our seats for hours. Cheyenne swears he makes them up, but I believe every word he says.

Since we can't watch TV while Grandpa takes his nap, we go into our room and everything is still the same as the last time I was here. It feels like I came home from bein' away a long time. Since Mommy likes to move at least once a year, I have no attachments or comforts in any place I have ever lived. And then there are The Sisters! But here I am safe. This family loves me like I am their own. I felt it the minute I walked through the door.

We climb up on the big bed and sink into the fluffy pillows. The ceiling fan is blowin' through the windows across the bed. We are full of food and stories, and after my long walk I fall asleep instantly. We wake up about an hour later and lie there on the bed catchin' up on all the things we missed over the past six weeks. I am happier than I have been in a long time.

I look at the clock and see it's five-fifteen. I know Normal has missed me by now, but I haven't cared all day. But now I am gettin' a little anxious about gettin' home. My feet have blisters and I know I can't walk the seven miles back across town. I also know it will be gettin' dark soon and I can't walk home in the dark. I have no idea what buses to take even though I saved enough money to take the bus home.

By the time Grand comes in to see if we are hungry I am sittin' on the bed cryin'. Cheyenne tells her what we have done.

"Oh dear," she says. "That's a problem. I can't drive at night, and Cheyenne's daddy has the car at work anyway."

We go see Grandpa and he says, "Don't cry, baby. We'll call you a cab."

I tell him I had only saved enough money for bus fare, but he says, "Don't worry your pretty little head about it, darlin'. Your company is worth more than a cab fare."

We hug and kiss and promise we won't go so long next time before we see each other.

The cab comes and picks me up, and then I am on my way home. I get home at six o'clock. The cab driver lets me off at the end of the street so I go around to the back of the house and sneak in the back door. I hear the TV on in the living room, but I go straight to my room. I pull my clothes off and get into a hot tub of water, waitin' for Normal or whoever to show up and kill me.

After I get out of the tub, I get dressed and go into the kitchen. It is a mess, so I start cleanin' it up. Normal walks in and asks where I've been? I tell her I was outside playin' and she says, "Well, you better get the kitchen cleaned up before Mother gets home."

I looked at her, amazed that she hadn't missed me all day long. "Okay," I said, and watch her walk out of the room.

What a relief! I have had the most wonderful day and no one knew. I had done it all on my own except for the cab part. And I hadn't even gotten a beating from Angry or a whipping from Mommy. I start singin', "Oh Happy Day!"

36

The Bible

When I woke up this morning and looked outside I saw a beautiful spring day with lots of fresh air and sunshine, and at twelve years old all I wanted to do was go outside and enjoy the lovely weather. But Normal said we had to do our spring cleaning today. I'm not sure why she said "we," 'cause she gave me a list of things to do and walked out of the house. Then she jumped on the back of Paul's moped and the two puttered away.

Paul lives down the street. Normal's been hangin' out with him since he moved in a couple of months ago. He's kinda cute, but he's as strange as she is. I'm sure they will make beautiful babies together 'cause it's obvious by the way she is French kissing him what they are plannin' to do today.

Bein' alone in the house is wonderful, even if I do have to do all of the work myself. I turn on the radio and my favorite song "Teen Angel" is playin'. I crank it up and start pullin' the sheets off all the beds and pilin' them in the hallway. I open all of the windows in the house and a wonderful breeze blows through the curtains and across the room. The gardenia bushes are in full bloom and fill the air with their sweet, heavy scent. I look outside and the azalea bushes are packed with pink flowers, and the yellow daffodils and paper whites are poppin' up everywhere.

I clean the picture window in the living room first and then move on to the bedrooms. Most people hate doin' windows, but I love lookin' out through a squeaky clean one. Mamie taught me to use crumpled newspapers and Windex for crystal-clear windows every time.

The list Normal gave me is long and I need to work fast to get it done before she gets back. I grab the can of Pledge from the utility room and find an old wash rag in the bathroom cabinet to use for dustin'. I dust every room in the house, singin' loudly with the radio. When I finish dustin' and look at the kitchen clock, I see it's half past noon already and realize I'm starvin'.

I fix myself a homemade pimento cheese sandwich on fresh white bread with crushed potato chips on top. Mommy says it's ridiculous to put potato chips on sandwiches, but I like the crunch. She also says it's ridiculous to eat dill pickles with BBQ Fritos, but that's what I have for breakfast every morning before I go to school.

After I finish eatin' my lunch, I go to our bedroom. Normal and I both push stuff under our beds all of the time, and we are runnin' out of space under there. I start with Normal's bed. I try to push all the junk out with a broom, but there is just too much to move. I pull the top mattress off and lean it against the wall. Even though it is a twin bed, it's hard to pull the box spring up from the frame. When I lift it up, a box drops out onto the floor. It looks like she had it nailed under the box springs but the jolt knocked it loose and it fell on the floor.

I can't decide if I should open it, but I'm much too nosey not to look inside. When I take off the lid, I sink to the floor and take out everything and spread it around me. There in the box are the horrifying pictures of demons and devils that she tortured me with for years when I was little. She sat me down in a straight back, wooden chair and for hours made me look at them and told me they were from The Book of Revelations and the pictures were from the Bible. But now I can tell these pictures were cut out of books, not the Bible. She obviously had cut the pictures the same size as the Bible pages and slipped them into the Bible to make me believe all of the horrible things she made me look at when I was a little girl. I guess I was too young to understand she was makin' it all up.

Then I see the verses she recited to me day after day about me goin' to Hell and Daddy dyin' for his sins. She had cut them out of books and pasted them onto paper, but over the years the pictures have fallen apart. How could anyone be so cruel to a six-year-old child? Even though it has been at least five or six years since I have seen these pictures they are still disturbin' to me.

I was pretty good about hidin' razor blades from her but I guess I missed some, 'cause it's obvious this stuff was carefully cut out of books with a razor blade. I remember Normal spent a lot of time at the library and now I know what Angry was doin' when she was there. I can't imagine how many books she destroyed cuttin' these pictures out of them.

I can't wrap my head around bein' traumatized for so many years by these pictures and scripture verses. And it was all a big, fat lie. Angry made it all up!

I pick everything up and put it back in the box. I go to the kitchen and find a box of matches and walk out into the back yard. I dump the whole box of pictures and pages into the large brick barbecue pit and pour lighter fluid all over them. I strike a match and throw it into the pit. Then I watch the pictures of the demons and the fake verses go up in flames. I don't know whether to laugh or to cry 'cause I'm still so traumatized by what she did so long ago.

I watch the last of the pile turn to ashes and think, *she's the one who should burn in Hell, not me.*

When the fire burns down, I drag more of her mess out from under the bed and then put the bed back together and finish cleanin' the room. I put the sheets in the washing machine, thinkin' about the bottles of alcohol and Valium I pulled out from under her bed. Maybe I'd feel better if I helped myself to some of it. But I won't. That's Angry's and Sad's game, not mine.

I go back to the bedroom and pull out the pills and the bottles of whiskey and gin from under her bed and sit there lookin' at it for a long time. While I'm sittin' there I realize I haven't seen Teddy Long in forever. As a matter of fact, I can't remember the last time I saw him. I push all of the junk back under the bed and go sit in the closet, but this time Teddy Long doesn't come. I cry 'cause I'm afraid I will never see Teddy again.

I walk outside into the beautiful spring day and decide to take a nice, long walk. I don't care that I didn't get Normal's list done. Let her do it herself.

37

Another Sad Day

I walk into the living room and see Sad sittin' on the couch. She is pullin' tiny handfuls of hair out of her head and puttin' them in a pile on her lap. She looks at me with her blank stare and turns her head the other way.

I try to talk to her, but she ignores me.

I slowly walk over and sit down next to her, but when I touch her arm she jumps up and starts screamin', "Don't touch me. I want to die. I need to die."

I'm so afraid of the look on her face I run out of the room.

She stops screamin' as soon as I am out the door. I hide around the corner and wait a few minutes before I sneak quietly back into the room. She has moved to the chair in front of the TV and she's watchin' "As the World Turns". She is calm and I think she is okay.

I ask her if she wants something to eat, hopin' I can get her to talk. She doesn't answer. Her back is to me, so I walk around to the side of the chair to see if it's Normal or Sad sittin' there. I am horrified by what I see.

It is still Sad and she is stickin' straight pins into her legs! There are dozens of them. I almost faint; my head is swimmin' and I think I am goin' to throw up. I beg her to take them out, but she looks at me with her tormented eyes and says, "Go to your room."

I have no idea what to do. If I stay, I will make her mad and Sad could switch to Angry. If I leave, what else will she do to hurt herself?

Fortunately, I don't have to make that decision. She stands up and puts her finger in my face and says, "Run." I know Angry is on her way, so I run to my room, close the door and pray.

I wait and wait. It's two o'clock and I am really hungry. I open my door and sneak down the hall to the kitchen. I see Normal standin' at the stove. She is stirrin' something and I think it's leftover chili from last night. She puts two bowls and a box of crackers on the table. I walk over to her and she looks at me and says, "Do you want some chili?"

I look at her and say no.

I walk out the door and down the street to the store. I sit in one of the rocking chairs and pretend I am sittin' on Cheyenne's porch with her and Grandpa, listenin' to one of his stories. I look up and see birds flyin' across the blue sky. I watch the clouds movin' into all kinds of different shapes like bears and dogs and lots of other things. They change from one thing to another in a matter of minutes. I think maybe that is what Normal feels like when she switches, like she is disappearin' from one person to another so quickly no one notices. But I do.

38

Boondocks

I'm in seventh grade this year at Bailey Junior High School. I had only been there a month when David decided to help us buy a house. I didn't really care 'cause I haven't made any friends here, either. Now I will be in another new school, another new house and another new neighborhood. I didn't mind leavin' Davis Elementary School last year 'cause I didn't bother to make any friends the three years I was there.

My first year at Davis I drove everyone crazy, including my teachers. I missed my best friend and I hated the world. I figured if Angry could be mean to me, I could be mean to everyone else. I didn't want any friends. I wanted my old school and my old friend. I wanted to be with Cheyenne again. I wanted my old life back and I knew it wasn't ever gonna happen.

I started cussin' and talkin' back to my teachers. I stopped turnin' in homework and I acted out in class. The teachers hated me and so did the kids, but I didn't care. I started failin', when before I had always been an A student. It felt like my life was over and maybe I wanted to die, too.

My sister was crazy and no one cared. I needed help, but I didn't know how to get it.

Then one day miraculously I heard Teddy Long ask me, "What are you doing, Patra? You can't change your life right now, but you don't have to turn into Angry! You are strong. You can turn this around before it's too late." He was right, this wasn't me.

After that, I pretty much kept to myself and tried not to be noticed by anyone. If I stay quiet enough and keep my mouth shut, I tended to blend in. At that point, that was about all I wanted to do. I pulled my grades up and stopped bein' a jerk. And before the end of the year I felt like myself again.

And then we moved to nowhere land.

David and Lola picked out a nice house in a nice neighborhood, and they say we will never have to move again. He says no more renting! It makes me very happy to know if I make friends here, I will never lose them by movin' away.

I do mind that we are livin' so far away from downtown Jackson. We have to drive thirty minutes and cross the Pearl River Bridge to get back to civilization. I'm a city girl. I've always been able to walk around town and go anywhere I wanted to. I never asked anyone and I was never asked by anyone where I was goin' or what I was doin'. I was pretty much on my own. I can't do that anymore and wondered how Angry would find ways to torture me now.

Normal lived in her own little world, and the older I got the more freedom I had. I could spend my days playin' in the parks, swimmin' in the public swimming pools and walkin' around downtown window shoppin'. I could even go to a movie by myself whenever I wanted to. I learned pretty quick no one cared I was a little girl on my own wanderin' around without any adult supervision.

Livin' in the city, I learned to be fiercely independent, determined to control my own life and not to depend on anyone for anything. That meant not askin' anyone for help, 'cause in the end it would cause me pain or rejection.

But here in this God forsaken place, I could wander for hours and still not be anywhere. Mommy says we are out of downtown where we can breathe fresh air and feel the sunshine, but I say we are out in the middle of nowhere where I have nothing to do and no one to do it with. I need to be able to walk to the store and buy Cokes and Twinkies and Almond Joys. I need to wander down Capitol Street and windowshop even if I don't buy anything. How will I ever survive?

Normal will be in tenth grade again this year 'cause she failed last year. I took quite a beating cause I passed from sixth to seventh grade and she has to sit through tenth grade again. She also failed fifth grade, so now she is two years behind and only three years ahead of me. I guess I shouldn't have been such a smart mouth, tellin' her that at least there would be all new people here. No one would know she had failed again! The remark caused me a punch in the back that took my breath away, leavin' a bruise the size of a baseball. But sometimes you just have to get a jab in no matter what the consequences are.

The first day of school is different from what I expected. I was prepared to be a loner and just try to survive the way I always have, but I really like it here. The teachers are friendly and the students seem happy to see a new face in the crowd.

Three really nice girls come up to me after first period and ask if I want to be friends. At first I am a little wary they are goin' to make fun of me if I say yes, but they don't. They are genuine and really want to be my friends.

I am stunned to say the least. I haven't had a close friend since Cheyenne and I have wanted one for a long time. Now I have three. They say that their names are Brenda, Linda Jean and Sue Carol. I tell them my name is Patra, and they say they would love to be my new best friends. I am so happy I could pee myself.

They spend the entire day showin' me around the school and introducin' me to everyone. Maybe junior high in a new school will not be so bad after all.

I have to ride a big yellow bus to and from school 'cause it's too far to walk. In Jackson, there are no school buses and you have to walk or take a city bus no matter how far you live from the school. Here, it takes an hour each way, but I love ridin' the bus 'cause it gives me more time with my friends, especially my new boyfriend, Ronnie and less time to spend at home alone with The Sisters.

Normal and I have to get on the bus at seven in the morning and Ronnie always saves me a seat on the first row 'cause he is the first stop on the route. We get off the bus around four-thirty in the afternoon. Lola and Mom usually get home by five-thirty, and it's our job to have supper on the table when they get home. If it's not cold or raining, I have figured out I can ride the bus around the block twice and get off at the other end of the street with my friends. Normal sits in the front of the bus on the way home and doesn't care if I don't get off of the bus the first time around. That wastes another fifteen minutes before I have to be at home alone with whatever Sister shows up that day.

The minute she stepped on the bus after school I could tell Sad didn't have a great first day. I can see by the expression on her face it's Sad, not Normal, and she has been cryin'. She keeps her head down and today she walks past me to the back of the bus. When we get off at our stop, I don't know whether to talk to her or ignore her, so I walk behind her up the driveway to the front door.

As we go into the house, she turns around and throws a book at me barely missin' my head. Sad has never been violent before, so I am standin' there with my mouth wide open like a hungry fish, but she could care less about my shocked face.

She flops down on the couch and in a high pitched voice starts screamin', "I hate school and I'm never gonna go back!" She pulls her hair out by the handfuls and throws it all over the floor.

I run to my room and lock the door. I change clothes and wait for her to stop screamin' before I try to leave the house.

Eventually I open the door and sneak down the hall, past the living room to the dining room. I hear nothing but silence. When I peek into the living room, I see Sad sittin' on the couch methodically burnin' the inside of her upper arm with a cigarette. I ease myself across the dining room and sneak out the back door in the kitchen.

I walk down the road to the store, if you can call it a store. It's about the size of a closet and only has six shelves of stuff. The door is always propped open 'cause there is no air-conditioning and only a small window high up on the back wall. They keep the candy in a small refrigerator with the milk and soft drinks to keep it from meltin' from the heat. I have to walk the half mile every day rain or shine to get my daily Coke and candy bar.

Today is a beautiful October day. I walk along the side of the road in the grass 'cause we live so far away from civilization there are no sidewalks out here in the country. I walk around a small pond with cattails swayin' in the wind like a bunch of hot dogs on a stick. The crisp, fall air and the thought of the new friends I have made at school makes me smile. I look up at the beautiful blue sky and watch the orange, red and yellow leaves flutter to the ground. I wonder why Sad enjoys hurtin' herself so much. And if she is so unhappy, why doesn't she do a better job of ending her own misery? If I was her, I would.

39

Lola

I am twelve years, six months and three days old. I have spent a lot of time over the past year piecing together the puzzle, tryin' to figure out when my life first spiraled out of control. I think between the age of twelve and thirteen most girls are livin' the good life, spendin' time with friends and thinkin' about boyfriends. But not me; lately I have become obsessed with the truth about my past. I also think I am grown up enough to stop callin' my mom Mommy. Mrs. Johnson, my English teacher, is a stickler about pronouncin' words properly and I am tryin' real hard to please her. She is like Uncle Durant. She says we will never get anywhere in this world without proper English. Believe me when I tell you this is one of the hardest things I have ever tried to accomplish.

So, with that bein' said, I need answers—a lot of answers—and if I have to be sneaky or if I have to lie about why I am askin' questions, I will. I keep my ears open and anytime I hear anything suspicious bein' discussed by an adult, I listen. You never know when you will hear valuable information that will close the gaps. It has also meant eavesdroppin' on conversations that are not for my ears. But I know if I am to survive this life I am trapped in that I need answers and no one else is goin' to give them to me. I have to dig them out all by myself.

I have lots of memories and lots of questions. One thing I have found out is that my mother divorced my father 'cause she caught him havin' sex with my sister, Lola, in her bedroom—my parent's bedroom. Lola was fifteen years old when it happened. I was six years old at the time and it was all so confusin' to me. I didn't understand but I knew something happened that was really bad. It was like an explosion went off in the house. My otherwise calm mother was screamin' and rockin' Lola in her arms. I remember Mom lookin' distraught. I hardly recognized her beautiful face. Her eyes were a stormy gray, not their usual light gray, almost a tarnished silver.

My sister, Stella, sat on the floor of the bedroom in a heap, bawlin' her eyes out. She beat on the floor, cryin', "No, no, no, not Lola." Normal sat outside the bedroom door, starin' at the wall. Lola was limp in my mother's arms. Lola's face was white and motionless, and I thought she was dead.

I was the only one who didn't have a clue about what was goin' on. The whole scene was devastating and at six years old I thought the world must be comin' to an end. I thought Aunt Lena would come, but Mommy said she didn't want anyone from *his* family here. I didn't know who "his" was until much later.

Normal and I were sent to our room to wonder what the heck was goin' on. I tried to get Normal to tell me, but all she would say was, "Daddy did it. I know Daddy did it."

Believe it or not, I was confused by what she said. I couldn't understand why Daddy would try to kill Lola. It would be years before I would connect the dots and realize it was about sex. That my father was a pedophile and what *he did* was incest.

It never occurred to me that he was molesting Stella, Lola and Normal. I know now that Hero kept him away from me. After that night in my bedroom, I suspected what he was doin' when he took her out of the room, but I was never one hundred percent sure. I blocked it out of my mind as soon as it happened. I don't know how I did that, but I got pretty good at it over the years. My friend, Teddy Long, helped a lot. Also, when it happened, I would think about other things—kinda like changin' the subject in a conversation. This would give me a small amount of peace for a short amount of time. But in my mind, the memory always came back.

And even stranger, it never occurred to me that the incident with Lola had anything to do with what my father tried to do to me. It was so confusing tryin' to put all the pieces together.

Around five o'clock that day, I heard voices I didn't recognize. I looked out the window and saw a strange car parked in front of the house. It was a black car with a white top, but it wasn't a taxi. It looked brand new with shiny hubcaps and it was as clean as a whistle. I can't remember knowin' anyone with a car like that.

I saw Mom leave in the black and white car with Lola, but I didn't know where they were goin' or who they were leavin' with that day. I was so worried about Lola my stomach hurt. It hurt so bad that I had to sit by the commode in the bathroom 'cause I couldn't stop throwin' up. No one would tell me anything. There was a lot of whisperin' goin' on, but if Lola was hurt why was it such a secret?

This went on all day long. It started on Saturday morning and by Saturday afternoon we were still waitin' in our room. Waitin' for what?

181

I had no idea. I needed to know if Lola was all right. I needed to know if Lola was dead or alive. Someone should at least tell us that.

Stella came into our room just after dark and said she had made us sandwiches for supper—bacon and grilled cheese sandwiches 'cause it's the only thing she knows how to cook. We hadn't eaten all day. I was starvin' 'cause I had thrown up my breakfast that morning.

Normal and I sat down at the kitchen table. I looked around the dining room and everything seemed just as it did yesterday. The red checkered tablecloth was the same and the dishes we were eatin' our sandwiches off of were the same blue ones we always used for supper. But to me everything was different. The air didn't feel the same. It was heavy, suffocating. I could feel everyone's mood, dark and heavy and hangin' over all of us like a wet blanket. I wondered if I would ever feel safe in this house again. I was hungry, but I just sat there and stared at the sandwich.

Stella walked in and sat down across from us. Her face was swollen and her eyes were as red as blood. I looked at her sad eyes and asked, "Is Lola dead?"

She glanced at me, clearly shocked by my question. "No Patra, she's not dead. She's with Mother."

She came around the table and put her arms around me and placed her face in my hair and mumbled, "I am so sorry I let you go all day thinking that. Something really bad has happened to Lola that little girls can't understand, but someday soon she will be back."

I asked if that meant she was not comin' home tonight, and she said, "No, Patra. She is not coming home for a while."

I started cryin'. Where is Lola going I asked, and Stella said she was going to spend a few weeks with our Aunt Dottie in Baton Rouge.

"How is she getting' to Baton Rouge? Why is she goin' so far away?"

Stella said she had no idea to either question, but that she was going tomorrow and that it would be OK.

How can it be OK when I didn't even get to say goodbye to my own sister? My mind was so confused. Who sends her daughter away when she is hurt and needs her family? I was so scared. Would Mommy send me away if she found out stuff about me, or if she found out about The Sisters?

All of a sudden, I felt like I was in a deep, dark hole with no one to help me out. The walls were closing in around me. I tried to take deep breaths 'cause it was so hard to breathe. I needed to get air, but I couldn't find a way out of the hole. I prayed, "Please God, let me be able to breathe." I kept tellin' myself, "It's OK, it's OK, it's OK." And finally my breath comes back to me.

When my breathing gets back to normal I look around the room, but no one seemed to have noticed I almost died. *How can that be? Did I disappear and come back and Normal and Stella didn't see? Am I goin' crazy?*

Stella and Normal just sat there eatin' their sandwiches. I took my plate to the kitchen and dumped it in the trash.

I went into my room, put on my pajamas and got into bed. I put my head under the covers. I knew I was just a little girl, but I wondered how could anything this horrible happen and no one told me anything? How was I supposed to feel? All of the secrets, not knowin' what everyone else knows. She is my sister, Normal and Stella's sister, not anyone else's, just ours. But I didn't know what was happening to Lola.

That night Stella came into our room and told us about Daddy moving out and Mommy and Daddy getting a divorce. Normal got up and walked into the bathroom and slammed the door. I was horrified. No one I had ever known had gotten a divorce. None of the kids from school in my class were from a divorced home. *They would find out,* I thought, *and I will be all alone.* No one wants to be a friend to someone from a divorced family. How long could I keep it a secret? I rolled over and cried myself to sleep, devastated by the news.

40

April Fool's Day

It's April Fool's Day and the pranks have been flowin' all day. I will be glad to get home to some peace and quiet. Normal, or I should say Sad, left school on the back of a motorcycle with some boy today I have never seen before, so I will have the house to myself for a change.

I walk into the empty house and turn on the TV. Then, I go in the kitchen to make myself a pitcher of iced tea and take a chicken out of the freezer to defrost for supper. I find a box of Pecan Sandies in the cabinet and head to the living room to watch "American Bandstand."

When I sit down in front of the TV, the phone rings. When I answer it, a woman asks to speak to my Mom. I tell her she is not home. She says she needs to leave a message for her. She sounds professional, so I say OK.

The woman says, "I need to inform her Mr. David Shelton passed away today. Mr. Shelton listed her as his contact person in case of an emergency and we need to know what she wants to do with the remains."

My knees buckle and I drop to the floor. *What did she mean by his remains,* and *he had passed away?* Then I realized it's April Fool's Day. Someone must be playin' a horrible trick on me. Who would call and tell someone something so terrible? And then I think, Angry; she would do it!

I hang up the phone as fast as I can. It rings again. I don't answer it. I sit there on the floor rockin' back and forth wonderin' *what if it's true? Should I cry or should I be happy?* If it's true that part of the nightmare would be over, but my daddy would be dead.

When Mom and Lola get home, I tell them about the phone call and they say it was probably a prank. That no one would tell a child his or her father was dead over the phone.

But we are all wrong.

The lady calls back at seven o'clock. Mom says she told her the same thing she told me. Daddy was dead; he died from pneumonia after falling into a lake while fishing. No other information was available and where did she want the body shipped?

Lola, Normal and I just sit there. None of us know what to say or do. Mom looks like someone slapped her. None of us cry.

Finally, Angry jumps up and says, "I'm glad he's dead."

She runs to our room and slams the door. Lola sits there stone-faced. Mom comes over and puts her arms around both of us and says, "We have to tell Grandmother and it won't be easy."

The rest of the week is a blur. We leave right after the phone call to go to Grandmother's house, and Mom says we will stay there until after the funeral. She called Uncle Billy and told him Daddy was dead and he'd better have Dr. Jones meet us at the house. She dropped me and Normal off at Aunt Karena's house because she knew this was going to be a bad afternoon and she didn't want us to have to be there.

The day of the funeral so many people drop off food that Miss Hattie, Grandmother's maid, has to go get her sister to come help in the kitchen! We have to be at the church by one o'clock for the service and everyone will go back to Grandmother's for lunch. Miss Hattie will have everything organized before noon.

"I have to be able to go to the service with Mizz Alexandria," Miss Hattie says, "'cause she can't make it through the service without me."

Grandmother does not come out of her room all day. Mom says she is heavily sedated and she just can't deal with Daddy's death. We all knew it would be hard on her, but Miss Hattie says, "Mizz Alexandria will never be the same again without her David being in this world." She had already lost the first love of her life, meaning Grandfather David, and now she had lost her beloved son.

The service is worse than a nightmare. The church is filled with flowers that smell like death. I recognized the smell from Lola's friend Elsie's funeral. She died when she was seventeen from cancer. We were not allowed to say the word *cancer*; we were only allowed to whisper it like it was some kinda secret. I guess pneumonia is different 'cause everyone was talkin' about it.

Miss Hattie wheels Grandmother to the front of the church and puts her at the end of the first pew. She sits there like she is in another world. She hasn't spoken to anyone and she acts like she is the only person in the church. Suddenly she stands up, walks over to the coffin and throws herself over Daddy's body. She starts crying, "I want to go with him."

Uncle Billy tries to take her away, but he can't get her off of the coffin. The preacher asks everyone to wait outside for a while until she can say her goodbyes.

Uncle Billy and Miss Hattie finally get her back into the wheelchair and wheel her out from the back of the church and to his car. He tells us Dr. Jones is going to meet them at the house and give her a shot to calm her down.

After they take her away, I walk up to the coffin and look inside. Daddy looks exactly the same except his skin is snow white instead of a tanned, golden brown. He has on a navy blue suit and a navy blue tie. And his baby blue shirt matches his eyes, if I could see them. He looks like he is sleepin'. How can someone so bad look so peaceful? I reach in and touch his face, and it is as cold as ice, just like his heart.

He tore our world apart and walked away like nothing ever happened. I want to hate him but I don't. I'm like Grandmother; I love him still and don't want him to be dead. I know he did terrible things to all of us, but I can't help how my heart feels. No matter how much I try to hate him, I can't! I can't believe how many times I wished he was dead, how many times I prayed he would die. And now he is gone and it is my fault. God finally answered one of my prayers, and I am so sorry he did! I am heartbroken, but it's too late. My prayers have already been answered.

I am bawling my eyes out next to the coffin when I feel someone put his arms around me. I look up and see my brother David. He puts my head on his shoulder and says, "It's time to sit down for the service, sweet."

I don't remember the rest of the funeral. Next thing I know we are on our way to the graveyard. I don't want to go there. I have never been to a gravesite before and nothing scares me more than bein' put in the ground.

I stand there frozen, lookin' at the deep hole. What if he's not dead and he wakes up? I know it sounds crazy, but Normal and I have seen movies about people bein' buried alive. They even put tiny bells above the ground so the people can ring them if they wake up. But Daddy doesn't have a bell!

They roll up the casket and put it over the hole. I cry so hard I get the hiccups.

Mom comes over and takes my hand. I look up at her and she doesn't even have tears in her eyes. She leads me away from the casket and sits me in her lap for the rest of the service. We sit on the front row and everyone else stands behind us. I just want to run away, I don't want to be here. Even bein' at home with The Sisters is better than this!

We are on our way back to Grandmother's house now and my heart is cryin' for her 'cause she is so sad. I am worried 'cause Normal refused to come to the funeral and she is at Grandmother's house alone. I know Miss Hattie is there, but she doesn't know about Angry. The last thing Grandmother needs is for Angry to pitch a hissy fit and tell her all of the horrible things Daddy did when he was drunk.

When we get back to the house there are so many people there you couldn't shake 'em with a stick. Food covers every table and the kitchen counter. Miss Hattie is sweatin' up a storm tryin' to keep everything cleaned up behind all of these people.

It is so loud I have to hold my ears; everyone is talkin' at once. People I don't even know are tellin' stories about Daddy when he was a little boy or when he was a rowdy teenager. They are laughin' and eatin' and I just want to disappear into the walls. I have never been to a funeral before, but I thought people were supposed to be sad.

I sneak up the stairs to Grandmother's room and slowly open the door. I peek inside and see her lyin' on the bed, so I tiptoe over to her and kiss her on the cheek.

She opens her eyes and says, "Patra, I know he wasn't always good but I still loved him more than life itself."

I sit on the side of the bed and hold her hand. "I know, Grandmother. I loved him, too." I crawl into bed with her and fall asleep.

* * * * *

I wake up in a cold sweat; dark shadows are floatin' around the room above my head. The moon casts an eerie glow across the bedroom floor. I sit up in the bed and try to scream, but nothing comes out. It feels like my scream is stuck in my throat.

I look across the room and see someone sittin' in a rocking chair blocking the only way out of the room. I look closer, and it's Daddy. I freeze! His icy blue eyes look straight into my eyes.

As he slowly rocks back and forth he says, "You are happy I am dead; you got your wish. I died."

I can't breathe. He looks so alive, but it can't be true. I saw him in his coffin. He was dead. I touched his face; it was cold and felt like wax.

I jump straight up out of the bed and scream. Grandmother pulls me into her arms and tells me I am having a nightmare. But I know better. It is his ghost and it will haunt me on April Fool's Day the rest of my life.

41

Lucifer

I *look back now at my life and wonder how my mom never knew what was going on in our home. Was she in denial, or was it so horrifying she couldn't face what was happening? Or was it just a time in history when sexual abuse was not acknowledged by anyone?*

I learned over my adult years that all of my siblings were abused and none of us knew that the others were abused also. I really wasn't sure Angela was being abused because I never saw it with my own eyes and chose to believe she was handling it some other way.

For some reason in this situation, you believe you are the only one and no one is talking. I have talked with many people in sexual abuse group therapy, which are the darkest therapy sessions I have ever endured, and everyone says the same thing. You feel too ashamed or afraid you will be blamed for letting it happen, even if you are a child with no control over what the adult does.

I believe my mom never believed Angela was possessed. Oh sure, she knew Angela had a problem 'cause she hurt herself so often. But especially given the times, Mom's way of dealing with all this was sweeping it under the rug. David always knew there was something terribly wrong with Angela and he tried his best to find a way to help her. We didn't know how, though.

When I was a child I didn't know what mental illness was.

I wondered if Angela was the only person in the world who had these other personalities inside her head. For the longest time I didn't have anyone to ask about it, and it was a lonely, dark place to live. Not until I started therapy in my twenties did anyone explain to me what I had been living through with Angela. That's how we met Father Joel and accepted his ideas about an exorcism.

* * * * *

Many days have passed since the funeral and Angry and Sad still scream at each other night and day. Angry doesn't seem to care if everyone knows about her. She's lost her mind and can't control herself. When I walk into the living room, I see her cussin' and throwin' things at Mom and Lola. They have no idea what's goin' on or what she's capable of. I try to tell them she's dangerous and to leave her alone, but Lola is determined to stop her from destroying the house. Lola has a hot temper and a stubborn streak as wide as a skunk's stripe. She is quiet and sweet until you piss her off, and then it's Katy, bar the door!

Lola loses it when Angry throws a book and hits Mom upside the head. She slaps Angry and tells her to go to her room. I can tell Angry is in full-attack mode. She grabs Lola by the hair and throws her to the floor. Mom is screamin' and I stand there frozen like a statue. I'm afraid Angry will hurt Lola. Even though she is the smallest of all of us—barely five feet tall—she is as strong as an ox, but Lola holds her own. They roll on the floor, punchin' each other in the face. Angry tries to bite Lola, but Lola punches her in the mouth. A tooth flies across the room. Angry screams like a wounded animal and blood spurts out of her mouth and across the floor. The two don't slow down. Mom and I stand there and watch punch after punch. We don't know what to do or how to stop them from killin' each other.

By now they have bloodied each other's faces and they are both a bloody mess. Mom and I don't know if all the blood is from the tooth or if they are bleedin' from other places, too. Their hair is messy and wild, and they've ripped almost all their clothes off each other's bodies.

The fight feels as if it has lasted for hours. I see they're both gettin' tired. Mom is upset and wants them to stop, but she knows they're both too stubborn to give up. When they can't hit each other anymore, but neither of them will give up they lie there on the floor tryin' to raise their hands one last time for a final slap.

Mom goes to them and asks, "Have you had enough?"

Neither says yes. But Lola rolls over and gives Angry one last shove with her foot.

"Yes! Finally someone has beaten her," I say aloud.

Angry stares at me. "It doesn't matter, you little bitch," she says. "I'm goin' to kill you anyway."

Then Angry is gone; Normal appears. She looks around the room and asks us what happened. Mom and Lola look at each other and don't know what to say.

Lola lets Normal get up off of the floor.

"Why am I bleedin'?" Normal asks, "Why are you covered in blood?" She doesn't wait for an answer. Instead, she walks into our room and crawls into bed.

After Mom calls David at work, he comes home and listens as Mom tells him what happened. That Angela acted like a wild, crazy person, that she tried to kill Lola and then she didn't remember anything about it.

"I've told you for years something is wrong with her," David says. "She acts like she is possessed by the devil."

Lookin' like she's goin' to cry, Mom mumbles, "I'll get her an appointment with a doctor this week."

After a week goes by, Normal is the only sister I have seen. Angry has not switched and I am nervously waitin' for her and my beating, or even possibly for her to kill me. Mom took Normal to the dentist and she has to have a false tooth.

I can't even imagine how mad Angry is! I'm worried about what she said 'cause when Angry makes a promise she keeps it. I know the first chance she gets I'm dead.

I stay as far away from them as possible so I don't trigger a visit from Angry. I even make it a point to stay at school even after the day is over and let Lola pick me up on her way home from work at the hospital.

The next week Mom takes Normal to a doctor. They tell her they can't find anything wrong with her physically and give her a name of a psychiatrist. He said he could prescribe Valium to keep her calm until the appointment. A lot of good that will do—she has a drawer full of Valium in her room. The doctor says that if Normal goes crazy again before the appointment he'll put her out at Whitfield so a psychiatrist can evaluate her mental state.

I ask Mom what the doctor said.

She explains, but then says, "I will not put her in a mental institution."

"But Mom, she's crazy, and if you don't want me dead that's exactly where she should be!" I said.

"She didn't mean that, Patra," Mom says. "She was just upset."

And I think, Mom, how stupid can you be?

Two weeks later we walk into the house and see that Angry has gone crazy again. She tore up the house and broke everything she could put her hands on. It looks like a war zone. I don't want to stay in the house and I tell Mom and Lola we need to wait for David to get there before we go back inside.

"We're not going to have a re-match," Mom says as she drags Lola out the door to the carport.

When David pulls into the driveway, Normal comes runnin' out of the house and falls into his arms. She begs him to help her. "The demons are tryin' to kill me!"

David tries to calm her down. I can tell it is Sad, not Normal or Angry, who is beggin' David for help. She must have been hittin' herself 'cause she has a bloody nose and it looks like she is goin' to have a black eye.

"Is there anyone in the house?" David asks.

"Him," she says.

"Who is 'him'?"

"Lucifer," Sad says.

"She's been reading Revelations again," I mumble. But no one hears me.

David gets her to settle down and go back into the house. They sit on the couch together. "Tell me about Lucifer," he says.

Sad explains that Lucifer lives in her head and tells her what to do. That sometimes he tells her to hurt herself and to hurt other people, especially Patra. "He wants all of us dead," she says, "and he wants me to do it."

David believes Normal is possessed by the devil, but I know she is possessed by other people. I don't think they'll believe me, so I don't try to tell them about Angry, Sad, Kind or Hero.

Sometimes when Sad is hurtin' herself she tells me Lucifer makes her do it. I thought she was makin' it up, but maybe he *is* real just like the others in her head. Just 'cause I haven't seen him doesn't mean he doesn't exist.

David asks a priest to come to the house to talk to Normal, who tells the priest she doesn't know what we're talkin' about. She's fine and we must be makin' this up. The priest says it's not unusual that a victim doesn't know about the demons inside them, but an exorcism will expel the demons.

Mom is so upset she can't stop cryin', "How did the devil get inside my baby?"

"We don't know how this happens or why a person is possessed, but she needs to rid herself of her demons," he says. The priest can arrange this and lets us know where it will take place.

Only me—and the good Lord—know an exorcism is useless for Normal. She doesn't have demons. She has other people inside her head.

I guess Angry is afraid of the priest 'cause she hasn't switched in weeks, but I'm still walkin' on eggshells waitin' for Angry's return. After the last incident when Angry tore up the house, Normal acted more like a zombie than a person. In the evening, she sat on the couch with a confused look on her face or locked herself in our room. She doesn't talk to any of us. After we go to bed, she goes to the living room and sits up all night long. Then she skips school and sleeps during the day when no one else is at home.

The Sisters are a senior this year and go to school only for alcohol, cigarettes and sex. I watch her hurt herself every day and wonder how much more her mind and body can take.

David keeps tryin' to get Mom to find help for Normal, but Mom pretends nothing ever happened. I keep my mouth shut and only hope Angry doesn't switch and kill me. I keep my distance and try hard never to do anything to provoke her. So far it's worked, but how long can Angry stay in the background and let Sad keep all of the control?

I didn't have to wait long for the answer. One day when I walked into the bedroom I know it is Angry sittin' there. She looks at me with her evil eyes and says, "I am not goin' to kill you, so you can stop runnin' away."

I start to back out of the room but she jumps up and closes the door. At thirteen, I realize I am not nearly as scared as I used to be. I stand up as tall as I can and say, "I will fight back."

She laughs. "And you will lose. You are not nearly as strong as Lola, and believe me, this isn't over yet. I will kill her for knockin' my tooth out." Then she says, "Sit down. Let's talk."

I've never *talked* to Angry. I just do what she says most of the time without sayin' a word. I don't know what to do or how to respond to her request.

She pushes me down into the chair and sits on the bed across from me. "I do not plan on bein' removed from my body or killed by a priest," she says, "but I do plan to remove all of these other idiots from my head so I can get on with my life, and you, dear little sister are goin' to help me!"

Why would she think I am goin' to help her, and how does she think I can?

"Stupid, when the time comes," she says, "I will tell you how. I will write down things you are goin' to do and when you are goin' to do them, and if you don't, I will beat you until you do!"

By this time I'm aware that all The Sisters know about Normal, but Normal doesn't know about any of them. That means Normal can't fight back. Kind and Hero can only switch when I'm hurt or someone is hurtin' me. But Angry can't hide anything from Sad. Sad knows what Angry is capable of doin' and she doesn't like Angry at all. Sad knows Angry is crazy and can expose all of them by actin' like a lunatic. It's all so complicated and I'm much too young to figure any of this out by myself.

42

Father Joel

David finally convinced Mom that she needs to make an appointment with the priest to discuss an exorcism. She's agreed, but made it clear she isn't making any promises until she has all of the information about how the exorcism would be performed. David called the priest and set up an initial meeting for a Tuesday evening at seven o'clock. Everyone who lives in the house needs to be there for the meeting. So, here we are waitin' for the priest to arrive. All except Normal. She made it clear she wants no part of what she called "this fiasco." She thinks we're all crazy—including the priest.

When we hear the knock at the door I almost jump out of my skin. I know this is a joke, but all this talk about people bein' possessed by the devil throws me off. That's 'cause I've lived with worse than the devil himself for the past six or seven years. Besides, I know Angry won't let any of this nonsense happen. She'll burn the house down first.

The priest walks in and Lola invites him to sit in the chair across the room from the rest of us. He tells us his name is Father Joel. I really like the name Joel. It sounds so godly to me. Father Joel is from St. Luke's Catholic Church in Jackson and he says he's done many exorcisms over the past years.

How many possessed people could there be in Jackson, or in the world for that matter? I wonder. Are there demons hidin' inside people, like The Sisters hide inside Normal's head? Are there any sane people in the world, or are we all possessed by some crazy beings that we are not aware of?

I stop my mind from ramblin' long enough to hear Mom say Normal is refusing to join us for the meeting. Father Joel says it's not important for her to attend the first meeting if she doesn't want to. He's just going to go over some of the formalities with the family members who will be in the room at the time of the exorcism.

After chattin' for a while, he opens his briefcase, pulls out a big leatherbound book and starts reading. He says his mysterious words in a strange voice that is hard for me to follow, but I heard him say that an exorcism is the act of driving out demons or evil spirits from people and places—even things. The demons or demon control the thoughts and actions of their victim for the purpose of evil. I didn't have any trouble believin' that!

He went on, sayin' that exorcisms are a proven technique that can help turnaround the effects of possession and then he added something that made my heart sing: "and restore tranquility of the human soul." Oh, how I hope this works. We could all use some tranquility around this house.

Then Father Joel said, "We'll use the exorcism of water and salt, and it will be prepared in the room using holy water blessed in the church." Next, the priest says he must examine Angela's faith.

Good luck with that, I think. He'll never know which Sister he's talkin' to and I can assure him Angry doesn't have any faith. She's intelligent enough to fool everyone in this house including Father Joel. She's been foolin' people for years. Now that she knows he's tryin' to kill her, she will fight back with every ounce of willpower she has left in her body. She will charm him and she will resist him, and I have no doubt that she will convince him she is as sane as he is.

Father Joel also mentions that he'll consult a church-approved expert on the paranormal for additional input. Plus, he wants a doctor or psychiatrist to talk to Normal and answer questions to make sure there's no other mental or physical reason she's behaving this way. At that time, if everyone concerned is satisfied that she's possessed then he will perform the exorcism.

About the time he's through answerin' Mom's and David's questions, Normal walks into the room and asks if everyone is done talkin' about her? I can tell she's been cryin', but I refuse to feel sorry for her. Father Joel introduces himself and tells her he's here to help her. I see Sad emerging before my eyes, but no one else seems to notice. Sad asks Father Joel if the process of the exorcism will hurt.

"I can't promise you it will be pleasant, but I can promise you I will be as gentle as I possibly can," he says. "Do you have faith in God?"

"Does God have faith in me?" she asks.

Father Joel assures her God has faith in every soul on earth.

"I'm not askin' about other people, I'm askin' about me," Sad says.

He looks at her sad eyes. "I promise you God loves you and he will protect you from the evil spirit inside you, but you have to let me help you get the demon out of your body."

With a look of determination on her face she says, "When do we start?"

She doesn't wait for an answer and instead turns away and walks silently out of the room.

Ready to leave, Father Joel stands up and approaches the front door. Then he says, "This will be a difficult journey, but in the end she will have peace."

After Father Joel leaves, David asks Mom how she feels about what he said. Does she think it will work? And does she really believe Normal has demons inside her body?

Mom says she's scared half to death to do something this drastic to a child, especially *her child*, but she feels we have no other choice. All of us are afraid of Angry and the things we know she is capable of doin' based on the last couple of weeks.

That night I am scared to go to sleep 'cause I know Angry is lurkin' close by, waitin' for a chance to switch. She heard Sad say she is ready to rid herself of her demons, meaning Angry, and if that happens Kind and Hero will probably be gone, too. At this point Sad isn't rational enough to realize if she rids herself of the rest of them she will still be alone and miserable. Her life is so depressing it's not worth living. I know if she has total control of her body she will probably be dead in a week.

The thing is, Angry and Sad don't know that an exorcism isn't goin' to affect either one of them. A priest can't do a damn thing about any of them. They aren't demons and the Catholic Church doesn't know how to deal with the likes of them. They will exist in the one body until they are old and gray and there is nothing anyone can do about it. I just hope I get old enough to leave this house and don't have to grow old and gray with them.

The next day I can tell Mom feels better and she and David have decided to move forward with the exorcism. David made the appointment with the doctors Father Joel recommended and everything should be set within two weeks. Now I just have to wait to see if Angry finds a way to put a stop to it.

The next afternoon before Mom and Lola get home from work Angry drops the bomb on me. If I don't help her convince all of them that they are successful ridding her of the demons, she says, along with keepin' her secret, she will suffocate me with my own pillow in my sleep. I tell her they will know she killed me, but she doesn't care 'cause she'll die anyway if I don't help her. I still have to sleep in the same room with her and there is no doubt in my mind she will follow through with her threat. So here is the same question I have had for years, *what choice do I have?* None.

The next week drags by with me tryin' to figure out how I am goin' to pull this off. Angry sits on my bed night after night askin' me what the plan is. I'm barely thirteen so *I* don't have a plan. Except for Sad or Angry, I don't have anyone to talk to about this.

Then it hits me. Sad is the only one who can help me. If I can make her believe Angry will be gone forever after the exorcism and I can convince

Angry to keep her mouth shut and not switch for a while, maybe, just maybe I can pull it off. That will give Angry enough time to figure out how to control Sad and the others. I know it won't be a permanent fix, but it will buy me some time, which is more than I have right now.

I start spendin' time with Sad describin' the exorcism I told her I read about in a book. I tell her she will feel the demon slowly exiting her body when the priest starts his prayers. Father Joel will do a lot of rantin' and chantin', but to stay calm, no one is goin' to hurt her. What a relief it will be when it's over. I also reassure her that Father Joel will be there to help her destroy Angry and that after she is gone all of our lives will be better. I have no idea if that's what happens in a real exorcism, but I also know there are no demons inside her to exorcise. From what Father Joel told us, she'll be strapped down on the table and it will be too late for her to do anything about the lies I've been tellin' her anyway.

Sad isn't the brightest of The Sisters and I think she will believe me as long as Angry stays away and does not threaten her. I make sure to spend some time with Sad every day. I tell her this is a family effort and I'm tryin' to do my part to help. I also slip her some Valium in a drink every day to keep her calm. As long as she's calm, she's not hurtin' herself and not causin' Angry any pain. She also needs to be rational when she talks to the doctors so they won't figure out she's mentally ill and not possessed by the devil.

In my wildest dreams I never thought I would be goin' to this extent to save Angry, but I help her or I'll suffer the consequences.

I write a note tellin' Angry that the only way this will work is if she doesn't switch for at least a month. I also say I have to be careful about talkin' to her 'cause I never know if Sad is listenin'. Besides, all of our conversations must be written in order to keep our plans hidden from Sad. I don't know if this will work 'cause Sad can read the notes, too. I tell Sad I have to write the notes to Angry and that she has to pretend she doesn't read them. Good Lord, this is gettin' confusing even to me.

"Keepin' quiet for a month is nothing compared to how happy you will be livin' a lifetime without Sad tryin' to kill all of you all the time," I tell Angry.

She doesn't like the idea of not switchin'. I can't be sure she will do it, but it's all I have to offer.

Since we need to know how she's supposed to act when the time comes, I tell Angry we have to go to the library in Jackson to check out the books on exorcisms. When Mom gets home from work we tell her we have to go to the library to do some research for a school project.

Mom looks at us funny. "I have never seen the two of you do anything together before."

"Don't worry," I say, "the truce won't last for long."

When we get to the library I tell Angry I can do the research by myself, that I don't need her help. She looks like she wants to spit on me, but she doesn't. She just walks away. I spend the next couple of hours writing down everything I can find on how she should respond during the exorcism. I know Angry can act like a demon so I just want to make sure she can convince Father Noel she is possessed and not just crazy.

When I'm finished I start searchin' for Angry, but I can't find her anywhere in the library. It's almost nine o'clock and they are ready to lock the doors. I know Mom will be worried if we're not home by nine forty-five and it takes about forty-five minutes to get home.

I walk outside to look for the car, but it's not in the parking lot where we left it. She must have driven away without me. I know I'm in for a long night. I'm afraid to sit on the steps to wait 'cause someone might ask me why I am still here. I go around to the side of the building and stand behind the bushes and wait. I don't have a watch so I don't know what time it is, and I didn't bring a heavy coat so I'm starting to get really cold.

I walk to a pay phone down the street, but then I see her pullin' up to the curb. She's drunk. I can tell when she talks and slurs her words. "I met a cute guy at the Tote-Sum-Store and we went to the beer joint down the street and had a few bottles of beer."

I look at her closer and know it is Sad, but Sad never parties. She asks me what I was doin' at the library anyway. "Research," I say, "but we need to get home 'cause we're late."

"You're such a party pooper," she says.

I ride silently with Sad, talkin' about everything in her life that I don't care anything about. I know if we make it home Mom won't say anything to her about being drunk. That's 'cause she's eighteen and she can drink if she wants to. She drives ten miles an hour across the narrow old Pearl River Bridge and still scrapes the side of the car a few times. Then she swerves from side to side on the two lane road. By the time we get home, my nerves are shot and I'm a wreck. As I get out of the car I vow never to ride with any of them ever again.

Sad sneaks into the house, but it doesn't matter 'cause Mom's door is closed and I assume she's already asleep. While Sad is in the bathroom I hide all of the information I gathered at the library in a cigar box and put it in the back of my closet where no one will find it. I climb into my bed and pretend to be asleep so I don't have to talk to the drunken chatterbox when she comes into the room. Thank God this night is over and I got what I needed to start my exorcism deception.

43

The Exorcism

I peek inside the room. It's dark except for the candles everywhere. They cast an eerie glow all around the room and make the walls seem like they are flowin' slowly in the breeze, but there is no breeze 'cause the windows are closed.

Father Joel prepared a small table with a purple satin cloth next to the long wooden table in the center of the room. There is a bowl of holy water, just like in the book at the library said there should be, and the long table has leather straps at both ends. I'm afraid when Angry sees the leather straps she's goin' to have a fit, and Lord knows what she is goin' to do when they start to tie her down.

In my notes to her, I told Angry she'd have to hide her true identity by pretendin' to be a peaceful spirit. She would have to lure them in looking lost and confused and she'd need to stay calm until the priest finished reading the holy prayers. No matter what he says or does, she has to stay calm until he finishes the prayers or she will blow it. Then she can let the real Angry come out kickin' and screamin'. Use profanity. Pretend he is Daddy and cuss him like a sailor. Then threaten to kill him the way she does to me. Hate him as much as she hates Sad. And then the hard part—get really calm.

She says she understands how important it is to do exactly what I tell her to do. "Don't worry little sister, I can do it."

The day has finally come. It is seven o'clock and we're all waitin' for Father Joel to knock on the front door. Even Sad is in the living room waitin'. Mom told her to wear comfortable clothes and no shoes. She didn't even put up a fuss about it; now she's wearin' her long, flannel pajamas and a pair of soft socks.

Sad and David stay in the living room and wait for Father Joel. Mom, Lola and I decide to wait in the den where we have our chairs sitting next to the wall on the far side of the room. When the doorbell chimes, the three of us sit deathly still. My heart is beatin' a thousand miles an hour and sweat pops out on my forehead. Mom is tearing up, but Lola sits stone-faced.

Father Joel comes into the room wearing his long, black robe with a purple embellished sash. A gold and black rosary is hanging over his sash and a gold cross at the end of the rosary sways from side to side as his heavy body walks across the den to the middle of the room. He's carrying a Bible and a large gold cross. He's chantin' and actin' erratic, or maybe he is speakin' in tongues. I can't tell.

David brings Sad in and situates her on the table. He puts the restraints around her wrist and I hold my breath and know *this is it*. If whoever she is right now can handle this we will be okay.

Thankfully she stays calm. She looks at David with her big, sad eyes and tries to smile. After he finishes restrainin' both her wrists and ankles Father Noel walks around the semi-dark steamy room, chantin'.

Mom, Lola and I are still in the chairs a few feet away from the table, but David is standin' beside Sad holdin' her hand. Father Joel asks Sad if she is ready to become whole again. She nods yes. He asks her if her faith in God is strong enough to carry her through this ritual. She nods again. He asks her if she is ready to rid herself of the demons. Another nod yes. Then he says, "Family, are you ready to get your daughter and sister back?"

In unison, we say yes.

Father Joel clutches his Bible to his heart and holds his rosary beads in his hands, then reads a prayer:

"God, You who are merciful and forgiving, please accept our prayer that this young woman, bound by the shackles of her sins, may be forgiven by your loving kindness. And in the name of God, I demand that the devil leave the subject's body.

"Depart, impious one, depart with all your deceits, for God has made man his temple and this young woman his loving servant."

I sigh with relief, thinkin' it's all over, but then he starts a new prayer to make the water holy.

"With this holy water, I cast out the demon from you in the name of God, the Father almighty, in the name of Jesus Christ, his son, our Lord and in the power of the Holy Spirit. May this water be purified and empowered to drive out the power of the cursed enemy and to banish this enemy, along with his fallen angels. We ask this through the power of our Lord Jesus Christ, who will return to this world to judge both the living and the dead. Amen."

I look over at Angry, hopin' she's got a halo on her head, but she's just looking down at the floor. I'm ready for this to start working, but then

Father Joel says, "Let us pray.

"O God, who for all our welfare created the mysteries in the substance of water, hear our prayer and send forth your blessings on this element now bestowed with purifying rites. Through Your grace, let this water serve to cast out the demons and banish all sickness within your servant. May all that this water be sprinkled in this home of the faithful and be delivered from all that is unclean and hurtful; let no contagion hover here, no taint of corruption linger. Through Your power, let all the evil of the lurking enemy come to nothing. By the sprinkling of this water, may everything work against the safety and peace of the occupants of this home and be banished. May they know the well-being they desire and be protected from every peril. Through Christ our Lord, Amen."

Father Joel walks to the small table he has prepared for the ritual. A brass bowl is filled with holy water and he pours the salt into the water in the form of a cross, saying, "May this salt and water be mixed together; in the name of the Father, and of the Son, and of the Holy Spirit. May the Lord be with you. Amen. Let us pray."

I can't believe there's another prayer, but when I think about all the evil Father Joel needs to drive out, this could go on for some time. He starts again, honoring God as the "source of irresistible might and King of an invincible realm," and then tells God to silence "the uproar of his rage and subdue his wickedness." Father Joel's voice is risin' and fallin' and just when I think he's winding things down, he starts up again.

"We beg you Lord, to bestow this humble salt and water with your grace, to let the light of your kindness shine upon it and create the dew of your mercy so that wherever it is sprinkled and your holy name is invoked, every evil of this tainted spirit may be foiled and the poison of the serpent's venom be cast out. We ask you to grant that the Holy Spirit may be with us wherever we may be; through Christ our Lord. Amen."

Thank heavens he seems to be finished with his prayers. Father Joel puts down his Bible and starts sprinklin' the holy water on Angry. I start thinkin' about what I'll do when this is over.

But it's just the beginning of a new round. Angry goes totally nuts. She jerks her arms and legs and screams, strugglin' to get off of the table. She's cussin' a blue streak and spittin' at Father Joel. He looks pleased and keeps sprinklin' the water on her body. He touches her arms with the cross hanging around his neck, then he takes it off and lays it on her chest. She starts screamin' louder. Mom tries to go to her, but David stops her and tells Mom she won't know who she is, that the demon has control of her but it should exit her body soon. I just hope he's right and that she remembers it's almost time to pretend to pass out.

Angry pulls loose from the arm restraints and sits straight up. Father Joel backs away from her but never stops chantin'. Again she spits and screams and flails her arms around, tryin' to hit anything within reach. She looks at me with wild eyes and I look at her and slightly nod my head. She falls back onto the table and pretends to pass out.

Father Joel tries hard not to smile, but I can tell by his eyes he is pleased with the way the exorcism went. "We have accomplished what we came here to do," he says. "I think you will see a different person when she wakes up."

Thank God Angry made it believable!

Father Joel tells Mom that Angry will sleep through the night and should be fine by tomorrow. Rather than moving her into the bedroom, though, Father Joel wants her there through the night.

Although Angry still isn't movin', leavin' her on the table all night will be a problem. While David, Mom, Lola and Father Joel are still talkin' I sneak close enough to the table to tell her I will be back when everyone has gone to bed to undo the straps on her ankles and let her go to bed. She doesn't move, but I know she hears me when she slightly moves her hand.

Mom, David and Father Joel go into the kitchen, but Lola goes straight to bed. Mom makes a pot of coffee and puts the pound cake she baked earlier on the dining room table. They sit around talkin' about how well they think the exorcism went and how easily the demons left her body. Father Joel thinks they won't come back, but he can't guarantee that. I'm glad to hear no one will be shocked when Angry returns.

After everyone goes to bed I slip into the den and unbuckle the straps. Sad jumps off the table and goes straight to our room and gets into bed.

"Father Joel is a creep," she says. "I wanted to punch him in the face."

I try to listen to her babblin', but I am so tired I fall asleep.

The next morning Normal is actin' like Normal and I'm hopin' Angry is goin' to keep up her end of the bargain and not switch for at least a month. Mom asks how she is feeling. "Fine," she says. "Why?"

"Do you remember Father Joel being here last night?" Mom asks.

She shakes her head no.

Mom looks at me and mouths, "Father Joel said she might not remember."

I keep eatin' my Sugar Frosted Flakes. I don't want to talk with anybody after the stressful night. Not that I doubt Angry still won't try to smother me in my sleep.

44

The Battle

It's my fourteenth birthday. I'm finally taller than The Sisters and almost weigh as much as they do. I can tell it makes Angry nervous 'cause she watches me whenever I'm in the room with her. When we had our little talk about her gettin' rid of The Other Sisters a few weeks ago I threatened her for the first time I'd fight back, and she said I would lose. *But would I?* I don't think so. I am much stronger now and more determined than I have ever been to stop her from destroying my life.

I spend a lot of time thinkin' about what I will do now that I won't let Angry control and abuse me anymore. I feel like I can defend myself and my daily life doesn't include pain, threats and physical abuse. I have long daydreamed about not waiting on her hand and foot. About spendin' time with my friends, and maybe havin' a life like other girls my age. And finally Angry is leavin' me alone. Maybe 'cause I told her I could just as easily put a pillow over her face while she is sleepin'. She ignores me and pretends I'm not even here most of the time. I love this new person I have become.

With my newfound confidence I wonder if it's time to tell Mom about The Sisters. I know she thinks Angela is a little crazy, but maybe Mom could get her help if she knows what's really wrong with her. Will she believe me or say I'm makin' it up? How do you tell your mother her daughter *is* a monster and not possessed by one? Or one of them is a monster. Or that there are five of them and only some of them are crazy. Who is goin' to believe that? I don't know that anyone will.

My only option is to stand up and defend myself. To not let her overpower me or hurt me anymore. I think, *God please help me remain strong enough physically and mentally. I deserve this peace and quiet in my life.*

Normal, Sad and Angry are around more and more, and I see Kind and Hero less and less. I haven't seen Hero since Daddy died, but sometimes I wake up and Kind will be sittin' on the side of the bed watchin' me sleep. At first it freaked me out, but then I think, *she is still my Guardian Angel checking to be sure I'm okay.*

Sad seems to be as strong as Angry now. She can switch whenever she wants to. Before this, Angry was the only one that had that much control. Angry doesn't even try to torment me 'cause she's tryin' to figure out how to get control of Sad. It's a daily battle between them. It's like they are at war with one another. It makes life easier for me, but I can feel the tension in the air.

Mom and Lola are both wary of every move Normal makes, as if they're waitin' for the demons to return.

I can see Sad becomin' more miserable every day. She is hurtin' herself more often and she always wants to be left alone. She stays in our room for days, only comin' out when one of the others switches with her. She never talks to me or anyone else. She just sits and cries and says she wants to die.

I ask her about Lucifer. "It's none of your damn business," she says. I think Mom is livin' in a bubble hopin' Normal is okay.

Normal never goes to school anymore, and Sad only goes to get alcohol from the boys. The girls at school call her a tramp 'cause she trades sex for cigarettes and alcohol. The boys she won't have sex with call her a whore. I ask her why she keeps doin' it and she says, "It's no worse than what I did with Daddy, and at least this way I get something in return."

Sometimes at school I see Sad stumblin' from the back of the shop building and I can tell she is drunk. It makes me want to cry 'cause she looks so lost.

On the other hand, Angry is happy when she is at school. I can always find her hangin' around the smoking tree with the rest of the thugs. The smoking tree is behind the shop classroom on the back side of the schoolyard. She only goes to school to hang out with the bad boys. My mom calls them juvenile delinquents and she says we should stay away from them 'cause they are trouble. She would have a fit if she saw Angry on the back of her boyfriend's Hell's Angels motorcycle every day, flyin' out of the parking lot and skippin' school.

I get off the bus alone and walk the two blocks to the house. I go into the kitchen through the back door and look in the refrigerator for a Coke, but there are no cold ones. The hot ones are sittin' in the wooden case on the floor in the pantry.

I grab a half-full ice tray out of the freezer and fill a Tupperware glass to the top. I open a hot bottle of Coke and pour it into the glass. Then I grab a jar of peanut butter and head into the living room to watch "American Bandstand" on TV.

At four o'clock I start fixin' one my favorites for supper: meatloaf with creamed potatoes and English peas. I mix the hamburger meat with bread, onions, ketchup and eggs and form a loaf, cover it with catsup and stick it in the oven. I made an egg custard pie last night before I went to bed and it is ready to take out of the refrigerator since I like it served at room temperature. Next, I cut up the potatoes and boil them with lots of butter and salt. I open the can of tiny green peas and add butter and cook them for a few minutes.

I start workin' on my homework. When I'm done, I want to go next door to Darlene's house. Darlene is a beautician and has her beauty shop in her closed-in carport. Her husband, Gary, built the shop for her so she wouldn't have to leave home to go to work. She's very nice and she doesn't charge me but a dollar to cut a couple of inches off of my waist-length hair once a month.

I go to Normal's room to ask her to watch the potatoes and not let them burn, but her room is empty. I call her, but she doesn't answer. I check the back porch where she normally goes to smoke. Empty. I go back inside and check the bathroom. She does not answer me, but I hear her arguin' with someone. She's talkin' in a high-pitched voice, then I hear Sad answer in her low steady one.

Sad calmly tells Angry, "It's over. I can't do it anymore."

Angry says what she always says, "You don't have a choice."

"I *do* have a choice," Sad says. "I have control of Kind and Hero and I will get control of Normal. You can't stop me. You are stronger and meaner than each of us, and I am the only one who can stop you. You are a very bad person!"

I hear a struggle and then water splashing and I think Sad is goin' to drown Angry! I run to my bedroom to get a paper clip to open the door.

When I get the door open, I walk into the bathroom. The water in the bathtub is red. In my confusion I think, *why is the water red?*

Sad is sittin' in the tub with a strange look on her face. I see the bloody razor blade lyin' on the floor. Sad looks down where she has cut her wrist in at least a dozen places. Angry is gone and I can tell Sad is in control. How did that happen? Angry always has control.

I look at Sad's face and see how miserable she is. I start to run to the phone to call an ambulance, but I stop in my tracks.

I remember all of the years of abuse I have suffered and all of the years of misery she has caused me. I look at her and she looks at me. I can't decide if she wants help, or if she wants me to walk away. I stand there hopin' Angry will surface, wanting my help so I can refuse, but she doesn't. Even in the end, she wins.

I ask Sad if any of the Other Sisters are comin', and she shakes her head no. I look at the water and it's darker red now. I look up at Sad, but she turns away. *Why should I help them after the life I have endured with them? How will I live with myself if I don't? I won't just be lettin' Angry and Sad die. Normal, Kind and Hero will die, too!*

I make a decision to look one more time. I turn around and see Angry tryin' to get out of the tub. Her eyes are wild and threatening, but she is too weak to stand up. She slips back into the water and tries to speak but nothing comes out. I expect to see tears or remorse on her face, but there is nothing but hatred in her hysterical eyes. I can see it in her face: she is desperate to live, but so am I.

I look at Angry one last time and with the determination to live a normal life, I turn away and slowly close the door.

Epilogue

I *know we all deal with childhood differently. I also know I'm one of the lucky ones. The trauma made me stronger. Angela was not so fortunate. Her mental illness destroyed her life.*

People often ask me how I survived such abuse and I tell them it's like the saying, "Sometimes you just have to put your big girl panties on and get over it." To me, that means you stop blaming your childhood for how you live as an adult. The blame game is a treacherous road to travel.

I'm not saying I'm happy about my childhood, but I know I would not be where I am today if I hadn't endured these character-building life lessons. And I'm grateful to the caring therapists and ministers who helped me along the way.

I want to add that Angela wasn't always a monster. Before the other personalities showed up, she could be loving and caring. I remember how summers in the south were too hot to play outside comfortably during the day. The house was just as hot, so we all looked forward to dusk when the neighborhood kids would get together to play hide and seek and chase lightning bugs. Angela always kept me with her and held my hand during the games because she knew I was afraid of the dark.

One night, we caught at least 50 lightning bugs and put them in a Mason jar. We poked holes in the top of the lid, hoping they could still breathe. After we finished playing, I snuck the jar into my bedroom and put them under the bed. When Angela went to sleep, I pulled out the jar and put it beside me on my pillow. I woke up sometime later and Angela was staring at all of the lights blinking all over our room. It felt like we were amongst the stars.

She reached for my hand, squeezed it and said, "See Patra, there is a God. Who else could make something so beautiful?"

Another time we were walking through a field on our way home and encountered a vast number of stickers growing there. I started crying because I was barefoot and my feet were covered with the tiny, prickly weeds. Without a word, Angela sat me down and pulled out all of the stickers. Then she picked me up and carried me all the way across the field and set me down on the other side.

Mental illness changed my loving sister into something that is hard for most people to understand. Her life was destroyed, and along with that she tried to destroy mine. Fortunately, I came out on the other side a better person, but I know that most people are not so fortunate.

After I finished writing my story, I researched DID and Multiple Personality Disorder (MPD) and the way they were dealt with in the 1950s and 1960s. Even though the movie The Three Faces of Eve *came out in 1957, no one really understood the disorder or believed it was real; it certainly wasn't recognized in rural Mississippi. That's why we thought that being possessed by the devil was the only option to explain Angela's behavior. I now realize the personality "Sad" was probably bipolar and that's why she was always so unpredictable and continually hurting herself.*

Most people in the Sixties, including Angela, were eating Valium like candy for a multiple of anxiety disorders and depression. This was before anyone knew how addictive tranquilizers were. The 1967 movie The Valley of The Dolls *seemed to open everyone's eyes up to the underlying problem of prescription drug addiction.*

DID and MPD are thought to be caused by separating yourself into another person to enable you to deal with extreme trauma, usually sexual or physical abuse. The Alters may be male or female, young or old, and most of the time you have no control over these other personalities.

There have been a multitude of movies and TV shows over the years about DID or MPD—some comedies and some dramas. For me, watching them has been both disturbing and amusing. It's hard to step back and remove myself from years of abuse and consider it entertaining, but on the other hand, movies for me have never been reality. In fact, they're just the opposite—my means of escape.

There is a very dark place these personalities live within someone else's body, and until you have experienced living within the realm of their mind and their world, it's hard to understand the horror of their existence. Angela's Others knew they were a parasitic part of her and could not exist without her. They also thought if she found out about them they would die. Death to them was very real. They were only allowed to live if she was alive.

Today mental health is uppermost in people's minds. We have a vast knowledge of mental disorders and treatments at our fingertips through the Internet. Very few people don't have a friend or family member who is bipolar or suffers from some sort of clinical depression. A Harvard study shows anti-depressants are prescribed and taken by one in ten people in the United States today, and my calculated guess is that some of these people have not been diagnosed and are suffering from DID. As far as I know my sister never was. Awareness of the disease is the only way to help people who may not even know they are suffering from the illness. Or possibly after reading this book someone will recognize these traits in someone they love. That is my hope. If even one person reads this book and realizes he or she can put the past behind and go forward or can help a loved one, it's worth the pain of dredging up my past and writing this book.

Please, I urge you to keep an open mind and help those with mental illness so they don't suffer the same way my sister did. We also need to help the abused put the past behind them and move forward. There are a number of foundations for mental illness out there, and after writing this book I hope to start one of my own.

Working in the movie industry for the past twenty-five years has enabled me to attend various award shows and presentations. The following photos are some of my most memorable.

Pam and Matt Damon

Jennifer Lopez and Pam

Rose McGowan and Pam

Pam and Quentin Tarantino

Pam and Billy Bob Thornton

John Corbett, Pam, and Rita Wilson

Anne Heche, Sharon Stone, Pam and Ellen DeGeneres

Ryan O'Neal and Pam

Julianne Hough and Pam

Jason Statham and Pam

Tom Selleck and Pam

Sylvester Stallone and Pam

Pam and Neil Patrick Harris

Pam and Clint Eastwood

Pierce Brosnan and Pam

Pam and John Travolta

Pam and George Clooney

Rob Lowe and Pam

Michael Douglas and Pam

Tyler Perry and Pam

Chris Hemsworth and Pam

Pam and Shia LaBeouf

Quinton Aaron and Pam
The Blind Side

John Candy and Pam

Jeff Bridges and Pam

Bobby and Pam Franklin

Acknowledgements

This past year has been quite a journey writing my first book at sixty-five years old and I'm hoping this is going to continue to be the next chapter of my life. With that said, I could not have done it without the support of family and friends.

Barbara McDaniel, my best friend for the past forty years, for giving me the encouragement I needed to write this book. Her faith in me is astounding. Debbie Brister Latham for all of her technical support and patience with my lack of computer skills. All of my closest friends, Carol Gray, Diane Melohn, Debbie Brister Latham, Jane Sunshine and Sandy Mulone for reading chapter after chapter as I was writing the book. Crying with me and encouraging me to keep on going when sometimes it was so hard I wanted to give up.

My wonderful brother and sister-in-law, James and Clydia, for understanding why I needed to put this story in writing after all of these years. My sisters, for the lifetime of love and devotion they gave me as sisters and friends.

Lynda McDaniel, Virginia McCullough, and Brittiany Koren at Written Dreams, for walking me through this journey of becoming a writer.

And to my husband, Bobby, for being there for me, supporting me with every word I wrote.

Coming in 2016!

*A journey through the mind of **The Sisters**...*

About the Author

Pam Franklin grew up in Jackson, Mississippi and lives in Celebration, Florida with her husband of twenty-five years, Bobby. When not working or writing, she spends time in Charleston, South Carolina with her daughter, Whitney and her grandsons, Teague and Crews. You can visit Pam online on her Facebook page at https://www.facebook.com/myfivesisters or on her website.

Printed in Great Britain
by Amazon

32769726R00127